SUBVERSIVE GIANTS

SUBVERSIVE GIANTS

WAR OF THE DAMNED™ BOOK SIX

MICHAEL TODD   MICHAEL ANDERLE
LAURIE STARKEY

DISRUPTIVE IMAGINATION®

LMBPN Publishing
PMB 196, 2540 South Maryland Pkwy
Las Vegas, NV 89109

First US edition, September 2018
Version 1.01, September 2018

SUBVERSIVE GIANTS TEAM

Beta Readers

Dorothy Lloyd
Tom Dickerson
Dorene Johnson
Diane Velasquez
Timothy Cox
Sarah Weir

JIT Readers

Mary Morris
James Caplan
Kelly O'Donnell
John Ashmore
Peter Manis
Tim Bischoff
Angel LaVey
Daniel Weigert
Larry Omans
Paul Westman
Micky Cocker

If we missed anyone, please let us know!

Weapons Consultant

John Kern
Proprietor
Spurlock's - Henderson NV

Editor
Lynne Stiegler

DEDICATION

To Family, Friends and
Those Who Love
to Read.
May We All Enjoy Grace
to Live the Life We Are
Called.

Tiamat was gravely injured. It was a new experience for her. She lay snarling and growling on the hard lava stones of hell. This was not her dimension and not where she was supposed to be. Moloch and Baal had had an agreement with her from the beginning. When she was done with the work they had asked her to do, they would send her back home. However, demons weren't the best at keeping their words.

"You need to release me. I belong somewhere else. You know this," Tiamat growled.

Baal looked at Moloch and shrugged. "I'm still stuck on what the fuck just happened."

Moloch snorted. "You and me both. I couldn't believe my eyes when Katie pulled Lilith out of her body."

Baal scratched his head. "Not just that, but Lilith took on her own body. She used all the magic she had here in hell before she was sent topside. That's not how it works. A human isn't supposed to be able to pull their demon out of them. They're not supposed to survive it, anyway."

Moloch looked down at Tiamat. She was beginning to pant, and blood was seeping out the side of her drooping dragon jowls. "Just when we thought we had seen it all? She walked over and took that Angel girl back to Earth through her own portal. She used all her energy here in hell, and as far as I understood, the power she had here doesn't necessarily transfer to Earth. If it had, we would've seen a lot more frozen demons over the last couple of years."

"Shit, I don't even remember her having that power in hell when she was here. It's not like we demons really like the cold. You would think the king would have put a stop to that immediately." Baal shook his head, completely exasperated.

Tiamat coughed blood. "I saw it from you before, and you did it again. You underestimated this demon. *I* underestimated her human and how ballsy she was. Of course, I wasn't aware that I would be facing an angel while on Earth. Just a note—next time you look for a Leviathan to do your dirty work for you, you might want to let them know the whole story."

Moloch ignored Tiamat's response. "That bitch flew right through the portal and didn't even care that it snapped shut behind her. I swear, this shit's getting old."

Baal put his large, scaled foot on top of a frozen demon and rolled him over. He snarled as he looked down at the face frozen in fear. "We aren't even safe within our own walls of hell. The bitch started a goddamned blizzard down here. *Now* look at this fucking mess. These were good demons, and now we have a pile of fucking demonsicles."

Moloch took in the mass of frozen demons still thawing on the floor of hell. Some of them were half-turned to dust and half-frozen in a sheet of ice. Others were still kicking and starting to break through the ice that surrounded them.

He wrinkled his nose. "There's nothing worse than the smell of wet demon. The sons of bitches don't keep themselves clean for anything. It's not like one of those human fucking dog pens."

Baal chuckled. "Well, *now* they're clean. If they can free themselves before they fucking die. I'm half-tempted to toss them into the lava and start over from scratch. There's plenty of humans up there that belong down here. We can build a different kind of army."

Moloch sighed. "There's no point in wasting good demons. Let them thaw and think about what they've managed to get themselves into. It's way too fucking hot for ice to last long down here."

Baal pulled his leg back and punted a frozen head. It sizzled when it landed in a stream of lava a hundred feet away. "The rest of this shit needs to be moved to the lava pits. I don't want to step in a pile of demon dust in the middle of the night when I look for a snack."

Moloch swatted Baal hard on the shoulder. "Next time I talk shit about Lilith, make sure she's still in her meatsack's body. I don't want to talk to her personally."

Baal put his hands on his hips and looked around. "No shit."

"I hate to break up this touching moment between the two of you, but you need to release me," Tiamat snarled.

Moloch and Baal turned to the giant beaten Leviathan. A small runt of a demon had become a little too curious. He inched closer to her, and she snapped at him and missed. The demon jeered, but Tiamat's tongue lashed out, wrapped around the demon and dragged it between her jaws. She pulverized the demon with her vicious teeth. Baal and Moloch glanced at each other, and both took a big step backward, out of Tiamat's range.

Baal mused, "She did her goddamned job. You know I'm not one who keeps my word. Kind of messes with my reputation, but I don't want her getting better down here. You know there's only one of us who can control a Leviathan in hell."

Moloch scoffed. "If you haven't noticed, it looks like she's about to bite the dust."

Several smaller demons started to gather around her. She swished her tail violently, smacking several off into the distance. Baal shrugged his shoulders. "If it were me, I might just let the demons kill her. Then you'd have a huge Leviathan soul chained in hell. That could come in really useful in the future."

Moloch waved his large, taloned hand. "There are six more. We don't go back on our word. I know most demons do, but remember that we hold ourselves to a higher standard. We were looked upon by Lucifer himself. He may be a demon, but he keeps his word almost every single time and expects us to as well."

Baal conceded the point. "I suppose you're right. The last thing I want to do is go through all that we went through today and then have to face an angry Lucifer. I need a vacation, a bowl of fresh puppies, and some wench to rub my tired feet."

Moloch chuckled. "I feel sorry for whatever soul you have rub your feet. I don't care what crimes they committed during life."

Baal raised a gnarled and knobby foot. "Hey! I take care of these beauties. All the lava and hot rocks really take a toll."

Moloch shook his head. "Come on, let's get this Leviathan back Earth-side so we can wash our hands of it. Doesn't look like she's gonna last much longer."

Moloch turned toward Tiamat and whistled in her direction. She grumbled and carefully lifted her head off the ground, barely able to move. The two demons slowly opened a gate right next to her. She took her time getting to her feet as they watched impatiently.

Baal looked down at his fingernails. "Anytime today, beast. I may have eternity down here, but that doesn't mean I want to spend it with you."

———

"I just don't understand what is taking so long," the general muttered as he looked out the window on the observation deck of the ship.

The captain peered at the island and tried to calm the general. "Sometimes these things take time. That was a big motherfucker."

"Anything on the video surveillance?" The general walked over and stared at the screen.

The petty officer adjusted the clarity of the screen and scanned the island. The trees swayed gently in the breeze, and water lapped quietly against the shore. Other than that, there was no sign of Katie or the Leviathan anywhere. The petty officer slowly shook his head, and the general rubbed his forehead. "It's been an hour since we've seen either one of them. We've got no view of them, no view of the Leviathan, and no idea whether we should be sending in more forces. Captain, what do you think we should do next?"

The captain took off his hat and wiped the sweat from his neck. "At this point, we have to assume someone is still left over there, whether it's the Leviathan or Katie. We can't sit by and do nothing. Our pants are down, here. I suggest we go ahead and send in the SEALs. They've been locked and loaded and ready to go since before this mission started. I can have them here within minutes."

The general walked back to the window and rubbed his chin. "I would hate for anyone else to get killed because I'm impatient. I've never seen Katie take on a demon and not be done in under an hour. She wouldn't just be hiding out there, that's for sure."

The captain cleared his throat and stepped closer to the general. He lowered his voice. "You have to be willing to entertain the possibility that Katie didn't make it out of this one. I know it's not something you want to think about, but we have to consider the greater good here. We don't have to send the SEALs onto the beach, but we can get them started in that direction so that if we need to deploy them, they're already on their mark."

The general wanted to argue, but the captain made a

good point. "All right. Get them on their boats and start them in that direction, but have them keep their weapons down and watch their backs at all times."

The captain nodded astutely. "Petty officer, call the lower deck and tell the SEAL team it's a go."

The SEALs gathered their gear and loaded it into the rigid-hulled inflatable boats the ship lowered into the water below. The captain and the general went down to the deck and watched as the SEALs sped off in their RHIBs toward the island. The ship was fairly far away, but the teams moved fast and with purpose. As they drew closer to the island, they began to slow down.

The general and the captain made their way back to the observation deck and waited for word. When the SEALs were a few hundred yards from the beach, they radioed in. "We are going to move in closer. There's some serious damage to the beach, the woods around it, and a plateau of rocks above. We don't see any sign of the Leviathan or the merc."

The captain took the radio. "Go ahead, but move carefully, and at the first sign of anything, move back."

The SEALs went onto the beach, and the general and captain watched nervously from the ship. The phone rang, and one of the seamen answered it. "General, it's for you."

The general cleared his throat and walked to take the phone. "Yes?"

"General, this is Timothy from Katie's base. I tried your cell phone, but it went straight to voicemail."

The general pulled out his cell and realized there was no service way out there on the ocean. "I'm on the ship watching the island. No sign of Katie."

"That's what I'm calling about. There's a new portal, and it's about to open right there on that island. If you have men there, you might want to get them off."

The general dropped the phone to his side and called to the captain, "Get your men out of there. There's a portal opening!"

The captain immediately grabbed the radio and called the SEAL team's lead officer. "A portal is opening. I repeat, a portal is opening. Get your asses off that island!"

The lead officer replied, "Copy that. Getting in the boats now."

The SEALs jumped in their boats and headed away from the island. When they were about a half a mile off, the deep, thundering rip of a portal opening echoed across the water. They slowed their boats and watched a tired and beaten Tiamat limp through the hole. She shook her body and stumbled into the sand, squinting at the bright sun overhead.

The team lead slowly pulled the radio to his mouth and whispered, "Fire on her. Repeat, fire on her. It's the Leviathan, and she's alone and badly injured. Take her down. It's your only chance!"

The team sat quietly in the boat, staring back at the ships wondering if they had gotten the message. Suddenly, the large weapons on the top of the ship began to rotate to point directly at Tiamat. The SEALs covered their ears and crouched in the boat as the weapons went off, sending rockets straight at the Leviathan. She looked up just as one of them shot across the sand.

"Oh, shit." The rocket struck her and threw her to the

ground. Before she could rise, dozens of missiles pummeled her already broken body, blowing her to shit.

The portal behind her started to close.

Moloch and Baal watched through it and chuckled as mounds of flesh blew off the Leviathan and into the ocean. Moloch stuck out his fist and Baal bumped it, both of them laughing hard.

Baal shrugged his shoulders. "Hey, we honored our word. We took good care of her."

Moloch snickered. "I knew the humans would be on the other side ready to beat the balls off her. I'm just surprised it wasn't Lilith and Katie getting revenge."

Baal wrinkled his nose. "I'm kind of glad it wasn't. I don't want a replay of what just happened. I really hate ice."

Moloch shrugged. "From the looks of it, the angel wasn't doing so well, and Pandora probably lost all her strength when she exited the portal. I'm not very worried about those two, at least not for a couple of days. They'll be back, sure. Until then, we get to watch the show from the sidelines."

A huge explosion rocked the small island, and the last chunks of Leviathan were blown every which way. Baal and Moloch both jumped back, a chunk of leathery skin barely missing them as it spiraled into the gate. Baal flicked a piece of flesh off his arm. "They didn't hold back, either. They gave her everything they had."

Moloch laughed loudly. "Did you see her body explode? Damn! I'm tempted to go get her skull later."

2

Katie groaned, her head throbbing. Slowly, her focus started to align. She realized she was on the inside. Pandora had taken over, and Katie was just watching at the moment. That was perfectly fine. She felt like she had been run over by a dozen garbage trucks and then kicked in the stomach by a Leviathan.

Where... Wait, where are we?

Pandora smiled and pulled Katie's knees up. *We are currently on top of a very tall building in the center of New York City. I figured the best thing to do was to hide for a bit. That would give you a chance to get your wits about you. Didn't want you looking all wobbly and drunk when we are walking around downtown with cameras everywhere.*

Thanks, Katie grumbled. *What the hell happened?*

Pandora was still busy trying to heal the wounds covering Katie's body. *Well, after you pulled me out of you, you collapsed onto the hot-as-hell ground of...well, hell. I fought off the demons and that giant bitch-ass dragon Leviathan thing, then I grabbed your passed-out butt and jumped out of the portal and wham! Here we are back to New York. I thought you might want to avoid a walk of shame, so I brought us up here. You need to heal, not go around looking like the Walking Dead.*

Is it bad? Katie was trying to look at herself, but being inside Pandora, that was a little bit difficult.

Bitch, you went down like a sorority girl, but I got you out. You had some broken bones, but none of the important ones. You had some burns from the lava rock, but nowhere important, and a bump on the head. I took care of most of it down in the alley where we came out. Now I'm just finishing up the scrapes on your legs and arms.

Katie took over her arms and patted her pockets for her cell phone. *I've got to call the general and let him know we're okay. I need to let him know the Leviathan isn't dead yet.*

Pandora chuckled. *First of all, you need to slow down because I need these hands to finish taking care of you. Secondly, I'm pretty sure I saw your phone in about a thousand pieces back there in hell.*

Katie sighed and relinquished control. *I'm going to need another phone.*

Pandora finished up patching the last of the wounds on her legs and got her to her feet. *Not perfect, but it will do. Once both of us have had some rest, I'll finish healing you the rest of the way. Now, would you like the honor of getting us home, or would you like me to do it?*

Katie grimaced at her bruised ribs. *I'm still too weak. I'll watch...and criticize, of course.*

Katie went silent inside Pandora, slightly shocked that she hadn't said anything snarky in return. Pandora stepped onto the edge of the building and spread her wings, flapping them once or twice before diving off. Katie decided not to joke around anymore. It was obvious Pandora wasn't in the mood, and she was having a hard enough time staying conscious.

Pandora flew around their building, running her hands down her sides. *Let me guess, you didn't bring the keys with you?*

Yeah. I didn't really think about it, I guess.

Pandora flew to the front of the building and aimed herself at the front doors. A crowd of people was standing in the street with signs, all of them now staring up at the flying woman. *Okay, looks like we're going to make quite an entrance.*

Everyone on the street made way, moving to the side as Pandora landed carefully on her feet. She flapped her wings a couple times, then allowed them to fold behind her and disappear. She posed for a moment, smiling and waving at those who were holding signs indicating their love for her. She snapped her head to the left, narrowed her eyes at the ones holding hate signs, and flipped them the bird.

They began to boo and yell. Pandora put up her hand. "Touch me, and I'll make you wish you were in hell."

One of the protesters growled and started screaming, "Who the hell do you think you are? I'm going to sue you for mental agony!"

Pandora tilted her head back, laughing. "Do it, bitch. But learn to spell first. Your sign looks like a first grader wrote it."

Those supporting of Katie and Pandora began shouting

at the others. Pandora chuckled and looked up when the doorman opened the door, his eyebrow raised.

Pandora eyed him and gave him a huge smile. "I'm the other side of Katie—the one who gives zero fucks about that shit." She jerked her thumb over her shoulder and added, "Except, if they start brawling, I'll bust out the popcorn."

The doorman stepped to the side, his eyes growing wide as he realized he was talking to Katie's demon and not Katie. Pandora walked toward the doors, but paused and looked over her shoulder. She flashed a smile to her supporters. "Give 'em hell, guys!"

Pandora slipped inside, and the doorman quickly closed the door and locked it. On the other side of the doors, both factions of protesters met in the middle of the street. Fists were thrown, signs were bashed, and an all-out brawl broke out. The doorman glanced over his shoulder at the concierge. "Looks like we have another brawl. You might want to call the cops for this one."

The concierge chuckled and picked up the phone. "This is becoming a regular thing."

As the elevator doors shut Katie shoved Pandora inside. She looked at her reflection in the doors of the elevator and grimaced. There was blood on her face, most likely hers, and a gash across her chest. Her clothes hung off her body in shreds. She leaned forward and carefully touched the purple and blue around her eyes.

Katie wrinkled her nose. *Oh, fuck, there goes that beautiful face.*

Pandora didn't say anything, staying quiet. Katie stood up and looked around. *Hello? Pandora? Are you in there?*

Just gathering my strength, that's all. Focusing on getting us into the apartment. The last thing I need is for you to pass out here in the elevator. I'm not outside your body anymore, and if you pass out, I can't take back over.

The door slid open, and Katie shook her head. *Fuck, what kind of inner injuries do I have?*

Whiny-bitchitis. Chill. I got this.

Katie shrugged and walked down the hall, stopping in front of her door and knocking hard. She could hear Angie running from the kitchen and unlocking the bolt. When she threw open the door, her face went from happy to shocked.

Angie tilted her head to the side. "Good God, woman. Do you ever come back here and *not* have something crazy going on? What happened this time? Did you get dropped in front of a freight train?"

Katie sighed and shook her head as she limped through the front doors. "Remind me next time that fighting Leviathans is a real fucking pain in the ass."

Angie followed Katie into the kitchen and stared at her as she took down a cup, filled it with water, and drank frantically. She downed glass after glass as if she had been stumbling through the Mojave Desert. After her fourth glass, she swallowed hard and put the cup on the table.

Angie lifted her eyebrows. "Are you okay?"

Katie coughed and grabbed her ribs, but nodded. "I'll be

fine. That's the beauty of having a demon. I only have to deal with pain for a little while."

Angie put the glass in the dishwasher before turning back to her. "I have to be honest, you look like you've been to hell and back."

Katie snorted. "I have, actually."

Before Angie could ask any more questions, Katie went to her bedroom and rummaged around for her other phone. Angie stood in the doorway, watching her throw her clothes out of a drawer and act slightly stranger than normal.

After a couple of minutes, Angie cleared her throat. "Can I help you find something?"

Without glancing up, Katie responded. "Actually, yeah. I'm looking for my spare phone. I kind of just disappeared on everyone, literally. I need to get in touch with the general before he thinks I'm dead and starts planning a memorial."

The general pumped his fist as the last of the Leviathan blew to pieces. There was no way that beast was coming back this time, not unless it was able to regenerate its body. As the smoke from the missiles cleared, he stared at the screen. He was watching closely for any sign of Katie. But as the breeze blew the smoke away, there was nothing except for burning embers and blood-spattered sand.

The captain put his hand on the general's shoulder. "We got her, General. We *got* her."

The general forced a smile and turned to shake the

captain's hand. "Good work, Captain. We've been trying to kill her for weeks. She sure as hell looked bad when she came out of that portal. I have no idea how bad hell must really be if she came back that injured, knowing we would be waiting here."

The captain nodded and turned back to the screen. "I'm assuming your girl had something to do with that. I'm sure she's okay. We'll keep searching for her."

The general nodded. "What about your teams?"

The captain held the radio up. "SEAL team lead, report."

For several very long seconds, there was only silence on the other end of the radio. Then a loud crackling came across before the captain heard a voice. "We're all safe and accounted for, sir. On our way back to the ship."

The general let out a sigh of relief. It was incredibly important to him that as few innocents died as possible. He took a step back and leaned against one of the chairs bolted to the floor. The phone on the wall rang, but he barely noticed. His mind was too far gone wondering what had happened to his merc—and his friend—Katie.

"Excuse me, General, but you have a phone call," one of the sailors interrupted. He nodded at the phone on the wall.

The general acknowledged and trudged his way to the phone. "Yes?"

"What I'm trying to figure out is why you haven't sent out the entire Navy to find me?"

The general smiled. "Katie, where the hell've you been?"

Katie chuckled. "Oh, you know, taking a little vacay in the deepest bowels of hell. The usual summer fun."

The general smirked. "We got the Leviathan. Another

portal opened on the island and she was severely injured when she came through, which I'm assuming had something to do with you or Pandora. We blew her to bits."

"Good. That bitch had it coming."

The general paused for a moment. "Where are you?"

Katie chuckled. "I'm actually back in New York. It's a long story, but I fell and was pretty much in a coma in hell and Pandora brought me back."

The general was shocked. "Really? Pandora was in hell? She had the option to stay where she came from, and she took the time to bring you back to New York?"

Katie smirked. "I told you. She may be a demon, but she's on our side. And I'm glad to hear you killed Tiamat."

The general relaxed. "I am too. One of seven down."

Pandora let out a whoop. *I was concerned. The last thing I wanted was that Leviathan on the loose again, pissed as shit at me for beating her ass.*

Yeah. Katie scoffed.

The general cleared his throat. "So, what's next? Back to the usual?"

Katie yawned. "I've definitely got some downtime coming. This was one of the hardest battles I've ever been in, probably because I took myself to hell. Unless there's some sort of crazy outbreak or incursion, I'd really like to have some time to myself. What I'm saying, in a nice way, is don't call me for at least a week."

The general laughed loudly. "You know you just jinxed yourself, right?"

Katie stretched an arm and grimaced at the sharp pain. "Unless the world is burning, I'm sleeping."

"Be careful what you say. We're dealing with demons

from hell, so setting the world on fire isn't one of the *least* likely things that could happen."

Katie groaned. "You have a point there, but I'm not sure how much help I would be. I'm an angel. I don't think any of my powers involve putting out fires."

The general shrugged. "You surprise us every single day, so I wouldn't at all be shocked if somehow you grew a firehose from your—"

Katie bellowed with laughter. "I would never live that down with Pandora. Also, I don't think the media would cover it. It wouldn't be appropriate for the primetime news."

Pandora giggled. *No, but you would have a hell of a lot of men in the world who were jealous of your...firehose. We might even be able to get you on one of those firemen calendars.*

Katie rolled her eyes. *Oh yeah, that would definitely get me laid. I have giant tits and a firehose. Not exactly what I was looking for.*

Hey, don't knock it until you try it.

Katie cringed. *Please don't put that on your list of changes to make to my body.*

She focused on the general again. "Are you coming back to land soon?"

"I am, but I would have one hell of a long helicopter flight from here. I might end up staying with the ship until we're close to land. I've never been fond of chopper rides."

"If I wasn't so beat up, I'd pick you up and fly you back myself."

The general laughed. "I don't think that would be much better. Falling into the open ocean isn't my idea of a fun time."

They both laughed, and then there was a mutual silent pause. Katie yawned again, and the general smirked. "It sounds like you need some sleep. I'll contact you if the world is on fire."

"Sounds good. I'll have my firehose ready."

3

"Y ou want to be careful with that. If you drop that box, you're gonna have to face Timothy, and you do *not* want to face Timothy." Korbin's eyes narrowed as he watched the soldiers carry boxes to the loading area on the base.

Timothy walked up behind them and put his hands on his hips. "Damn straight. One scratch and I'm coming after you."

Korbin chuckled. "I'm pretty sure that at this point he's not going to let it slip one inch."

Timothy nodded but wrinkled his nose. "Am I really that scary? I mean, how scary can I be in Marc Jacobs and Valentino?"

Korbin rubbed his face as Timothy did a little pirouette to show off his outfit and asked, "Is everyone ready to move on?"

Timothy turned to Joshua, the government consultant, and the other people. They all nodded, trying to hold back smiles or laughter. Joshua stepped forward with his notebook and looked at Korbin. "Tell us about where we're going?"

Korbin nodded. "Right. We're moving near Groom Lake. Obviously, we won't be able to be directly at Groom Lake because it's a landing site for Area 51. Several of the locations around it have been closed to the public since '95 so they couldn't get shots of the installation. Groom Lake and the area around it is a salt flat, but there is an airfield in the area we're looking at already, which was decommissioned from Area 51 and sold off. Nothing has changed much, and there's a lot of defense still in place. We're to build it up. They will bring up more defenses and consultants to learn from the last attack and make sure that if another one happens, we're ready. We also chose this area because it's far from civilians. Area 51 has their own protection, and the general has written down where we'll be, so he knows exactly how close we are to them."

Joshua nodded as he took notes in his book. "Will there be a place for the armory?"

Korbin tilted his head back and forth. "Yes and no. We're going to make a place for you. It isn't set up for that right now, but neither was this place. I remember everything now, but it's taking me a little bit of time to get back on my feet. The consultants are here to help me and help you until that happens. The armory is obviously very important to us and the world, so it'll be the first priority after defense."

One of the consultants stepped up. "This is supposed to be temporary, a place to go that isn't here, and the demons aren't aware of. Most likely, it'll only be until we're able to hollow out a large enough area inside a mountain."

Korbin put up his finger and shook his head. "I'm thinking that might not be the best. What happens if the demons open a portal to hell inside the mountain? Not only will we be right next to the portal while demons are pouring out, but the intense heat will take out our communications. We can't afford that."

The consultants looked at each other and nodded. "That's a good point, Korbin. We'll put our heads together and think about it. We don't want to put the base or you folks in unnecessary danger."

"I second that," Timothy put in. "It's a shame they figured out where this place was. I feel like having everything underground was perfect. It kept us safe from any roving eyes and allowed us to put our communication efforts above ground but not be obvious with some huge building with the satellite dish on it. On top of that, it was damn quiet, which was nice."

Joshua closed his notebook. "The only thing that would've been better was if the armory had been underground too. The demons could have walked right over this place and never known we were here. I was really hoping this was going to be home for a long time."

Korbin put his arm around Joshua. "I know you've moved a lot in your life, kid, but just remember, it isn't the physical building that makes it home. It's the people who are there with you. You're part of a family, and we're all in this together. We will make the next place just as awesome as this one."

Timothy wiped a tear from the corner of his eye.

"You're getting right to the heart of it. I sure as hell am glad you're back, Korbin. And I have to say, being married to Stephanie has softened you up quite a bit. I can't imagine the old Korbin saying anything that sweet."

Korbin chuckled. "I'm thinking it's more the soap operas than anything else."

Timothy put his hands on his hips. "You don't have to be ashamed of your femininity. Embrace it, boy. Embrace it."

Everyone laughed and then Joshua looked up, his shoulders tensing. "Well, it looks like it's beginning."

Korbin smiled at him before turning to the road behind them. Dust clouded the air as several large trucks headed toward the main part of the base. Korbin sighed. "I remember this."

I seriously don't understand how you're still sleeping. It's been two days, and you act like you're no better than you were before. I've taken care of all your wounds and put a pain blocker on you so you wouldn't feel the soreness from your muscles healing. Pandora wasn't having it anymore. She was starving.

Katie groaned, rolled over in the bed, and opened her eyes. *You have been bitching at me for hours now. I told you, and I told the general, that this is my goddamned vacation. I just want to get some sleep.*

Pandora narrowed her eyes. *Don't you get fucking snappy with me, bitch. You got your sleep, and now I need to be fed and so do you. You'll never regain your energy if you don't get out of bed and eat something.*

Katie rolled onto her back and slapped her hands down on the bed. *Fine! Just stop complaining. Why don't you remind me again how I pulled you out of my body?*

Oh, sweetie, you do that right now, and I can promise you won't get back up again. It just about killed you, and not because you were standing in the depths of hell.

If I'm dead, do I get to sleep? Katie shoved herself up and swung her feet over the edge of the bed, taking a minute to collect herself before walking to her dresser.

She put on a pair of jeans, a black tank top, and a light leather jacket, then sat down on the edge of the bed to tie her shoes. She grabbed a small pistol out of the bedside table, placing it in her inner jacket pocket. There. She was ready.

Pandora wasn't sure what she needed a gun for when she was going to get donuts, but she figured it was better not to ask. Katie headed out of the apartment and downstairs, deciding to walk to the Krispy Kreme instead of worrying about catching a cab. She'd pulled her hair back in a ponytail and put on a baseball cap before she left the apartment, so none of the protesters outside paid her a bit of attention.

It's good to see them not fighting each other today.

Pandora laughed. *I find it amusing when they fight each other over you. Got a bunch of people defending your honor.*

I feel like that's what I'm constantly doing with you— defending my honor.

Katie turned the corner and stopped to stare into a small ice cream shop. Her stomach rumbled, prompting her to walk inside and order two scoops of rocky road in a waffle cone.

Pandora was confused. *Uh, I thought we were getting donuts.*

Yeah, yeah. I'm getting this for energy. It'll help me get to the donuts, which will give me even more energy.

Pandora was impressed with her thought process. *I like that. Keep moving, I don't want to miss hot, recently glazed donuts.*

You know, everything about this day screams I'm not taking a vacation, though I have to admit, a dozen donuts right about now sounds absolutely delicious. Of course, not as delicious as those firefighters over there.

Katie licked her ice cream cone, watching several New York City firefighters clean their truck. She whistled at them and they looked up, smiling at her. She winked and kept walking toward the donut shop, talking about men, her boobs, and everything else she normally wouldn't talk about.

Pandora narrowed her eyes but didn't say a word. She wasn't used to Katie talking like this. She also wasn't used to Katie talking so much. In fact, everything about her was a little bit off. It made Pandora wonder if she had a different Katie. She had gone to hell and then come back to life after pulling a demon out of her soul. There were so many ways something could have gone awry.

As they turned the corner, Katie stopped to watch three guys leave a van and walk into a bank. They were pulling masks over their faces as they entered. The short guy in the back was holding a silver gun tightly in his hand. It was obvious they were going in to make a withdrawal.

Pandora was excited about it, but she knew Katie wouldn't be. *Hmmm, what do we have here? Three little piggies* entering the wolf's den. They picked the wrong bank on the wrong street on the wrong day.

Katie leaned her head back and groaned. "For fuck's sake, really?"

She started munching her ice cream cone as fast as she could, talking out loud to Pandora. "I'm noth in anthy mood for thith shith."

Pandora winced. *Slow down on the ice cream, meatbag. You're giving both of us a brain freeze. And aren't you supposed to be excited about things like this? This is your whole angel side, remember?*

You're the one on the superhero kick, not me.

I would've been perfectly happy to chill at the house and eat donuts. But no, you have wings, which means you have to protect the innocent. Or at least that's what you *think it means.*

Katie swallowed the last of her cone. *I had no choice in the matter, remember? One day, I'm just Katie the volleyball player, the next day I'm Katie the demon, and the day after that, I'm Katie the angel-demon. I blame all of you, but for right now, I get to take my anger out on those assholes.*

With that, Katie began trotting toward the bank. She checked her pistol and stuffed it into her side pocket.

The general leaned back in his chair and stared at the ceiling, listening to the people on his conference call talk. He was back in his office, and very glad to be. He was pretty sure he'd spent enough time bobbing up and down on the ocean to last the rest of his life. He was in the Army, not the Navy, and his people kept their feet on the dirt.

One of the officers on the phone was talking about finding the other Leviathans. "We want to make sure those beasts aren't going to start coming out of the woodwork. We killed this one with bombs and heavy artillery. It took everything we had, and the beast was already half-dead when it came out of the portal. We know what it was like to try to kill it when it was in good health. We need to start building a strategy for when the next one comes, or better yet, when we *find* the next one. We want to be able to take it out quickly and efficiently."

One of the other officers spoke up. "Sure, but what are we going to do? Send that merc into hell every single time and have her beat the shit out of the Leviathan until we can blow it to bits? I think that's a little bit dangerous, and pretty much not an option."

The officer replied, "What do you propose, then? We can't just sit here and do nothing. We don't know anything about the other Leviathans. They could be weaker than the first one, or they could be ten times as strong. I think sitting here doing nothing is ridiculous. Are we waiting for them to track us down and eat us for an afternoon snack?"

The phone erupted as everyone began talking all at once, and the general sighed. He leaned forward, took the mute button off, and barked at the phone. "Gentlemen! Fighting amongst ourselves isn't going to solve this problem. I need everybody to calm down for a minute. I agree, we don't know if the others are stronger or weaker than Tiamat."

A voice spoke up. "Great, so we're fumbling in the dark here. All we can do is hope the next one is less fierce than that weird Godzilla creature. We need to start tracking them with sonar and find them before they know what hit them. This Leviathan was living on our planet this whole time, but we had no idea. We could've dropped a nuke on the bitch a long time ago and saved ourselves this trouble."

The general chuckled and let out a puff of air. "You know, gentlemen, we could always just let them sleep. Just because one was sent after us doesn't mean the others will rise. But I know one thing for sure. If we start hunting them down and wake them up, they're *all* going to come after us."

4

K atie ripped the bank doors open and stomped inside. She scanned the bank for the three men and realized that they probably hadn't pulled their masks all the way on. After all, no one was screaming or hitting the ground. The bank was busy, just like any other bank in New York City, with most people not paying attention to anyone or anything around them.

Katie spotted the three of them bunched together in a corner. *Lookie, lookie. Found you.*

Pandora was the one advising caution for once. *Careful. They have guns, and there are a lot of people here.*

Please, it's me. *None of these people are going to get hurt. And since when did you* become the voice of reason?

Since you decided to act like a gunslinger from the Wild West, saving the day in the local bank.

Katie scoffed. *My angel senses are tingling. Either those three assholes are going to go down, or they will take a whole bunch of people down trying to rob this bank. I'm making a logical decision here.*

She took a step toward them, and her eyes flashed from red to blue, tingles flying all over her body. She could feel her angel power pulsing through her from the top of her head to the bottom of her feet. The wings she kept hidden from sight shivered invisibly on her back. Katie swallowed hard and twisted her neck from side to side, still staring at the three men. Her eyes went from red to blue and back again, as if the angel and the demon inside her were fighting.

Pandora felt the rush of energy through Katie's body, but Katie didn't react the way she normally did. Her attention was locked on those men; she wasn't going to let them get away with what they were about to do. It was anger flowing through her.

The short man looked up, and his eyes immediately fell on her. She was hard to miss, especially since her eyes were glued on them. He shouted to the other two.

They grabbed for their weapons, but they were too slow. Katie already had her pistol at the ready, and her eyes blazed red as she fired directly at them through the crowd. Everyone in the place dropped to the ground and started screaming. Katie's bullets found their mark, and all three men went down. Katie scanned the crowd, checking to make sure no one else was hurt. Everyone seemed to be fine. They were terrified of the woman firing into a crowd but fine.

She walked toward the three men on the ground but stopped when a guard came around the corner and pointed his gun at her. "Freeze!"

Katie lifted an eyebrow and started to laugh. "Put your popgun away before I take it from you."

Pandora was taken aback. Katie was usually the nice one. *Hey, that's* my *line!*

Katie rolled her shoulders and willed her wings out, flaring them to each side. The crowd uttered a collective gasp. The guard froze and nodded slowly, gaping. He carefully put his gun back into the holster, leaving one of his hands up so Katie could see it.

He swallowed hard as he watched Katie walk past. "You're Katie from Katie's Killers."

Katie lifted an eyebrow. "What made you think that? Was it the wings, or the way my eyes flashed red?"

The guard took a step back nervously. "I don't understand what happened here."

Katie ignored him and stopped in front of a little boy and his mother. She bent down to lift the boy's chin. "You were really brave today. Good job."

The mom held tightly to the boy's shoulders, staring at Katie. She was obviously afraid of her, even as she tried to give Katie a smile. The guard took a step forward, and Katie turned her head fast, narrowing her eyes at him. He stopped in his tracks and put both hands up. "Are they dead?"

Katie walked to the three men and kicked one in the ankle. "These guys might need a medic or a coroner. It depends on whether or not they give me any shit."

The sound of sirens echoed through the bank. Katie turned around when the flashing lights pulled up in front. She yawned and stared at the guard, who was now joined by two of his buddies. She shrugged and started walking out. "You guys got this. I need donuts."

The guards looked at each other nervously as she put her pistol back into her jacket. Her wings folded up behind her and disappeared as she walked to the door. She tugged on the front of her leather jacket and ran her hand across her ponytail, pulling it through the hole in the back of her baseball cap.

One of the guards put up his hand and stepped toward her. "Hey, you can't leave! You need to explain yourself! What were these men doing?"

Katie didn't look at them. "I'm pretty sure that between the guns, the bags in their hands, and the ski masks on top of their heads, you can figure out their motivation. You're welcome. I just saved you from a bank robbery that prob-ably would've killed a bunch of people."

The other guard stepped forward with one hand on his pistol. "That doesn't mean you can leave. You have to stay and answer questions from the police."

Katie showed him her middle finger. "I've had a shit couple of years. I'm getting donuts!"

The Krispy Kreme under Madison Square Garden was a lot less busy than it normally was. Still, after collecting her donuts, Katie went next door to the pizza place and sat at her normal table in the corner. She began shoveling donuts into her face, not caring who might be staring at her. She was starving—even hungrier than she'd thought she was— and glad Pandora had woken her up to get some food.

Slow down, hooker. You're gonna get indigestion. Pandora groaned as Katie shoved another donut into her mouth.

Katie chuckled, not seeming to care. *Just use your voodoo and make my tits bigger or something. Besides, you're the one who wants to eat donuts so bad. Why are you complaining?*

Hey, calm down there, sister. I'm not complaining. I just know how you are when you get so full you can't move, and I can't fix you fast enough. Usually, you're *the one saying this, not me.*

Katie rolled her eyes. *I'm starving. I was unconscious and dragged out of hell, and then I slept for two days. I feel like I could eat this entire restaurant. In fact, I'm thinking about a piece of pizza right now.*

You hate their pizza.

Katie nodded. *Good point. I'll just stick with the donuts.*

As she ate, the bell on the door to the pizza place rang. Detectives Travers and Schultz walked in, obviously looking for her. She slowly slid the last bite of a donut into her mouth and grabbed a napkin to wipe the sugar from her lips. Detective Travers looked down at a chair. "Mind if we sit?"

Katie swallowed. "Of course not. Have a seat."

She turned the box of donuts toward them and opened the lid. Both detectives took a napkin and picked a donut out of the box. It was silent at the table for several moments as they each took a bite of the confections. Noticing how quiet they were, Katie put her hands on her lap and cleared her throat loudly.

Travers chuckled and put his donut on his napkin. "Understand you were at the bank today?"

Katie laughed. "I'm sure there's a video. I told them where I was going."

Schultz smirked. "That you did. You told them a couple times. Personally, I didn't think you were running from it, but you know we had to come down here. You had a hell of a lot of witnesses and it was in a bank, so you know every single second of the incident was taped. Not only that, but we weren't the only ones to see it. It's not like we can just brush this under the rug."

Travers leaned forward. "Katie, we're just worried about you, as police officers and as friends. We've known you for a while now, but we've never known you to handle a situation like that. You're usually very diplomatic, and if you do get involved in a civilian affair, you do it discreetly and contact us. This was quite the opposite. You walked into a busy bank in the middle of New York City and shot three men standing in a corner. You threatened a guard and walked out when they told you to stop. We just want to make sure you're not overworking yourself. This partnership is great for both the police force and for the citizens you protect, and we want to keep it that way. We want to make as few waves as possible."

Katie wiped her mouth and sighed. "You guys. I've been to hell...literally. I fought monsters that can take out this whole city with one swipe of their ugly-ass tails. I fought droves of demons, more than I've taken out on the ground here during an incursion, and I was almost all by myself when I did it. As you might imagine, I didn't want to dick around with three bank robbers. I could've kept walking, but I decided I wasn't going to let them get away with it."

Schultz nodded. "And it's a good thing you didn't. They

had some serious firepower on them, and a couple of them were wanted for murders in other armed robberies upstate. It's not that we're not glad you did it. We just want to make sure you're okay. And for the paperwork, we do have to take a statement."

Katie agreed. "Easy-peasy. I saw the three guys going into the bank with masks. One little guy had a gun. I walked in. I scanned the room, and I saw him hiding in the corner waiting to attack. When he saw me, he alerted his idiot partners, and they pulled their weapons. Of course, I was a lot fucking faster than they were, so I shot all three of them before they could hurt anyone. When the guard came at me, he caught me all amped up, and that's why I said what I said."

Travers wrote down what she said and had her sign the bottom of the statement. When Schultz was finished with his donut, they stood up and stared down at Katie. She kept her eyes on the table. Schultz leaned over her and put his hand on her shoulder, feeling her tension. "If you need somebody, you can call us any time. You're part of our family, and we won't leave you out in the rain."

Katie forced a tight-lipped smile and nodded at them, and they walked back out the doors.

Once outside, Travers stopped and looked back into the shop. Schultz shook his head, looking at her statement. "She's acting weird. I haven't seen her be that violent toward anyone in a long time."

Travers nodded his head. "I think we need to get in touch with her boss."

Schultz chuckled. "Who the hell is her boss?"

Travers scratched his head. "Good point. Let's try the general unless you know how to get hold of…God?"

Schultz laughed. "Not fucking likely."

Pandora held it in as long as she could, but after that showing with the cops, she couldn't keep her mouth closed any longer. *I want to talk to you about something.*

Yeah?

It might sound a little strange, but ever since we got back from hell, you've been acting a little bit off.

Katie took another bite of her donut. *What do you mean by "off?" Shooting three robbers in a bank robbery?*

Pandora took a moment to choose her words, knowing she had to keep her cool. *No, not necessarily that, but yeah, kind of that. I'm talking about the way you're handling everyone right now. You're snappy, quick to point the finger, and you have no problem telling anyone off.*

Katie laughed. *I feel like you're describing yourself just a week ago.*

That's true. And it's not that I have any issues with it. I think telling everyone to go fuck themselves is the proper response. But the Katie I know, she doesn't do that. The Katie I know handles everything with kid gloves.

Katie closed the empty donut box and wiped sugar off her face. She tossed the box into the pizza place's trash can and went back to Krispy Kreme. The girl behind the counter smiled. "Back already?"

Katie smirked. "Hell, yeah! You know I can down the

damn donuts. Let me ask you a question. Do you like working here?"

The girl at the counter shrugged. "We're not demon-angel mercenaries saving the world or anything, but it's not a bad gig." Two more employees came from the back, cautiously peeking around a rack of donuts.

Katie wiggled her finger at the cashier. "How long have you guys known about me?"

One of the guys hiding behind the rack of donuts laughed. "Probably since the first time you came in here. Maybe the second time, after we saw you on the news."

The other guy chimed in, "We try to keep it on the DL for you, though, because we knew you wouldn't want to come in here to enjoy a dozen donuts around a whole bunch of people holding signs."

Katie clapped her hands. "I like you guys. Now, pack me up three dozen, and I'll be out of your way."

They went to work packing up three dozen assorted donuts, and Katie paid them quickly. She took two hundred dollars from her purse and stuffed it in the tip jar with a jaunty wink. Before she left, she flashed her eyes red. She heard the cashier gasp and call the guys over as the door shut behind her.

Pandora cleared her throat. *Are you going to answer me?*

If you want to know my heart, you have to promise to open yours.

Pandora sighed. *Well, fuck.*

5

"Did you pack up all the tablets from the guardhouse?" Calvin asked Joshua.

Joshua looked down his clipboard. "Yep. All packed."

"You're always on top of it, dude."

Calvin's phone buzzed in his pocket, and he pulled it out. The general's name flashed on the screen. He turned his back to the group and put the phone to his ear. "General, everything okay?"

The general walked to his office door and closed it. "Yeah, how's everything going over there?"

Calvin watched as several people carried boxes toward the helipad. "It's going. A little at a time but we're getting there."

"Good, good. And how are Korbin and Stephanie doing? I know they got their memories back, but how are they adjusting to the mercenary lifestyle?"

Calvin took in a deep breath and blew out his cheeks. "They're adjusting faster than I thought they would.

Korbin's kind of falling back into things, but he recognizes that it's been a while and things have changed. He's taking it one step at a time. He's using the consultants whenever he can and listening to us about our concerns. He's good about learning what we know about being mercenaries."

"That sounds promising. And how's Stephanie?"

Calvin chuckled. "Loving being a merc again."

The general sat down in his chair and leaned back, taking a pause. "I'm glad to hear it. I was actually wondering if you had a few minutes to chat?"

Calvin pointed to a group of men and directed them to the next item that needed to be loaded onto the plane. "About?"

The general didn't beat around the bush, just got straight to the point. "Katie."

Calvin pointed to Joshua and then to his phone. Joshua gave him a thumbs up, he had everything under control. Calvin walked away from the noise, putting one finger in his ear. "Okay, I'm all yours."

"Today was an interesting day. I got a call from the NYPD. There was a robbery, or I should say an attempted robbery. Katie took care of things before they had a chance to go downhill," the general explained.

"And that's a bad thing?"

The general chuckled. "No, it's just that the way she did it was a little bit odd. She was aggressive. Even brutal. She threatened a guard after the robbery was dealt with. I guess I'm kind of worried about Katie and the possibility of PTSD after her last fight."

Calvin was shocked, but he recovered. "She's been through a lot of tough things as a mercenary. It would surprise me if this was what broke her, but I guess I've seen stranger things."

The general shook his head. "I know that. I also know that I asked her to fight the Leviathan. Maybe I asked too much of her this time. I'm starting to think it might've been a mistake. She seems to have come back a bit changed."

Calvin sat quietly for a minute, thinking about the general's words. He had not touched base with Katie since she had finished that mission. "Changed how?"

The general put his fingers to his lips. "It's hard to explain. She's a lot harder. She's not the Katie I know."

Calvin considered carefully before responding. "It's still Katie. I've seen something like this a couple of times. Listen, I can talk to her, but I would have to go to New York to do it. It's not really a conversation I want to have over the phone."

The general grumbled, but he had to agree. "No, it's not a conversation you can have over the phone. At the same time, I need that base moved. The demons know where you are, and there's no concrete evidence to suggest they won't attack again, especially now that they know your weaknesses. That armory is what's going to keep us alive right now, and I can't have it taken by Moloch and his cronies, not after what I just saw."

Calvin could tell from the general's voice that he was extremely stressed. He softened his tone. "General, you trusted her to save the world, so why is this so much harder?"

"I don't know how to explain it. I guess I don't have an answer for you. Katie's become a very important person to me, both professionally and personally. I've never seen her act like the Katie I saw today on those tapes. I've only seen her act that way when Pandora takes over. To be honest, even Pandora didn't seem as rough-and-tumble as Katie looked today." The general hated to say it, but it was true.

Calvin looked at the others, remembering what it was like for him and Katie after Korbin and Stephanie had left the team. "General, I hate to hear that she's going through this and I can't be there. However, I've seen her ups and downs. I've seen the worst and the best, and I'm pretty sure she's going to be okay. Whatever happened between her and this Leviathan in hell, I'm sure it took a serious toll on her, but I don't think it broke her. Give her some time to come around. My guess is that Pandora is already working on her. If *you* noticed it, you can be damn sure Pandora did too."

The general nodded. "I appreciate you taking my call, Calvin, and I'll give your words some thought. Good luck with your move. If you need anything, let me know."

The general hung up, and Calvin stood there in the sand, watching one of the choppers take off. He hoped whatever was going on wasn't as bad as the general thought.

Katie stood in front of the mirror in her bedroom. She fastened the catch to a long dangling necklace and adjusted the pendant so that it sat in her cleavage. She swished her hair back and forth on her shoulders and tugged the edge of her miniskirt. Her tight black top stopped just above her midriff, and her skirt came up snugly right above her waist, leaving a little bit of flesh showing around the middle. Her breasts were pushed upward by a French lace bra that was a size too small.

Angie walked past her open door and glanced in, stopping in mid-stride. She let out a loud whistle and walked into the room with her hands on her hips. "Somebody's looking to score tonight!"

Katie laughed it off with a shake of her head. "Just felt like a little sex appeal was in order after being covered in soot and cuts."

"Well, you hit it right on the head."

Before Angie could turn away, Katie stopped her. "Angie, did I leave my keys here the other night? You know, the night I…" Katie paused, then continued, no matter how insane it sounded. "The night I went to hell and came back."

Angie furrowed her brow. "No, you always put your keys on your belt. You took them with you that night."

"That's what I was afraid of. I must've left them in the other dimension. Would you make me a new copy of the condo key?"

Angie chuckled. "Sure, though I don't think I'm going to tell the front desk that I need a new key because you left the other one in another dimension."

Katie smirked. "Probably a smart move."

Katie breezed through the condo to the front door, pausing when she realized Pandora hadn't said a single thing, not even one snarky comment about her sex appeal. She shrugged her shoulders and closed the door before taking the elevator downstairs. When she stepped off, the doorman was standing there with his hand out and a smile on his face. Katie let him take her hand and help her off the elevator. "You look lovely tonight."

Katie smiled. "And you know just what to say to the ladies."

The doorman led her to the concierge desk and then down the hallway. "I think it's best that you go out the side door tonight. Maybe we can keep from having another fight in the street."

Katie looked at him abashedly. "Sorry about that. Oh, do you think I could get a new set of keys?"

The doorman held up a set of keys for her. "Angie already called down."

Katie took the keys and nodded. "Sorry about losing the other ones, but I wouldn't worry about it. I don't think anyone's going to find them where I left them."

The doorman gave her a funny look as she walked outside. Almost everyone walking past eyed her, not because they recognized her but because of how hot she looked. She slid on her dark glasses and grabbed a cab. She was on her way to a nightclub, and she was really surprised Pandora hadn't asked yet where they were going. In fact, it was absolutely silent in her head.

When she reached the club, a bouncer took one look at her and her six-inch heels and immediately pulled the rope from the VIP section, welcoming her in. She didn't look at the hipsters waiting in line or the doorman, just walked straight up to the bar. The bartender stopped what he was doing and walked to her. "What can I get you?"

She kept her glasses on. "I'll take a whiskey on the rocks."

The bartender shot her with a finger-pistol and walked off. Katie turned and leaned against the bar, staring at all the people dancing and talking around the club. The bartender slid the glass across to her and inclined his head. "It's on the house."

She smiled and turned back to the crowd. *Look at these men. I'm going to play a game. Let's see. That one in the corner over there, with the tight jeans and tight black shirt. At first glance, I'd say he's at least an eight, but after you watch him for a while, it's obvious he hasn't gone shopping in about a decade. It's the same with the guy across from him. I give him longer since he's gone because he has a dragon on the back of his shirt. They haven't made those shirts since 1993.*

Pandora could hear everything she was saying, but it wasn't like Katie. Katie didn't seem to care that Pandora wasn't responding. She picked up her drink and walked across the room, standing on the edge of the dance floor. *Now, that guy, however, is definitely at least a 9.5. Those muscles are huge! Fuck it. I don't want to be here any longer than I have to, so why not make it an early night and grab him now?*

Pandora was torn. This was her scene, but she knew whatever was going on wasn't healthy. She wasn't going to let Katie go home with some random guy. She started to fight against Katie's movement toward him, making her struggle as she walked. *I don't think this is a good idea, Katie. It's not the night for that, and I can sense he's not worth it.*

Katie pouted. *But I want to get some!*

Do you really, or are you just being destructive? I think you should go home and think about this. I'm not trying to be Debbie Downer, but seriously, you're making some very drastic moves here. *You know me. I'm all about you getting laid, so you know that if* I'm *saying no, there has to be something to it.*

She stutter-stepped across the dance floor. Katie strained with all her might, but Pandora fought her to a standstill. *You want to fight me on this? I'll make you wet yourself.*

You wouldn't.

Try me.

Katie finally gave in and allowed Pandora to take her back across the club. She wasn't happy about it, though. *You're such a bitch. All you do is moan because I don't get any, but when I finally want to get a little sweaty, you throw a fit.*

Pandora got her out of the club and onto the sidewalk. *Trust me, you'll thank me for it in the morning.*

I really don't think I will. I think I'll be just as horny as I am now. You're a goddamned hypocrite. You can't push me to be who you want me to be and then pull back when I finally become her.

Pandora sighed. *All I'm saying is that you need to think about it. You're on some crazy streak right now, and I'm saving you from yourself. Stop being a damn asshole and just hail a cab.*

Katie stomped her foot. *You know what? Why don't you just take over? I'm going to sleep.*

With that, Katie's voice faded into the background, and Pandora found herself in the driver's seat. She looked down at her heaving breasts and shook her head. That hadn't been her intention, but if that was what it took to get her out of destructive mode, she wasn't going to complain about it.

I guess it's just me by myself now. That's fine. I need to think about some stuff anyway.

"Would you like another glass of wine?" the waitress asked Pandora.

Pandora gave her a kind smile. "Yes, please."

The waitress poured the wine into her glass and walked away, leaving Pandora alone. She was sitting in a cafe on the roof of the very tall building in the middle of town. She was right on the edge of the roof and could see the whole city, including the dark river to the east. She watched the specks of light from the boats, and her mind began to wander. Until that moment, Pandora had only focused on one thing—being a badass demon inside Katie.

Sitting there in the hot summer air watching the twinkling city lights, she began to wonder about her future, and she couldn't help worrying about Katie. Katie was only human, even if she did have angel DNA and a demon inside her. If Pandora didn't have Katie, she couldn't go back home to hell. She was too different now. She'd changed.

Pandora took a sip of wine and sat back in her chair, listening to the conversations around her. People were talking about business, relationships, and everything else normal human beings would talk about in a rooftop restaurant late at night. It was almost refreshing to Pandora. In fact, she was so lost in her thoughts that when she heard the voice next to her, it made her jump in her chair.

"May I sit with you?"

6

Pandora turned and found herself looking at a silver belt buckle. *Interesting.* She ran her eyes up the man's body, which included a flat stomach and a broad chest under a white shirt and suit coat. His shoulders bulged under the coat. On top of it all was Gabriel's smiling face. *Aw, shit.*

He was wearing a bright silver tie that almost perfectly matched his hair, which was pulled back into a ponytail. His shimmering blue eyes let her know he meant her no harm.

Pandora gestured at a chair across from her. "If you must."

Gabriel sat down. "Good to see you, Pandora."

Pandora took a sip of her wine and lifted a skeptical eyebrow. "Is it?"

Gabriel waved his hand, making it so no one around them could hear their conversation. He smiled at her, staring with his penetrating angelic eyes. "Yes. It's not every day that I'm surprised."

Pandora tilted her head. "It didn't use to be for me, either, but I find myself shocked more and more. What did I do to surprise you?"

"You had an opportunity to stay in hell."

Pandora barked out laughter. "You saw that, did you?"

Gabriel picked up an empty glass in front of him. By the time it reached his lips, it was filled with water. "No, but I was told about it. I'm not omniscient."

Pandora snorted, not at all impressed by his magic tricks. "When has that stopped you from assuming what happened?"

Gabriel shrugged his shoulders slightly. The waiter smiled as she came over, and Pandora quickly tipped back her glass, finishing her wine. "I'll have another. One for my guest as well, please."

"Right away." The waitress hurried away.

Pandora glanced at Gabriel. "Unless you want to transform your water into cabernet?"

"That wasn't me."

"Oh, right. It's been a while since I read anything. They have movies here. Very exciting."

Gabriel nodded calmly. "Where is Katie?"

Pandora snorted. "Sleeping off a bender, believe it or not. I made her leave a club, and she threw a hissy fit. She just gave up and told me to take over. Before I knew it, she was fast asleep. If I hadn't been paying attention, we would have face-planted right there on the concrete. I wasn't ready to go home, so I came here for a nice glass of wine and some peace and quiet. Apparently peace and quiet are in short fucking supply."

Gabriel ignored her last line. "This is a lovely restaurant. The view is absolutely gorgeous. I'm surprised to see you in a place like this. I would have assumed you would still be at the club, doing whatever it is that you do."

Pandora smirked. "You know what it is I do."

The waitress came back over and poured two glasses of wine. Gabriel thanked her and lifted the glass to his lips to take a sip. He closed his eyes as he swished it around and swallowed. "Good stuff. You always knew your reds and whites."

Pandora shrugged. "After all the time I've spent here, I should know the good from the bad." Gabriel smirked at her and Pandora cut her eyes at him. "Wine-wise, at least."

Gabriel set his glass down. "Michael asked me to tell you hello."

Pandora snorted. "You can tell him to go fuck himself."

Gabriel chuckled. "That was the expected response. It seems you know how to hold a grudge."

Pandora snorted, exasperated. "It's only been ten thousand years, give or take a few. What does he expect?"

Gabriel shrugged, not thrown off by Pandora's outburst. "Not much, really. He just wanted me to pass along his greeting."

"Greeting received and reply given." Pandora gave him a side glance. "You done here then?"

The two of them sat there for several minutes, not saying a word to each other. Pandora took in the dark skyline, all kinds of thoughts running through her head. She was in a strange place, not physically but mentally. She quite simply was not herself. It was apparently going around.

Finally, she looked him straight in the eyes. "Gabriel, when did this become too much?"

Gabriel pursed his lips. He could tell she didn't expect an answer, so he allowed it to slide. He could see in Pandora's eyes that she was struggling with something, but she wasn't ready to admit it to him. A crisis of conscience wasn't something that usually happened to a demon. She lost herself in her glass of wine for a moment, and finally just asked the question. "What's wrong with her? And I don't mean what's wrong with her, as in she's infected with a demon or that she has angel DNA, but how did she change so quickly? One minute, she's the Katie I know, the one I'm trying to talk onto the wild side. The next minute, I'm trying to pull her back from the edge so she doesn't jump off a cliff."

Gabriel waited calmly, knowing she wasn't done speaking.

She set her glass down and rubbed her hands over her face. "She's acting out of character. Hell, she was grading studly men tonight. It took everything I had to stop her from jumping one right there on the dance floor. She was like a completely different person. The way she spoke to me was so odd. I hate to say it, but it was like I was talking to myself, only she gave zero fucks. Sometimes, albeit rarely, I actually do give a fuck. Shit, at least when it comes to *her*, I give a fuck. She's the girl who gives a fuck about everything and everyone, but tonight she was ready to take on whoever would take her."

Gabriel gave her a surprised look. "And you did not

encourage that?"

Pandora agreed. "Usually I would have, sure. But this was unusual. She's been acting all weird since we fought Tiamat in hell. Since she came back, it's like she's trying to be me."

Gabriel hid a smirk. "As if."

"I know, right? Seriously, do you know what's wrong with her?"

Gabriel took a sip of his wine and nodded.

Pandora looked surprised and leaned toward him. "Well, what the fuck is it?"

Gabriel set down his wine and steepled his fingers in front of his face. "She's willing to tell you."

Pandora sneered at him. "Yeah, but she expects something from me."

"You know what I think?"

She finished her wine and set the glass down hard on the table. "No, but I'm sure you're gonna tell me."

Gabriel chuckled. "I think for the first time in thousands and thousands of years, you're feeling again."

Pandora huffed. "Oh, fuck you. It isn't about feeling."

She stopped. She could tell that he was baiting her, and he could tell that he was starting to get to her. She wasn't going to give in to the feelings Gabriel wanted her to have. "I'll deal with it. If you have another message, I'll pass it along. If not, scram."

Gabriel took another sip of his wine and shrugged. "Can't I just want to chat with you for a moment?"

Pandora scoffed. "You could, but we both know that isn't how your schedule works. We also both know that's not how *you* work."

Gabriel nodded. "Most of the time I'd agree, but I was heading to Canada when I noticed you here. I couldn't let you sit here all alone. You looked so contemplative. I thought I'd come down and have a glass of wine with an old friend."

Pandora rolled her eyes. "Right. An old friend, sure. What you mean to say is that you're keeping tabs on me because… Well, we both know why."

Gabriel feigned shock. "What? You? Lucifer's wife? Why would you ever think that?"

Pandora grumbled, "I'm divorcing that asshole."

"I mean, I'm no expert on hell or how its legal system works, but is that even possible?"

"Usually it only takes a kick to the balls, but I'll settle for someone serving him with papers. I'd rather not go back and have a personal discussion with him. He isn't the most logical person to talk to, as you can probably imagine. Nor is his temper conducive to a conversation like that."

"Yeah, I guess he might be a little pissed."

Pandora shrugged. "He's probably replaced me with five others."

Gabriel cleared his throat. "Twelve."

Slowly, Pandora looked at Gabriel, her eyes wide. "*Twelve?* Damn, I'm worth twelve hos? I mean, he's a total asshole—and most of them were probably around before I was gone—but I thought that a half a dozen was pushing it. Shit. He liked me a little bit more than I thought, even with all his extra fiery soul-whores rolling through the kingdom every night. Maybe I should be impressed with myself."

"Maybe."

Pandora smiled. "Okay, do your angel business. I have

to think this through. Once out the lips, I can't take it back."

Gabriel looked at her with a smug face. "Worried?"

"Yeah, I am." Pandora looked away from him as she said it.

Gabriel scoffed. "I've seen you stare Michael down and call him names he had to go look up later. I mean, there were words I didn't even know. I'm pretty sure they made the big guy blush. And the fact that I had to sit in a room with Michael while he looked them up was absolutely mortifying. I wanted to wash my brain afterward and forget everything. Sometimes I wonder how demons and humans come up with this stuff."

Pandora snickered. "That was funny as hell."

"For you to tell me you're worried really surprises me. I've never seen you worried about anything in your life. Well, maybe your shoes or your clothes, but definitely not another person or an angel or anything in between. You are Lilith, the Queen of the Damned, Lucifer's wife, the keeper of the bodies, the tour guide to hell."

Pandora leaned forward and whispered, "Did you know that she pulled me out of her in hell? She totally turned to me and told me to do whatever needed to be done. She knew I was a demon, Gabriel. I am the Queen of hell, and she brought me there and collapsed. Left herself to my mercy."

Gabriel didn't seem surprised, but he still asked the question. "How did she get back here?"

"Me, of course. It seems I love donuts too much to stay in hell."

Gabriel took one last sip of his wine and stood up. He

put his hands on the back of his chair. "You keep telling
yourself that, and someday you might believe it. When you
get a chance, tell Katie I have something for her."

"Another riddle?"

Gabriel smiled. "Hardly. But if I told you, then you
wouldn't have a reason to bitch about angels so harshly."

"Try me," she retorted.

His lips curled, and he shook his head. "See you around,
Pandora."

Pandora gave him a half-smile. "You too, Gabe."

Pandora watched Gabriel walk away, then she was
alone in the crowded restaurant, surrounded by all those
innocent faces. She knew she was using the word "innocent" lightly, but they were nothing like the demons she
knew or the souls that had been trapped in hell. Her
thoughts wavered between her former home and everything that had happened.

She thought about the fight with Tiamat, and how
much Katie had trusted her. She replayed the scene over
and over in her head. Katie had pulled her from her body,
given Pandora her own form, and trusted her not to
abandon her there in hell. Pandora wasn't even sure what
had come over her, but when she'd looked down at Katie's
body, she knew she wasn't done with the woman. She
wasn't done with that adventure. It had turned into more
than an adventure for her, and whether she wanted to
admit it to Gabriel or not, she *was* feeling things again.

The waitress walked over to the table, bringing Pandora's attention back. "No more wine for me, thank you. I'll
take the bill."

"I'm sorry, ma'am, but the gentleman paid it already. Including a very nice tip."

"Of course he did." Pandora rolled her eyes. "That ass."

The waitress giggled before walking away from the table. Pandora smirked, took off her glasses, and stuck them in her cleavage. It had been one hell of a night, and she knew she couldn't let it end by walking nonchalantly out of the restaurant. After all, she was Pandora, and Pandora always went out with a bang.

She bit her lip, grabbed a spoon, and tapped her wine glass with it. She stood and tapped harder, grabbing the attention of the entire restaurant. When they had quieted down and were staring at her, she smiled at them. She reveled in their gaze, slowly putting the spoon back on the table and milking the tension for all it was worth. "Hey, just wanted to make sure you all get to see something you don't see every night."

With that, she stepped onto the ledge of the building and leaped off. She heard a collective gasp and someone screaming behind her as she plummeted. She wanted her audience. Once the crowd had made it to the edge of the building, Pandora opened her wings wide. They flapped up and down, sending a whoosh of air back up toward the crowd. A round of applause and whistles erupted from above her as she headed toward the river and into the darkness.

She always did like a fucking audience, and humans were so damn impressed by the little things.

Pandora chuckled and shook her head as she glided between the buildings. "Momma still has it."

7

Katie rolled over in bed and uttered an acrid groan. Her lips smacked together. She wiped her hand across her cheek, streaking makeup and drool, the remnants of her deep, dreamless night. She opened one eye and looked around, not really sure what she would find. She couldn't remember anything from the night before. She had been forced from the club, and then nothing. She had definitely been wasted. She'd only had one drink at the club, but while getting ready she had helped herself to four glasses of wine, three beers, and three shots of whiskey.

Well, I seem to be alone. There's no soreness in any region of my body, so I know I didn't have some hot and sweaty orgy.

Katie waited for a sarcastic reaction from Pandora, but nothing came. Apparently, Pandora was still asleep inside her. *Hell must have frozen over.*

Slowly, she stretched her arms high over her head. The morning light was cascading into her room, and the smell of cooking bacon drifted in from the kitchen. She sat up, waiting for the inevitable throb from deep in her head that signaled a truly hellish hangover, but the pounding didn't come. She only wobbled in bed. Not hungover, then, but not sober, either. She put her hand down on the bed to stabilize the spinning. "I need to slow the hell down before I fall out of this bed and break something. I don't think I've drunk that much—ever."

Still nothing from Pandora.

Katie shrugged and walked to the mirror, where she grimaced at her reflection. The remnants of her dark makeup were now streaked down her cheeks, and her hair was twisted into some sort of matted beehive. She half-expected a small furry animal to stick its head out. Katie shook her head at her reflection and pointed at herself. "Get it together, bitch. Shower and food, then we can figure out what's next...like not standing alone in my room talking to myself."

Katie turned the shower to scalding hot and slipped out of her lace panties and bra. She almost sank into the stone walls as the hot water ran over her. Cloudy water ran around her feet as she lathered up and washed away what she assumed was a collection of embarrassing moments from the night before.

She tried to ignore the feeling of loneliness in her chest without Pandora there to chide her and push her along.

You know, even if you're not going to respond, I'm going to talk. What good is having a demon inside me if I can't have a conversation?

Nothing. Just silence. Katie climbed out of the shower and stared at herself in the mirror. She bounced up and down for a moment, trying to get a response. Any response. *Maybe I should have a breast reduction.*

She lifted her eyebrows and smiled, thinking that would for sure get her demon's attention. After a couple of moments of silence, Katie sighed and dropped her hands to her sides. *Fine, whatever. I don't need someone else in my head all the time. I can be on my own.*

Katie brushed out her hair and pulled it back into a messy ponytail. She rummaged through her drawers until she found a comfy pair of old sweatpants and a Las Vegas T-shirt from back in her college days. The smell of coffee wafted to her nose, and her stomach grumbled. She made her way out of the bedroom and shuffled into the kitchen, where Angie was standing in front of the stove finishing up breakfast.

Katie plopped down at the table, her wet ponytail dripping down her back. Angie looked at her with a smile. "I barely heard you come in last night. Did you have fun?"

"I guess. To be honest, I don't remember a lot about it. I was drunk and got into a fight with Pandora pretty early in the evening. I just let her take over. I passed out after that, nice and comfortable in the dark abyss inside my own body."

Angie plated the eggs and bacon and looked at Katie with surprise. "But you didn't get in until really late. What did Pandora do?"

Katie shrugged. "I have no clue. She's not talking to me right now. I think she's still asleep, but she could just be shutting me out."

Angie giggled and poured their coffee. "I had two little sisters growing up. They annoyed the hell out of me. I can't imagine walking around with one of them in my mind. No matter how much I love them, I need my space."

Katie shoved a piece of bacon in her mouth. "I used to feel that way, but I won't lie, it's a little weird in my brain without her yammering on about food."

Angie gave her a comforting smile. "I'm sure. You know, everyone needs a sleepy day once in a while. I'm sure she'll be up and jamming your frequencies in no time. For now, though, we can talk about life. The project is still full speed ahead, and I got a call from Calvin saying the move is right on schedule."

"Oh good. I almost forgot about all of that. My trip to hell and everything kind of threw me for a loop. I think it was the oppressive heat. Or it could have simply been me hitting my head when I passed out."

Angie wrinkled her nose. "You need to get that looked at?"

Katie tapped her head. "Nah. Remember, I have my own personal MD inside. She fixes anything that has gone awry, or at least she does when she's awake."

I'm awake, Pandora responded quietly.

Holy hell, you live! What did you do last night, fly all over the city? I've never seen you sleep later than me.

Pandora's voice lacked any emotion. *I was up late with my thoughts, that's all.*

Do you feel better now? Katie looked at Angie and nodded to let her know Pandora was up and around.

I do. I think we need to talk, though.

Katie couldn't help feeling nervous. It was like a boyfriend telling her they needed to talk—never a good sign. *Sure. You mind if I finish my breakfast and conversation with Angie?*

Nope, not at all. The bacon is hella tasty today.

Katie glanced at Angie. "Pandora says you did a good job on the bacon."

Angie laughed. "Oh, you know, I take my time slaughtering and butchering my own pigs."

Katie raised an eyebrow at her. "You pick up a new hobby?"

Angie shook her head, rolling her eyes. "Man, you *are* off. I was kidding. Thank Hormel for packaging it and putting it in the supermarket. All I did was throw it in a pan."

Katie chuckled abashedly. "Sorry. Not sure why I thought you had opened a slaughterhouse. It's been a long couple of weeks."

Angie picked up their empty plates. "I know it has been, at least for you. I'll take care of all the lingering details and contact you if I need an answer to anything. You go do whatever it is you do. Try to relax. Get your mind straight. It's just as important as physically being there."

Katie finished her coffee and handed Angie the mug. "I will. Thanks for breakfast. I'm probably going to head out for a bit. I have my backup cell, so you know how to reach me."

Angie nodded. "Yep. I got ya, girl."

Katie walked back toward her room so she could get changed. *I'm assuming we aren't having a leisurely talk in the bedroom. What's the attire?*

Get dressed for success, and that means the big guns too. Those boys haven't been out in a while.

Katie clapped her hands together excitedly. *Yes! Tom and Harry have been stuck in the drawer for far too long.*

Pandora snickered. *Nobody puts Harry in the corner.*

Katie paused as she pulled out her spandex outfit. *Nice reference!*

I've been working on it. Pop culture is all the rage now, apparently.

That it is, my fiery devil friend. Katie chuckled and pulled on her outfit, straightening the bust and noticing the top was a bit tighter.

Pandora giggled. *I heard you this morning, so I decided to move you up a quarter of a cup size. Don't joke about the titties, dude. That's sacred territory.*

Noted. Katie smiled.

She pulled Tom and Harry from the drawer and carefully slid them into their holsters, tightening her straps. *I forgot how heavy these bad boys were.*

Worth the weight.

She pulled her hair back in a tight ponytail and walked to her balcony doors, taking a step out into the cool morning air. She leaped off the balcony as easily as she would step off a street corner, spreading her wings.

"Katie, we love you," several people yelled from below.

Katie smiled and began flapping her wings, soaring high above the buildings and the city. People ran to windows in the skyscrapers, waving and gawking as she flew by. She took a sharp right and dove, skimming just above the water of the river. People on the running trails and in small boats pointed and took pictures as she hovered over the water.

Pandora spoke softly in Katie's mind. *You know, I once*

thought everyone bowing down to me was the emotional connection I needed.

Really? I mean, it's not that big of a surprise. I always assumed that those things were changing. Do you still feel like that?

I have my moments, I guess.

What's different?

Pandora took a moment to think about it as Katie blew past a couple of boats and arced higher into the air. *I've been alive for a very long time. In that time, I've met a lot of different people, some good and some not. There were times in the past that I sought love. I looked for it from both men and friendships.*

Katie was surprised. *Then you do know what it means to love someone.*

I thought I did. But now that I look back, I don't think any of them ever really loved me. It was infatuation. Lust, even. None of it was pure love, the kind where you would give up anything for the other person. I hear a mother's love is like that, and I know there are higher beings who have that kind of love, but no one close to me.

Katie was saddened by this revelation. She realized that she had never thought about the concept of love in connection with Pandora. Katie spent so much time focusing on the fact that she was a demon, she'd just assumed Pandora never cared about the love of strangers.

Pandora chuckled. *Imagine my surprise when I'm down in the bowels of hell, my bastion of power and authority, and an angel pulls me out and gives me my freedom! And then asks me to save her. I'm a goddamned demon, Katie. But you told me to do what I wanted with you.*

Katie stayed silent, not really sure what to say. This was a light bulb moment for her, an emotional moment that Katie hadn't seen before. She didn't want to scare Pandora away from it. She wanted her to get out what was in her head and her heart. Katie knew it might not ever happen again. Pandora had held this inside for so long that it had taken action on Katie's part for her to finally open up.

Pandora had finally said fuck it. She wasn't going to hold onto it forever.

Pandora stayed silent as they soared past the bridge and over the cars honking and creeping toward the city. *You told me to do whatever I wanted, and I defied everything about being a demon. I surprised myself, but not at that moment. At that moment, there was no question. I picked you up and saved your life. It wasn't because I couldn't stay in hell, or because I was afraid to be there alone. I'm a badass bitch who can take care of my own.*

Amen to that. Katie smiled.

I don't know how exactly to explain it to you. There wasn't a second thought. I simply couldn't let you die down there. I couldn't give those two morons what they wanted, sure. But it was more than that.

Katie made her way to the Statue of Liberty, waving at the tourists on the boats as she approached the grand woman holding the torch. She spiraled all the way to the top and landed for a moment on the statue's crown. She crouched and watched as the sun sparkled over the water, looking one way toward the crowded metropolis and the other toward New Jersey and beyond.

Pandora blew the air from her lungs. *It's damn beautiful*

out here. I remember when they put this statue up. There was barely a skyline to look at. Everything changes so fast.

For Katie, the view was a representation of her life before Pandora and after. Although up here it was open and quiet, if you looked closely, there was garbage and turmoil. After, the city was filled with craziness, people, excitement, and lights. It was overwhelming at times, but when the seasons changed, the sun set, and calmness fell over the twinkling lights of the buildings, it was the perfect place for her. It was her sanctuary. It was home, and that was something she hadn't had in a long time.

When she woke up that morning and Pandora wasn't speaking to her, things weren't right. So in a way, Katie knew what Pandora was saying without having to hear an explanation. She had spent a long time not only with this woman in her head but even more importantly, with this woman having her back at almost every turn, no matter what.

Katie cleared her throat and stood up, feeling the wind on her face. *You see all those people down there? Some are tourists, some are New Yorkers, and others are just passing through. They all have something strong and vibrant in their lives. They all have something that pushes them. I have someone who pushes me. You do, every single day of my life. I wanted to pay that back, show appreciation, and stop fighting you so damned hard on every single thing. I wanted to give you everything you gave me.*

What?

I wanted to give you something for doing what you did. You want guys, so I went out to find them. I was going to find the best dick I could to fill you.

Pandora cackled loudly. *You were paying me back with dick?*

Katie blushed. *Well, it's either sex or donuts, and I tried cramming in five dozen as a start. I figured sex was next, and who knew what else? You not only saved me, but you chose to stay with me. I've never been wanted that badly by anyone, Pandora. Only my mom, and she doesn't count because she's my mom.*

Pandora couldn't believe she was letting it all out, but since it was on the tip of her tongue, she knew it just needed to roll. *Katie, I got thrown out of heaven for wanting something I couldn't have. I was forsaken because of a soul that was breaking. I was told that hell wasn't my place, but I knew heaven wasn't either. I felt like I was sailing the sea with nowhere to land, searching for something I couldn't find. Something I couldn't even name.*

Believe it or not, minus the hell and heaven thing, that's not uncommon for us mortals either. We tend to spend our whole lives stumbling from one fuckup to the next. Some of us meet that person who changes it for us, but the rest continue to stumble until the end.

Pandora listened. She realized she was a lot more like humans than she liked to admit. *You know what they told me after I left heaven? They said God cried storms into existence when I left.*

Thanks for that.

Pandora smirked. *The thing is, we all have determination, and I needed to see and feel more than my role in heaven. How are you supposed to be that good and that pure if you don't understand why you're doing it? I've spent over ten thousand years roaming to find the acceptance you gave me. Your strength, your honor, and your loyalty are beyond any relationship I have ever experienced. At first, I thought it was the angel in you, but then I realized it was just who you were. That touched me from the beginning, and not in the gropy way I was used to. I was just me, and you were just you, and that was enough.*

Tears were streaming down Katie's cheeks. They slid off her chin and cascaded over the side of the statue and down into the water below. Ripples of blue angel magic shimmered in the river every time a tear dropped in.

Katie wiped her cheeks and stood up, letting the wind whip around her.

Pandora sent a comforting feeling through Katie's body, almost as if she were hugging her from the inside. *You are my sister, Katie. When you freed me, I chose to come back to you. I guess that means we're together forever.*

Katie's lips curled into a half-smile, remembering what Pandora had said when they were in hell. *I so swear it.*

Just then, a huge flash of lightning blasted through the sky, and the frightened screams of tourists below filled the air. Katie lifted an eyebrow and looked around. *Pandora, there aren't any clouds.*

8

Pandora sighed. *I'm glad we talked.*

Me too. Now that the mush fest is over, I figured we could take a little swoop-swoop around New York to find out what's going on in the Big Apple today.

Pandora wrinkled her nose. *More angel crimefighting, I suppose. I guess you're feeling better.*

Katie smirked. *A thousand times better, both physically and mentally. And shit, I'm glad I don't have to go out tonight searching for tail.*

Whoa, whoa. I laughed, but repaying a debt with dick isn't the worst idea you've ever had, sister.

Katie turned down Broadway but stayed high above the buildings. *Yeah, let's just say you loved me when I was sensible, so you'll still love me when I say no.*

Pandora grumped. *I knew it was a bad idea to say anything. Now I gotta go back to coercion. That's fine. You asked for it.*

Katie laughed and shook her head. *It's good to see things are as they should be.*

Pandora agreed. *Speaking of being back to normal, what's going on one street over? That's like three cop cars heading somewhere at high speed.*

Katie hovered for a moment, looking down each cross street as she passed. She took a quick left and tucked her wings slightly to avoid hitting the windows on either side of the narrow street. She glided gracefully around the corner and looked ahead, keeping to a normal speed to see what was going on.

Sure enough, rolling fast down the street ahead of her were three cop cars, their lights flashing and sirens blaring. Pandora was excited. She was tired of the bullshit, and it had been days since they'd seen any real action that didn't involve their own sad feelings. She may have opened up once, but that was going to be the extent of her emotional outbursts for a while. *Hot damn, we gots ourselves a real-life car chase.*

Katie sighed. *I don't ever want you to use that accent again. You sound like a cross between a Southerner and an Irishman. I'm not Southern, but I'm offended.*

Pandora ignored her and continued with her accent. *Come on, little lady. Pick up that pace. Move that ass. We gots tractors that move faster than you.*

Katie rolled her eyes and flapped faster. Ahead of the cops was a car flying down the street, barely missing pedestrians, cars, and anything else stupid enough to be outside. It looked like someone was hanging out the passenger-side window.

Katie swooped lower and picked up a bit more speed,

flying right on the cops' tail. *I need a closer look. I think they're doing something in that lead car, but I can't quite make it— Whoa!*

A bullet whizzed past Katie's shoulder and took a couple of feathers off her wings. Pandora growled. *Oh no, he did not! Motherfucker almost hit my wings. Let me have him. He won't have a hand to shoot with or a dick to piss with by the time I'm done with him.*

He's shooting at the cops, but shit if he isn't going to hit someone on the streets. Remember, we can't go off half-cocked.

I know. I'll rip his whole dick off.

You know what I mean. Playing the loose cannon didn't go too well for me at the bank, and now that I'm over impressing you...

Oh, I get it. We have one talk, and now it's back to pissin' on my parade.

At that point, Katie was no longer listening. Another round of shots rang out below, and the cop in the lead lost control of his car, ramming straight into one of the buildings. Katie's eyes flashed red. She folded her wings and went in for the kill.

The two remaining police cruisers followed the runaway. The new lead officer called in the accident. "Dispatch, this is One Adam Six. I've got a 902, officer involved, crashed into the Vietnamese restaurant on Erwin and Main. Can you send an ambulance? We're still chasing the suspect."

"Hold one. We have several calls coming in from that area," dispatch replied.

The cop in the passenger seat, Drew Whitfield, began waving his hands wildly. "Left! Watch out for the puppy!"

Jason started swerving left and then right. "What about the old lady?"

Drew shook his head, his emotions heightened. "Fuck the old lady. She's had eighty years. That should be good enough. That puppy just started to see the beauty of goddamned life here. So help me, if that bastard gets that puppy run over, you're gonna have a homicide on your hands, and I'll have blood on mine."

Jason chuckled, shaking his head. "Drew, you need to work on your empathy. People are people, too. I'm pretty sure they told you that in school. And again at that special school they sent you to after the incident involving the pig and the farmer."

Drew snapped his head toward Jason. "Hey, that farmer got himself out from under the tractor just fine. That piglet was trapped in the field, and his bacon would have been splattered everywhere if it weren't for me. Piglets are smarter than dogs, you know."

Jason laughed. "I have to be the only motherfucker stuck in a high-speed chase with Dr. Dolittle."

Drew ignored his comment and picked up the radio. "Dispatch, are you out there? This is One Adam Six. We have a car down. Suspects are fleeing north on— *Holy shit!*"

A body plummeted from the sky, wings wide. The cops slammed on their brakes, trying to keep the car under control. Katie slammed into the hood of the assailant's car feet-first, stopping the car in its tracks. The tail end flew up and then crashed back down, showering the street in broken glass. Jason grabbed the wheel and swerved to the side, coming to a complete stop.

"What the hell did she just..." Drew pressed his face against the windshield, his hat having fallen off.

"Was that a she? That was one fucking powerful *she*." Jason gaped at her.

"You don't see those huge tits and that tiny waist? Yes, that's a fucking she. That's Katie," Drew replied, not taking his eyes off her.

The assailant in the passenger seat hung out the window and cursed the driver. "Go! Go! Fucking go!" He screamed with joy as the driver slammed his foot on the gas, shocked when the car started moving again. It sputtered and smoked, but they crawled away from the police. Katie launched herself into the air, rolling into a ball and dodging as bullets cut the air around her. She swooped right and left with a huge smile on her face.

"What the hell is she gonna do now?" Drew asked.

Jason couldn't turn away. He couldn't blink, and he could barely move his lips to answer. "Fuck if I know, but I don't think she's too happy about being shot at."

Drew slowly looked at Jason. "She has fucking wings, and she's a human."

Jason slapped him on the shoulder. "If she needed saving I'd say she was right up your alley, but she's the chick who does the rescuing."

Drew looked at Katie as she rose high into the sky. "She can save me any fucking day of the week."

Katie looked down at the assailants, who were still firing at her. The bullets whizzed around her, but she paid them no mind. Instead, she bared her teeth and extended her hand, summoning her sword. Onlookers were momentarily blinded by the huge flash of light as her angelic sword appeared in her hand.

Her eyes flashed red. "Oh, boys, you picked the wrong street on the wrong day."

Get 'em, Momma, Pandora yelled.

Katie gripped the sword with both hands and turned the blade down. Her wings folded behind her and she dove, moving faster than anyone could see. She slammed into the car at full speed.

A ring of raw energy exploded from the point of impact. The cops held on tight as their car rattled and slid backward. Windows within the radius of the energy ring burst, showering the street with glass.

The angelic sword cut the runaway car completely in two. Katie stood behind the halved car, her blade embedded in the street.

Drew and Jason were absolutely silent as the woman yanked her sword out of the blacktop. She sheathed it, jumped into the air and turned, her wings catching air. Her eyes were shining brightly, and her lips were curved into a malicious smile. The assailants hunkered in their ruined car. Cockeyed headlights lit the buildings on either side of the street.

"What's your status, One Adam Six?" The voice of the dispatcher crackled.

Drew grabbed the radio, still staring at Katie. "You won't believe this, but Katie just came out of the sky and went all Thor on their asses. The car has stopped, and she's walking toward it. We better get over there, or we might not have suspects."

Drew, Jason, and the other two cops drew their weapons and began to walk over. Katie drifted lazily to the ground and went to the car. She pulled the drivers-side door off and grabbed the guy by the throat, lifting him from the car.

Katie looked at the guy, her narrowed eyes red. "You could have killed that fucking puppy back there."

Drew snapped his head toward Jason. "See? I told you. I am not the only one."

Meanwhile, the passenger stupidly reached into the console and pulled out a massive revolver.

Katie's eyes flashed, and she dropped to the ground with her prisoner as the passenger began firing wildly in her direction. Katie put the tip of her boot in front of her prisoner's crotch and hissed, "Move an inch, and you won't have your manhood in prison, my friend."

She launched herself high, flipping over the halved car and landing on the ground in front of the passenger door. She ripped the door off and threw it behind her before reaching inside and grabbing the passenger. She dangled him three feet in the air. The guy whimpered for a second, then snarled and shoved his gun at her and pulled the trigger over and over. His revolver just clicked, spent. Katie snatched it from his hands.

She looked at the pistol and tossed it toward the cops before grabbing Tom from her waistband. "You think you're a big man with a gun? Well, I'm a small bitch with a very, *very* big gun."

The passenger put his hands up and swallowed hard, closing his eyes. Katie smirked and grabbed both of his hands in one of hers. She flapped her wings and lifted him,

MICHAEL TODD

crossing back over the steaming car and landing next to the other criminal. She dropped the passenger on top of his teammate and landed in front of them, and her eyes glowed red as she drew her other gun.

Immediately, the two of them scrambled to their feet and ran toward the cops. They screamed like little girls. "Save us!"

Katie laughed and nodded at the cops as they cuffed the guys, and flew away.

Katie put her feet up on the chair across from her and folded a piece of sausage pizza in half. She took a big bite and set it down, the grease dribbling down her chin. Pandora groaned, smelling the donuts just a foot away. *You could at least have some fucking manners and wipe your damn chin.*

Katie grabbed the napkin. *Can't you see I'm busy here? Who would have thought? I come in here in full getup, and they give me pizza on the house?*

Pandora scoffed. *Yeah, because they're afraid of your ass.*

Nah, they just appreciate my service to their city.

And they're scared of you.

Katie glanced back at the counter toward the two guys watching her nervously. *Okay, and they're scared of me.*

You don't even like *pizza. Why aren't you eating the donuts?*

Katie frowned. *I like pizza. I'm just usually trying to get you to stop bitching. It's all dicks and balls and murder until I shove a donut in your mouth. This time you can wait a hot minute.*

The door to the pizza place opened, and Detectives Shultz and Travers walked in. Pandora groaned. *Great, now they're going to take up valuable donut-eating time. You better not stop eating just because they're here.*

Calm down, Satan. I got this.

Pandora snorted. *As if. I would not be in this dive if I were Satan. I'd be franchising Krispy Kremes in hell.*

It would take some damn strong air conditioning to keep them from melting. Katie looked at the detectives and smiled, taking her feet off the chair.

"Hey, guys! Have a seat."

Schultz looked skeptical, but the two men sat down in front of her. She wiped her hands on the napkins and slid a dozen donuts across the table. "I got you guys a twelve-pack to take back to the office. Figured the other guys would appreciate it."

Travers nodded excitedly, but Schultz remained impartial. "Katie…"

Katie put her hands up and sat up straight in the chair. "Look, I know. But seriously! There was no way I was dicking around at the accident. I attract way too much attention. I figured you would find me here, so here I am."

Schultz relaxed and chuckled, shaking his head. "We know. You did a good job. Maybe a little less rough next time, but good job."

Travers shrugged. "I think those sons of bitches got what they had coming to them. Our guy will be in the hospital for a week. Concussion, broken leg, and luckily, that Vietnamese restaurant was closed for renovations."

Katie grimaced. "Gonna need a lot more renovations than they originally thought."

Travers waved his hand. "They got insurance."

Schultz slid a piece of paper across the table along with a pen. "You know the drill. Write your statement and sign the bottom."

As she wrote, Katie noisily chewed her pizza. She re-read her statement and waved the pen at them. "You know, we can find a more efficient way of getting my information."

Schultz raised a brow. "Yeah?"

Katie finished signing her name and pushed her statement to the detective. "Oh, for sure. I mean, my guy came up with a whole system to detect portals before they open. You don't think we could figure out something as easy as getting this info without a face to face? Shit, a cell phone could probably solve that problem. I can fax you a fucking John Hancock."

Schultz laughed. "Better yet, we could get a stamp made of your signature and just stamp the fax."

Katie wiped pizza grease from her lips and nodded. "I like the way you think, detective. Work smarter, not harder. Now I just gotta figure out how to implement that theory in my work. Some kind of criminal-catching magic with a wave of my finger."

Pandora cackled. *We're an angel-demon, not Harry Fucking Potter.*

Travers reached over and grabbed a donut. "But how does that get us out of the precinct building and into a donut shop?"

"Touché, my friend." Katie laughed, pointing at Travers.

"We could make it a payment for every time you make us contact you for a statement. You just fly through with boxes of donuts attached to tiny parachutes. We'll come outside and grab 'em." Travers was obviously happy with his plan, but Schultz just stared at him.

Schultz turned back to Katie. "Like cops don't get enough hell with the donut stigma. All we need is a picture of it raining fucking Krispy Kremes over the precinct. We'll never live it down."

Katie picked up a donut and shook it at Schultz. "Yeah, but you'll be the ones with Krispy Kremes. Bet you a thousand bucks that other cops start sending me tips on things happening around the City. They may hate on you, but they won't hate on the free donuts."

Pandora gasped. *We could put our superhero symbol on the parachutes.*

We don't have a superhero symbol.

Pandora scoffed. *Please, like that would be the toughest thing to come up with. Slut Girl's symbol could be two huge tits with wings.*

Katie choked on her donut. *Nope. Not even going to give you a reason. Just no.*

She laughed and glanced out the doors right as a guy wearing a plaid shirt, dirty pants, and boots ran toward the entryway. He headed for the doors at full speed, and he had a purse in his hands. Katie dropped her donut. "Son of a bitch stole a damned purse. Fucking get a goddamned job."

Katie jumped up, grabbed a chair, and dragged it behind her to the door. Schultz's eyes went wide, and he spun around. "No killing!"

"Blah, blah, blah." Katie kicked the door open and pushed the chair out on the sidewalk. She watched the guy race toward her. She squinted one eye and stuck her tongue out of her mouth thoughtfully, calculating the trajectory and adjusting her aim. In one fluid motion, she picked the chair up and hurled it down the street. The chair tumbled end over end, arcing through the air. The detectives winced when it hit the thief in the side. Thief and chair tumbled to the ground.

Katie smiled and nodded, brushing her hands off. A little old lady wearing thick glasses ran up and shook Katie's hand vigorously. "Thanks, honey. You should play for the Mets." The old lady ran to the thief, grabbed her purse, and proceeded to kick the shit out of the guy with her orthopedic shoes. Katie grimaced and walked back to the cops.

"See, he isn't hurt."

The old lady had her fill and walked off. The thief groaned and sat up, cursing at her. He looked around until he found Katie and the detectives inside the pizza place staring at him. He put up his fist and started yelling. "You fucking bitch. What the fuck? You hit me with a goddamned chair! See how tough you are hand-to-hand with me, cunt!"

Pandora perked up. *Nope. He said the C-word.*

You want?

I want.

Katie glanced at the cops. "Excuse me just a second."

She kicked the door back open and stomped to the thief. Katie grabbed him by the collar and slammed him back down on the ground. She put a foot on either side of his body and bent over him, their noses touching. Her eyes flashed as she let Pandora take over.

Her voice became a growl. "I'm going to make this

really clear. The one who threw the chair? She was the docile one. Me? I'll grab your nutsack, tie it to my belt, and take you for a little flight. Either you will fall, balls not attached, or you will have to strap those babies to your shoulders to walk around. Now, lie here till my friends come and get you, or you know what's next."

The thief's eyes grew wide. Katie turned and strutted back into the pizza place. Travers and Schultz were already halfway out the door and ran over to take the guy into custody. He looked at the cops, freaked out. "She…her eyes. She's a… Take me to jail, please."

Travers chuckled and put the cuffs on him. "Don't worry, buddy. You're on your way there."

As the detectives hauled him off, they waved at Katie. She waved back and gathered her pizza and donuts, ready to go home. She nodded at the Krispy Kreme employees but figured the pizza guys were hiding in terror in the back, which made her laugh. As she exited the shop, a little girl with long dark hair tugged on her mom's hand. "Mommy, it's the angel!"

Her mother looked up and smiled broadly. "So it is! Katie is her name."

The girl wriggled free from her mom and ran up to Katie, tapping her on the leg. "Excuse me. Can you sign an autograph for me? You're my hero."

Katie grinned and knelt. "It would be my honor, little lady. What would you like me to sign?"

"Oh." The little girl looked around.

Katie laughed and ripped a piece of the Krispy Kreme box off. The little girl's mom walked up and handed her a pen. "Thank you. My daughter loves you. We all do."

"Aw, that's so sweet. What's your name?" Katie asked.

"Abigail," the little girl proudly proclaimed.

Katie signed the box, *To Abigail, Keep flying high and never look back. The angels are on your side. Love, Katie*

Pandora snickered. *Oh, brother. That makes me want to vomit on myself. You should have signed it, Dear Abigail, the world will eat you whole. Grab a demon and make it your bitch.*

Angie grimaced as Katie walked in the door. She muted the television and turned toward her employer. Angie was curled up on the couch with her knees to her chest. "Hey, there. You had quite the eventful evening."

Katie glanced at the television. The local news was playing cell phone footage of Katie plowing into the car and slicing it in half. There were multiple angles. Katie wrinkled her nose. "Those citizen journalists never let me get away with anything."

"I think you did a good thing."

Katie laughed, laying her guns on the table. "Thanks. All in a day's work. Got a purse snatcher too, but it wasn't as epic. I tossed a chair at him as he was running. You should have seen his ass topple over. Then an old lady kicked him silly. It was fucking priceless."

Angie giggled. "That sounds good, but watch this."

She turned toward the television and backed up the TiVo. She pressed Play, and the shaky video showed Katie flying over the halved car holding the passenger in one hand. Katie leaned forward, squinting at the television. "Wait...did he?"

Angie wailed with laughter, nodding her head. "Yep, he pissed not only on himself, but you can see it splashing on the forehead of the guy beneath him."

Katie slapped her knee. "How did I miss that? That is amazing shit. I should have put that in my report. Caught assailant, made him piss his pants...and on the other guy's face."

Pandora guffawed loudly. *God, that is amazing. That right there makes the whole night worth it. They're going to be sitting in jail covered in that one guy's pee. People pay money to watch shit like that. Weirdos, but still.*

Katie shivered. *That's two girls/one cup kind of shit. That's disgusting, my friend.*

Hey, I don't give 'em the ideas. Humans are freaky creatures. They'll do anything for fame, money, and an orgasm or two.

Angie clicked off the television, her eyes watering from laughing so hard. "You in for the night?"

Katie leaned back in the chair. "Yep. Done for the night, hopefully."

Angie looked surprised. "No sexy rendezvous and pass-out session at the local club tonight?"

Katie laughed. "Nah, I'm hanging up my slut shoes for a while. They don't really fit. They're Pandora's, and they're huge on me."

Pandora grumped, *That was uncalled for.*

9

Baal fidgeted with a wide-brimmed black hat as he trekked across the hardened lava toward Moloch. The other demon stood in front of two ironwood chairs and a long table filled with food. Moloch looked over his shoulder as Baal approached. "What the hell is that thing on your head?"

Baal ran a talon across the brim of his hat. "Do you like it? The humans on Earth say it's all the rage."

Moloch curled his lip. "You look ridiculous. In fact, you look like that priest mercenary. What was his name?"

Baal's eyes grew wide. "Damian?"

Moloch nodded. "Yes, that's the one. Ridiculous bow tie. God-loving idiot."

Baal shook his finger at Moloch. "He was pretty crafty."

"Lord Lucifer, please don't tell me you have an inter-species crush on that man-child."

Baal looked away, took his hat off, and set it at his feet. "Don't be stupid."

Moloch arched an eyebrow. "How did you find one to fit your gigantic head, anyway? It's the size of ten human heads."

Baal shrugged indignantly. "They make them special-order in Colorado. What is all this, anyway?"

Moloch clapped his large paws and stood up, putting his back to the table. "We're going to have some fun today. We're going to take a little European tour."

Baal pursed his lips. "Oooh, I love that idea. I've always wanted to vacation in Europe. I wouldn't fit on the trains, though. And forget about any of the Asian countries. I would stick out like a sore thumb."

Moloch sighed. "Yes, yes. Well, in honor of our tour, I have set up a delicious spread representing our locations. I have guinea pigs in croissants, wiener dogs on a stick, rabbit and potato pierogies—still fresh—and my favorite, Slovenian gerbil stew."

Baal licked his lips, looking at the table. "That sounds delicious. You went all-out."

Moloch waved his hand nonchalantly and plopped down into his large wooden chair. "Yes, well, I figured we would mark the next era of destruction with a little celebration. I'm so tired of doom and gloom. I figure there's no way Katie has found out about our little plan, even if she did come out of hell alive and well. This should be nice and sneaky and entertaining."

"Are you using the small demons?" Baal grabbed a guinea pig sandwich and chomped down.

Moloch flicked off a piece of fur that flew onto his shoulder. "You will see. Remember, we decided to go with minor inflictions of pain and death instead of full-on destruction. We want to be in and out as quickly as possible, just like the Leviathan. She taught us a lot about making a statement without getting pulverized…at least up until the end."

The demons laughed loudly. Moloch spread his arms wide, opening a window that allowed them to view anywhere on Earth. "We will begin our tour of Europe in the quaint little town of Manarola, Italy. There are no cars or roads, just a bunch of disgusting humans enjoying the beauty of their fishing town."

Baal leaned forward. "Nice, but it will be much nicer once it's been renovated."

"Mwahahahaha." Moloch chortled maniacally.

The window moved as Moloch swished his hand, giving a panoramic view of the town on the Mediterranean. The skies were bright blue, and the ocean gently lapped at the tall stone cliffs. Bright, colorful houses peppered the side of the cliff, etched right into the stone face once thought impenetrable. Small boats bobbed in the small inlet below, which opened to the vibrant blue sea.

Baal laughed giddily as he pointed at the town. "Look at all those little Italian people. Hanging their laundry, talking to their neighbors, and shopping at the market, all with no clue of what's coming. Give it to 'em, Moloch. Give it to 'em good."

Moloch chuckled, cracking his knuckles. "As you wish."

He clapped his hands and a crack of lightning shot from the sky. Reality groaned and split in the small seaside village. The air shuddered, and a gate opened in the picturesque harbor. A dozen large demons came barreling into the harbor at full force. Each of them carried two huge wooden mallets that they swung with fervor. Boats exploded into shards of wood, and human bodies went flying over their shoulders into the water. They stomped up the hill leading to the town, smashing and crushing anything in their path.

The stone of ancient buildings crumbled easily. Houses generations old fell at the demons' feet. They dropped their mallets and began grabbing people out of their homes pulling villagers apart limb by limb and taking their time to have a bit of a snack before moving on to the next house. One large demon walked through the center of the pathway, his broad shoulders scraping the colorful houses. A small dog ran out and barked loudly, nipping bravely at the demon's ankle. He slowly bent down and picked it up, putting the small dog in his palm.

A woman ran from the house screaming. *"Mio Mitzi! Il mio povero cagnolino. Lasciala bestia!"*

The demon looked down and lifted his thick leg. With a hellish chortle, he slammed his foot down on top of the woman, squashing her flat. He pivoted through the blood and bones and turned toward the ocean. The demon lifted the yapping dog to his eye. It growled fiercely. The demon cocked his fingers back. *"Arrivederci."* He chuckled as he flicked the dog away. The pup's squeal grew faint as it flew into the distance, eventually landing with a small splash in the sea.

Moloch clapped his hands and laughed. "All right, that's enough, my beasts. Let's move on."

At once, the beasts dropped the mangled humans, marched back through the rubble, and leaped into the gate before it snapped closed behind them. They hadn't decimated the town, but they had definitely done some damage. Moloch cleared his throat and popped a wiener dog into his mouth.

Baal clapped excitedly. "Where to now?"

Moloch swallowed and waved his hand, changing the view. "Give yer best round o' applause. We ur gawin` tae Portree, Scootlund!"

Baal raised an eyebrow. "Huh?"

Moloch rolled his eyes and sighed. "Portree, Scotland. The largest town on the Isle of Skye. Home to some twenty-five hundred people. A booming port, and quite nice on the eyes."

Baal laughed at Moloch's spiel. "If you ever get tired of being an evil demon dictator, you could open a tour company on Earth."

Moloch snorted. "And eat all my customers."

He flicked his fingers, and the two watched as a gate opened in the hills above the brightly colored port town. Two dozen smaller demons poured out of the gate, hissing and snarling, and ran frantically toward the town. One of the demons became separated from the group and rushed into an open field. A flock of sheep began bleating loudly as he flew through them, jumping from sheep to sheep and taking a bite of each. Moloch and Baal laughed loudly at the wool flying everywhere. The stray demon left a string of mutilated mutton in his wake.

The other demons descended on the town and began attacking those in the streets. A dozen of them grabbed boulders and hurled them at buildings, blasting large holes in the colorful walls. Tourists screamed and poured from the restaurants, trying to get away as fast as they could.

The demons were faster. The cobblestone streets were littered with severed legs and arms, and one head rolled down the hill.

Moloch and Baal focused on the head, and they chanted as it rolled all the way down the street and plopped into the water below. They bellowed with laughter, tears filling their eyes. Baal wiped his cheeks and focused on a Scottish barkeep. The red-haired brute burst out into the street with a shotgun.

Baal pointed at the guy, taking a big gulp of his drink. "Uh-oh, watch this asshole. He's got a shotgun."

The man pointed his gun at one of the demons and pulled the trigger, taking its head right off its shoulders. He lowered the gun with a smile, proud of himself. Before he could bask in his triumph three demons were on top of him, tackling him to the ground. The man fell back, his shotgun going off. The buckshot flew through the gate into hell, and Baal and Moloch hit the floor as the pellets whizzed over their heads.

Slowly, they climbed back into their chairs. They glanced at each other and burst into laughter. Moloch wiped his eyes and clapped his hands, signaling the demons to retreat. They made a run for it, dragging human snacks behind them and into the gate.

Moloch sighed and slumped in his chair. "Oh, that was good. Two down, four to go."

He swiped his hand, and the picture changed. The gate was now showing rolling green hills studded with foliage. Bordering a lush forest was a medium-sized town at the edge of a large lake. Baal oohed and sat forward.

Moloch smiled. "This is my favorite. Dobrodošli na

Bledu, Slovenija. Or for the less worldly, welcome to Bled, Slovenia. This town is about double the size of the last. It was established in 1004."

"When?"

"Long ago, by human standards."

"So?"

"They take that shit seriously. The humans will take this town's destruction personally."

"Got it."

"It's also considered the most beautiful town in the world. At least, it will be for a few more moments. But my favorite part is that castle right there. It's situated on a small island in the middle of the lake. Too bad it doesn't have any protection."

Moloch rubbed his hands together and gathered hellish energy in them, then pushed them outward quickly. The air around the small village shimmered, and two gates opened simultaneously. One of the gates was right on the shores of the tiny island, pouring six medium demons out. The other was at the edge of the town, this one releasing four demons so large that they trampled the trees as they walked.

Sirens sounded as the six medium demons went to work. They ran through the droves of tourists climbing to the top of the castle to see the panoramic views of the mountains. They tossed humans from hand to hand, ripping their bodies in half just for fun. Four of the demons focused on the people, rending and biting their flesh for their afternoon snacks. The other two began climbing the tall tower atop the castle.

The demons wrapped their thick arms around it and

began to sway back and forth. Moloch sat on the edge of his chair, nodding his head wildly. "Yes, yes…and there it goes! Excellent."

The tower toppled, crashing to the ground in an explosion of debris and dust. People caught beneath the rubble screamed, and the demons did nothing but laugh. On the mainland, the large demons swung their long arms through the village, toppling the old stone buildings. They grabbed any living being they could reach and ripped each in half in their rage. A trail of blood led from the middle of the town to the gate. The demons destroyed everything in their path.

Baal narrowed his eyes. "If I remember correctly, one of the heads of the Holy Roman Empire gifted that place to the Bishop of Brixen. He was an infected member of the church. I loved his sense of style. Torture was so unique back then. He introduced them to so many ways of dismemberment."

Moloch nodded. "Oh, yes, I forgot all about him. Well, it's no longer the most beautiful place on Earth. Sorry, bishop."

Both demons cackled, and Moloch gave the signal for the demons to return to their gates. He closed the gates to hell but frowned and quickly counted the returned demons. One short. He had left one of the medium demons behind. He spotted it easily, thrashing around in a sea of mangled tourists. Moloch shrugged and clenched his fist tightly. The demon grabbed his head in pain and exploded in a shower of blood and guts.

Moloch stood from his chair and did some stretches,

readying himself for the last three towns. His talons nearly touched his toes.

Baal wandered back to the table and tapped his claw against his lips. "Hmmm, I really like those wieners. Delicious!" He selected a few more snacks for the next part.

Moloch groaned as he stretched his back. "Thank you. I learned a few things from the old days. All converted to much tastier proteins, of course."

Baal nodded. "Of course."

They both got situated back in their chairs, and Moloch swished his hand, bringing up the next location. It was beautiful, with lush green grass and stone cottages with thatched roofs. A gentle river ran straight through the center of the village. The whole scene was perfectly manicured, and the residents were all out enjoying one of the few sunny days.

Moloch smirked. "Bibury, England. It's one of those places I can't wait to wipe out of existence or at least cause considerable damage to."

Baal considered the town. "Crappy little place with crappy little houses. What's your beef?"

Moloch groaned. "In the 1000s, late I think, a book was written about this town. Or at least the town was in the book. It was called the *Domesday Book*. I wrote the original *Domesday Book*, but that bastard William the Conqueror got hold of it and ended up using it to gain enormous power over much of medieval England. I'm still bitter. Anyway, this town was in it."

Moloch waved his hand and rested his chin on his fist. The gate opened outside the small medieval town. The demons poured into Arlington Row, sniveling and snarling. People, both residents and tourists, began screaming and running. The demons jumped and dove over old stone walls and onto thatch, taking the roofs off the houses. They burst from doorways and tackled people in the center of the streets. Moloch chuckled as a stream of blood ran down the main street, trickling into the River Coln.

Baal clapped his hands. "The streets will run red with their blood. Take that, William the Shithead!"

Moloch looked at Baal and chuckled. The demons ripped through the small town quicker than Moloch had thought they would. He raised his head, realizing they were doing more damage than he wanted. He snapped his fingers and sent the demons back toward the gate, shutting it quickly behind them. He leaned forward as he scanned the remains of the town, satisfied with what he saw.

Baal grabbed one of the guinea pig sandwiches and tossed it at him. "Hey, wake up. We've got two to go, and I'm enjoying myself much more than I thought. You did your deed and wreaked havoc on England. What's next?"

Moloch picked his nose thoughtfully, trying to remember. Finally, it came to him, and he smiled. "Let's do these two simultaneously, shall we?"

Moloch swished his hand to the side and opened a second window. The one closest to Baal showed a wide-open plain with lush green grass. Perched atop a tall hill was a domed palace with a gold roof and cylindrical yellow towers. Moloch chuckled. "This was one of Lilith's favorite playgrounds centuries ago. It is Sintra, Portugal, and is known as the Moon Cult City. They worshipped the moon goddess Cynthia, and when Lilith arrived there, she used her demon powers of persuasion to make them all believe she was the goddess in the flesh. It was actually pretty funny to watch. I chose this place because I know it will chap her ass."

Baal laughed. "You're asking for trouble by picking on Lilith. I like it."

Moloch snarled, "That bitch is going to know she messed with the wrong demons. If she likes Earth so much, she can watch me destroy it piece by piece. I will take down every beautiful place she loves. Besides, there is no damn moon goddess. We all know that. The people are a bunch of nutbags running in the streets, throwing flowers and lighting candles. It's ridiculous."

Baal smirked. "Am I sensing a bit of jealousy? Perhaps because there are no cities for you?"

"No. Besides, when I take Earth, *all* the cities will be for me. If they don't worship me out of desire, they will out of desperation."

Baal was silent for an awkward moment. "Okay, then. Where's the other place?"

"Giethoorn in the Netherlands, also one of those places close to the bitch's heart. During one of her quarter-life crises, when she was trying to figure out who she was, she lived there. She thought it was quaint and sweet. It's one of those places that doesn't have roads. You have to get everywhere on foot or by boat through the little canals. It's a fucking joke. Supposedly, she fell in love there, but Lucifer found out and ended up filleting and frying the guy in the pits of hell or something." Moloch tried to look bored at that point, but Baal knew he was trying to cover his spite.

"So you selected these two to pick a fight with Lilith?" Baal asked.

Moloch shook his head. "No. I selected these two to get under her skin. By the time she finds out they both will be ravaged, and there won't be a damn thing she can do to save them."

Baal thought about that, looking carefully at Moloch. "And don't you think that will bring her wrath to your doorstep?"

Moloch shrugged. "Meh, who cares? What's she gonna do, come back down here and do her ice queen magic? What is this, fucking *Frozen* on tour?"

Baal was obviously apprehensive about taunting Lilith, but Moloch quickly changed his mind. "Go on, Baal. Be my guest. You can open the gates to both of those. It's not often that you get to do the fun part. I'm tired anyway. You know how opening a gate takes it out of me."

Baal smiled and jumped up. He cracked his fingers. "Don't mind if I do."

He closed his eyes and began to sway back and forth as if a symphony were playing. He brushed one arm to the right, opening a gate at the top of the hill where a castle stood. He waved his left arm, opening a larger gate in the middle of the small village of Giethoorn. Moloch chuckled as Baal danced around, his large feet shaking the ground beneath them.

In Sintra, tall ogre-like demons poured out of the gate carrying all manner of weapons. Three of them immediately attacked the castle, bashing their spiked clubs into the stone walls. Chunks of buildings fell, and people began to run. The ogres squashed them right and left with their large horned feet. One of them stomped down on the walkway, killing at least a dozen humans. He bent over and picked up a screaming woman, staring at her with his big red eyes. She screamed even louder, and he grimaced, quickly biting off the top half of her body.

The other ogres ran down the mountain, taking boulders and trees down with them. They picked up the large stones and rolled them at the city below like bowling balls. One smashed into several houses and then proceeded through the center of the town, rolling right through a church where service was being held.

Moloch threw his hands into the air and cheered. "Strike! Eleven more to go for a perfect game."

Baal was relieved to see Moloch coming out of his bad mood. He pointed at the Giethoorn window, laughing. "Look at them swim!"

Several of the people ran from their homes, screaming as demons chased them out. They dove over the wooden bridges into the canals and began to swim as fast as they could. Little did they know that demons didn't mind the water at all. The water boiled as though it was infested with a swarm of piranha, and soon the canals ran red. The water calmed suddenly. The only thing that came back to the surface was a dress shoe and a clump of hair.

Terrified people ran in all directions as demons piled out of the gate. It was a grand finale to the European Tour of Horror. Beautiful towns all across the continent were just pawns in Moloch's game. They had captured the imagination of humans everywhere, and their destruction would strike a deep blow. Their destruction would move humanity to fight back. It would draw the mercenaries from their homes. It would even bring Katie from hiding. Moloch was getting really tired of her. He hated to admit it, but he was actually afraid of her. He was ready for change, and only he could make it happen.

By the time Moloch stepped in and called his demons back to the gates, the beautiful landscapes of Sintra and Giethoorn were covered in blood and gore. The streets were empty, and the only sounds that could be heard were the moans of the wounded and the echoing cries of the orphaned. Sirens blared, but no one came to help. The terror had been real and poignant, albeit short—exactly what Moloch and Baal had been trying to achieve.

Moloch waited for the gates to shut before waving away the windows, and a smile moved over his lips. He collapsed into his chair and gazed at the volcanoes and moaning souls of hell. An explosion in one of the lava rivers shook him from his trance. He clapped and put his large feet up on the table. Baal laughed jubilantly, still shoveling food into his mouth.

Moloch yawned and stretched his arms over his head. "That was a beautiful trip, don't you think? Though I *am* disappointed. I didn't come back with any souvenirs."

Baal nodded with a mouthful. "I think the highlights for me were the rolling heads, the drowning humans, and... that one pub guy in Scotland who had the shotgun."

Moloch nodded. "Hmm, yes, those were good. Personally, I would say the pub owner was definitely on the top of the list. I also like the way that castle in Bled came down, the beauty of the falling stones crushing the bones and limbs of the people below it. I love watching history crumble. People get so emotional about it, as though the buildings hold meaning. It's pathetic."

Baal laughed. "Maybe we should start naming some of the places here with historical references and let the idiot humans come to us. It would save Lucifer a lot of hard work. Just let the souls collect themselves."

Moloch shook his finger. He stood up and grabbed one last bite of the stew. "I like the way your evil little mind works, Baal. Though I'm pretty sure His Majesty loves his job. The look on those poor bastards' faces when he arrives to bring them to hell. They always wonder what they did to deserve it."

They both laughed. Moloch snapped his fingers, and several of his demon servants appeared. "Clear this out and take the leftovers to Baal's home. I'm not going to want any more of this stuff."

"So, what is our plan now?"

Moloch put his arm around Baal and walked with him across the molten stone. "We wait and see what happens next. You know I always have a trick or two up my sleeve. Lilith will get word very soon, and so will the rest of the world. They will wake up to carnage, and unlike you and me, they don't enjoy that. It's going to be a shit show for certain, one I cannot wait to see."

10

Pandora was fidgety, and she was transferring that restlessness straight onto Katie. Not that she didn't mean to do it. *Rise and shine, sunflower. It's a new day and a new chance to eat donuts, kick ass, and...eat more donuts.*

Katie grumbled and turned over in the bed. She was trying her hardest to push back against Pandora, ignoring the rush of energy that was starting to flow through her. Her legs were starting to tingle, a jolt running from her toes up to her hips. Katie kicked out petulantly but only succeeded in winding her legs up in the blankets.

Pandora chuckled. *Try all you want, but you have yet to master the ability to ward off my energizing vibes.*

Katie took her pillow and slammed it over her head, wishing it would somehow stop Pandora's constant chatter. *Is that an option?*

Pandora sighed. *No. But it's a nice thought, isn't it? Come onnnn. The sun is up, the birds are fucking chirping, and one just landed on the windowsill like you're Cinder-fucking-ella. I'm not going to remind you how many chores you have to do.*

Katie yanked the pillow off her head and turned in bed. She opened her eyes wide, hoping that Pandora could feel her icy stare. *I thought we had a damn agreement.*

Pandora tsked. *No, we didn't. We know we love each other, and we know I love to get up early. That is the compromise.*

That's not a compromise. That's you getting what you want.

It is? Weird how that happens.

You suck at friendships. And relationships in general. You know that, don't you?

Pandora shrugged. *So I've been told. But I've also heard 'a happy demon, a happy life.'*

Katie sat up in bed and pulled the covers up to her chest. *First of all, that is not how the saying goes. It's, 'Happy wife, a happy life.' I am not your wife, and my life is not very happy when I have to wake up at the ass-crack of dawn. Why can't you just sleep or doodle or something?*

Doodle? On what? Your liver?

It might be better than this medieval torture. Seriously, I think you do it to make your mornings brighter.

Pandora thought about it for a moment. *On a normal basis, I might agree with you. In fact, on most mornings, I would agree with you wholeheartedly. This morning, though, there's actually a purpose.*

What? You want donuts? You smell bacon? You're thinking about men? You have an itch? What is so important that you have to wake me up this early in the morning?

Pandora snickered. *Good lord, relax. Your blood pressure is shooting through the roof. I'm trying to talk to you and control you from stroking out at the same time.*

I was relaxing, then you woke me up!

The truth is, I've got more to tell you.

Katie picked up her head and looked around. *Really?*

Yes! Now get up and dress for war!

Katie sighed but pulled herself out of the bed. She went to her closet and pulled out a fresh outfit of black spandex and a low-cut top and got dressed. She strapped her guns on her hips and rolled her shoulders. A twinge in her neck spiked, then became warm, then was gone. That was Pandora. *Thanks.*

I'm a licensed masseuse.

No, you're not.

I've massaged some crazy stuff. Stuff I should either get a license for or get arrested for.

Now, where are we going?

Pandora whistled in excitement. *I'm pumped about this. Jump out, do your wing thing, and head north out of the city. Just find some nice, quiet place out of the way to chill.*

Katie nodded and ran right out of her open balcony doors. She leaped off the side of the building and enjoyed a moment of free-fall. She spread her wings far and felt them catch air. She swooped high, not wanting anyone to see her leave that early. Luckily for her, the protestors and counter-protestors weren't early risers.

She glided along through the cool morning air and in minutes she was out of the city. She soared over the countryside, looking for a pleasant place to land. Katie spotted a large wooded area with a clearing in the center. She circled around to make sure no one was there and carefully landed in the soft moss.

Pandora approved. *Perfect. Now, let me drive.*

Katie sighed and sat down on the edge of a fallen tree. *All right, go ahead.*

Katie dropped into the background, and Pandora took over. She experimentally rolled her neck. *Man, I did a piss poor job on your neck. I'll fix it later.*

I wasn't going to say anything, but maybe you should have your license revoked.

Pandora laughed as she stood up. She stretched her back and touched her toes, limbering up.

Okay, is this yoga in the park?

Leave the witty banter to me, bitch.

Pandora concentrated hard. She extended her hands in front of her and demonic claws formed on her hands. She swiped her claws through the air, and reality tore with a guttural sound. A shimmering portal opened in front of her. She smiled at her handiwork, and before Katie could protest, she carefully stepped inside.

Oh, boy, my favorite place.

I can work better here. You know that.

The energy seemed to roll through Pandora, and even in the background, Katie could feel it. Katie looked around, feeling a bit nervous. It was a desolate place, covered in dark, shimmering stone. She scanned through Pandora's vision and realized they were high on top of a black mountain. Lava ran in rivers far below them, though the heat still managed to reach them.

Pandora waved her claw through the air and a smaller portal appeared, almost like a window. The edges of the window wavered and flickered as though it was unstable. The window showed a calm, peaceful place.

Where is that?

Not where, but when.

What?

Angels and demons appeared on the peaceful plane, destroying the scene. They raised wing and claw and crashed together. The battle played out like a movie in front of them. Katie was getting more and more confused by the moment.

Pandora put her hands on her hips, watching the angels and demons brawl. *The demons have been fighting the angels for so many millennia that we lose track of the exact dates. Hell, I'd say it's been about ten thousand years, but that's what we all say when we mean a time long ago. We don't know how long it was really.*

On the screen, angels donned their version of armor and wielded weapons forged by the hands of God himself. They came in waves of silver and gold. They swung their weapons mightily, and many demons fell before them. Then demon reinforcements arrived in vast hordes, screaming and wailing and slashing with claws and crude weapons. Katie winced as a lava ax cut a glorious angel in two. She felt the pain in her heart as she watched a row of angels perish at the hands of the vicious beasts. As many died, more were called to the killing floor. The battle continued.

Kate heard a sharper sound over the sounds of war. *What is that?*

The wailing?

Yeah, it's horrible.

Pandora sighed, waving her hand and muting the window. *Those are the sounds of the angels crying. Every time one of theirs is lost, it strikes them in their souls. It's the pain you're feeling, only its much stronger at the moment. God cries, too, when his angels are lost. That wasn't just reserved for me, although I like to pretend that it was.*

Katie scoffed. *Figures.*

Pandora ignored that. *Anyway. When the humans came along, we demons saw how much God loved them. And we realized that hurting them was a way to hurt God. Like any good demons would, we jumped at the chance. We did horrible physical things in the beginning. The angels tried to protect them, of course. The battles we fought felled mountains and created canyons on Earth. The more we went after the humans, the harder the angels fought us.*

Katie listened patiently, astounded by the stories. *But why don't you fight like that now? We don't see those battles. We don't see those fights. If the ground shakes, it's because of an earthquake or volcano. We definitely don't go hiking in the mountains and find a bunch of glowing angels beating down the demons.*

Pandora chuckled. *You don't, and that's for a good reason. The demons found out there were rules to God's efforts, there were rules to what he could send the angels for. And there were rules regarding what types of punishments the humans could receive. He loves you all very much, but the bible isn't joking. He can be a spiteful God. He created those rules himself, to protect your kind, but also to keep you in line.*

Katie looked through Pandora at the screen. *Because he loved us.*

Pandora nodded. *Right, because he loved you. Anyway, we figured that out. So no more direct assaults. We started possessing you meat sacks and using the humans to do our dirty deeds. When humans did them, even if it was through our* control, the angels wouldn't come down and kick ass. They knew if they killed us, the human would die too. Quite the conundrum. The humans ultimately became the perfect buffer between us and the wrath of God.

Katie sighed. *There's always a loophole. Even when it comes to the creation of the universe and the essence of life, there's a damn loophole. Is God a lawyer? He is, isn't he? Or she?*

Pandora laughed. *You know as well as I do that God is neither he or she.*

You keep saying "he."

That's the patriarchy talking. I'm working on it.

Okay. You were talking about loopholes.

Right. No, God is not a lawyer. Lucifer has dabbled, though. Anyway, everything has limits. Your all-knowing God protected you from everyone with his rules, that means from demons and God himself. But we demons weren't as dumb as he thought. The whole meat sack idea is pretty ingenious, really.

Katie scrunched Pandora's forehead. *What does that all have to do with the war now? The demons aren't even using humans that often. They are literally busting through portals and demolishing shit.*

Pandora crossed her arms over her chest and walked to the edge of the mountain. *I know. For whatever reason, it seems that the angels are allowing the humans to get harmed pretty grievously. I fully expected to see them coming down in droves and battling the hell out of the demons. I expected that even before Incursion Day. It never happened, though. The only two angelic beings I've seen down here are you and Gabriel. That's it.*

Katie let out a deep, frustrated breath. *But they're supposed to protect the humans. I know it because I feel that surging need to do it every time something bad is happening. Why aren't they coming?*

Pandora shrugged, turning back to the window as Gabriel sliced through a demon on the playback of history. *I don't know, maybe because they can fight back? Perhaps they don't have quite enough faith in this modern age, so the big man upstairs is offering up a little proof?*

A rock crumbled overhead and rolled past them. Katie watched it plummet over the edge. *Where are we? This is nothing like the last two times. Even the heat is a bit less than before.*

Pandora looked around them. *Yeah, it's hell, but not the same as before. We are in one of the outer rings. There aren't as many demons all the way out here. It's not hot enough, and there's really nothing to do. Demons are not quite the adventurers that you humans are.*

Katie was a bit worried. *But they can still tell when an intruder is here, right?*

Pandora bit the inside of her lip and nodded her head. *Mm-hmm. But it will take some time for them to realize anything's happening. I'm able to block myself well enough to throw them off the trail for a bit. Then it takes time for them to get out this far. Of course, unless Lucifer suddenly starts to give a shit.*

Uh...and how likely is that? I really don't want to meet your ex-husband for the first and last time today.

Pandora waved her hands. *I doubt he's even thinking about me. He's probably three hos into a twelve-ho night by now. Shit depends on when he started. Old Luci isn't as full of stamina as he was back in the day, if you know what I mean.*

Katie grimaced. *Gross. I'd rather not think about Lucifer*

dicking anything, thanks. So which way to Baal or Moloch from here?

Pandora smirked. *Nice try. Their area is in the innermost ring, just before you enter the final circle.*

That sounds full of doom.

You think? It's not something we can do right now. Besides, I've never known an angel who could handle being in hell for that long. The heat coupled with the hatred, suffering, sin, and damning kind of gets to them. It's not really their playground.

Katie scoffed. *I remember. Trust me, I remember. It's not terrible up here, but that's probably because you're shielding me.*

Yep. That is precisely right. When I take over, my demon body acts as sort of a bubble for your human/angel body. You sit comfortably out there, and I take the brunt of it. I can feel your angel hurting a bit, but that's more because of the inner turmoil and the suffering souls below than anything. Angels know the rules. They know the damned and sinners go to hell, but that doesn't mean they like it. They tend to have soft hearts for that kind of thing. It makes them sad.

Katie chuckled. *Why do I feel like that's the punch line for a lot of demon jokes?*

Pandora smiled. *We don't tell a lot of jokes. Demons are either raging assholes or self-loathing emo types. But yeah, you're right. Every joke does end with some variation of "Angels are pussies."*

Katie stared at the shimmering window through Pandora's eyes. *So we have fought wars, humans have fought wars, and now humans and demons are fighting a war.*

That's exactly right. It's been happening for a very long time.

Katie thought for a moment, looking around. *The problem is that we aren't...*

Pandora perked up. She growled and slashed open a portal. *Sorry, girl, time to go! Whoops, that didn't take as long as I thought it would.*

Pandora stepped through the portal and slashed her claws, shutting it quickly behind her. Katie immediately switched places, taking her body back. She took in a deep breath of the cool air and watched the steam cascade off her hot skin. The breeze immediately cooled her down, but it was strange to her that until that moment, she hadn't even noticed how hot it was in hell. Pandora really was a bubble for her human body.

Katie let herself get her center of gravity back and suddenly realized she was standing on top of her apartment complex. *What was that back there? Was it Moloch or Lucifer?*

Pandora laughed. *No. If it had been Luci, we wouldn't have been able to leave before he shut down the gate. Moloch is too slow to get there that fast. Think of him as a porky politician who used to be in the military way back when. He's grown accustomed to fattening foods, comfortable chairs, and luxury. He still knows the tactics but getting up and running might take him a minute.*

Okay, so what was it?

Oh! It was just a dire. Somehow, we caught one's attention. They aren't necessarily too bright, but they tracked you pretty damned fast. They must have been out on patrol after you and I were in hell last.

Katie looked over the city. *Should we be concerned that they'll track us here?*

Pandora yawned. *No, they can track inside hell, but they can't track where gates open up. They may be able to smell that I was there, but other than that, nothing. They probably won't tell anyone important either. They know if they reveal they were on my tail but let me get away, they will end up in the torture chamber for a good decade or so.*

Katie sneered. *That sounds charming. Well, thanks for the trip and the information. Why don't we go down and see if there are any leftover donuts? If not, we'll run out and grab some.*

Hell, yeah. You know the way to my heart.

Katie shook her head. *Yeah, through my stomach.*

They both laughed as Katie opened the door to the roof. She headed down the stairwell and out onto her floor. One of the guards poked his head around the corner, and Katie smiled and waved at him. He gave her a shy smile and nodded his head, quickly disappearing back around the corner.

Katie walked into the condo and immediately took in the smell of coffee. "Angie, I'm home! You're the master at coffee making. I swear, how would I live without you?"

Katie stopped in her tracks. Angie was sitting on the couch, frozen in place. She had the news on, and tears were streaming down her face. Katie hurried into the room, put her guns on the table, and wrapped her arms around Angie. "What is it?"

Angie pointed at the television. "The demons. They attacked six places throughout the world."

"*What?*" Katie looked at the destruction and gore on the television.

The newscaster came back on the screen. "Major incursions happened all over Europe last night. Portals opened one after another, releasing demons, causing death and chaos, and then closing again. Right now, we have reports from Manarola, Italy, Portree, Scotland, Bled, Slovenia, Bibury, England, Sintra, Portugal, and Giethoorn, Netherlands. The death toll is in the thousands and climbing. We will have more for you right after this commercial break."

Katie stood up, her eyes flashing from red to blue. "Those sons of bitches. They attacked all those places, knowing we wouldn't be able to get to them in time. Goddamn it!"

Pandora sniffled and then let out a high-pitched growl. *Those bastards! This will not go unavenged, Moloch!*

Korbin stood on the salt flat around the entire base. To the right was an old runway, long enough to work for small planes. On the base were an older hanger bay and a helipad, perfect for when the general and the others flew in.

In front of him were six large buildings, all made of brick, all square and boxy like the old military installations used to be. Stephanie walked up to Korbin and kissed him on the cheek. He smiled and put his arm around her.

The guards were repairing one of the security outposts. Joshua was scanning the grounds around the new but temporary armory. There would also be a new supply building for all the ammo and weapons that were on backorder.

Stephanie elbowed Korbin lightly. "What's on your mind?"

Korbin smiled. "This just reminds me of the old barracks and base when I was in the military. It's crazy to me how much things don't change. But I do have to say, after being in the underground bunker, I'm feeling really exposed."

Calvin walked up next to them. "That's why we're planning the perfect defense system here. We have to be ready for these bastards, even more so than before."

Korbin nodded. "I agree. We need ammunition, traps, better fencing around the perimeter, and reinforced defensive shields for all these buildings."

Calvin chuckled and crossed his arms over his chest. "Well, if we want to do all that, then we better get on it, boss."

Korbin shook his head and turned to Calvin. "I'm not your boss. Not anymore. You know that. I'm just doing what I'm best at."

Calvin smiled kindly and put his hand on Korbin's shoulder. "You're a leader, and for all of my infected life, you've been mine. Even when you were gone, I remembered all the things that you had taught me. I can't help but follow you now."

Korbin glanced down at Stephanie. "How about this? How about we walk side by side into all of this? There are foggy things in my brain, and things you know I haven't learned yet. The world is so different from when we left. Even this war is different, and we need everyone to help us ease into it."

Calvin agreed. "You got it. I'll be right by your side the whole way. Now, what are your thoughts on the first line of defense systems?"

Korbin turned to face the fence to his left. "I think we learned from the last incursion that we need several lines of fire, way more than we had before. We need them to come way in toward the base and trap them. A good killing floor. Most of the demons won't even realize it's happening until we're right on top of them."

Stephanie rubbed her hands together. "I like that idea. Fucking pricks need to learn their place is in the depths of hell, and I'm ready to send them back there."

The general stood at his desk and looked at the blueprints of the base the mercs were moving to. He had the base's master armorer on the phone, going over the best place to have the entrance guard area. They would be fortifying it and making it basically impenetrable by anyone not authorized by the MA on duty.

"So, what you're saying is we need to lay concrete spikes all along the east side of the front line." The general ran his finger across the length of the blueprints.

"Yes, sir, that would be good, along with the firepower Korbin is relaying to us during the meeting later," the MA replied.

The general stood up and caught his secretary motioning to him from the door. "All right, chief, sounds good. I'll be in touch, probably later today. Good work."

He hung up the phone and stared at the call blinking on his phone pad. "Who is it?"

"It sounds like Katie, sir."

"Oh, good," he replied, sitting down and grabbing the receiver.

He pulled the phone to his ear and heard a loud gnashing sound. He chuckled. "You eating donuts?"

Katie swallowed hard. "Sorry, sir. I was on hold for a hot minute."

The general smiled. "Not a problem. What can I do for you?"

"I want to come and meet you at your base."

The general raised an eyebrow. "You know that's like coming into the mouth of a lion."

Katie laughed. "Do they really want to harass a person who can open portals to hell?"

The general snorted laughter. "Sometimes. I do wonder about them and where their common sense is."

Katie sighed. "Well, either way, I'm coming down there to meet you. No one is going to limit what I can do for the good of the world. I don't care if they're afraid of me or not. I have done nothing but prove my loyalty time and time again. They should know I'm on the right side by now."

"Yes, well, you have to remember that most of these guys, whether they're in fatigues or suits, are politicians at heart. The right side might be a bit foggy for them. When are you planning on coming to see me?" The general opened up his calendar.

"Tomorrow at lunch okay?" Katie asked with a grin.

The general grimaced and scratched out his lunch plans on the calendar. "That's fine. Didn't have anything planned."

"Perfect, then I will see you tomorrow. It'll be good to see a friendly face."

The general couldn't help but smirk. "I agree."

Katie hung up the phone, looked at Angie, and nodded. Angie immediately got on the line with the airport and started making arrangements to have her plane ready the first thing in the morning. Katie walked to the window and stared at the city lights.

Pandora cleared her throat. *You know what you're doing, right?*

Katie shook her head, her eyes fixed on the horizon. *I sure as hell hope so.*

11

Moloch cracked his knuckles and leaned back in his chair. Baal munched giddily on a bucket of teacup Chihuahuas as they watched the news from Moloch's office. The newscaster was visibly rattled, which made it all that much more exciting for the two demons.

The carnage played on the screen. The horrified screams of humans echoed through the office. "As you can see from this footage shot by one of the people in the town, the demons didn't hold back. Ravaging through the small historic village in England, they managed to demolish some of the oldest standing buildings in Europe. The carnage left in their wake is unimaginable and hard to watch. It seems these days, the news is like a horror movie."

Moloch chuckled. "She's got that right. We are the original horror villains."

Baal smiled, grabbing one of the dogs by its tail and popping it into his mouth. Moloch cringed from the incessant barking but tried to ignore it.

The newscaster continued her report. "All across Europe, including towns in Portugal, Scotland, Italy, and the Netherlands, we saw wide-scale destruction. Images and videos from the events have been flooding the internet, though we don't know who out of those capturing video actually survived. Specialists in the field of demonology are still trying to piece together the details, as many of the places were too remote for any professional footage to be captured. The President of the United States has sent aid to those in need in these locations and was quoted during a press conference as saying, 'We will stand by the world as we work through this tragedy and this ongoing war.' After the speech, the President's approval ratings hit an all-time high."

Moloch snorted. "He means they will send out the bitch, but unfortunately, she's too late."

Baal nodded. "It was a fantastic day. They had no idea what hit them. The only demon fatalities were the one lit up by the Scottish barkeep, and then the one you exploded."

A shit-eating grin grew on Moloch's face. "Yes. And no Pandora and Katie to fuck things up. Good tactics. Terrorize the populace and get them to come to the table. We sign all sorts of agreements and then renege on them. Love it."

Baal was beside himself. "I just don't understand the humans. Why would they think they could ever trust us? Hell, they sign agreements between each other all the time and never fully commit to them. They're constantly backstabbing each other. What makes them think we'll hold true to an agreement? We live on immorality and broken promises."

Moloch slammed his hand down, catching one of the Chihuahuas as it ran across the desk and nipped at his knuckles. He threw it at Baal, hitting him in the side of his head. "Please keep your lunch in the bowl. Those little bastards always make a mess, and they're never potty-trained. The little bastard peed on my French Heritage oak desk. It took a lot of work to get this thing delivered to hell. I had to send a whole team. Not to mention the fireproofing bill."

Baal grabbed the puppy and swallowed him whole. "Sorry, Moloch, these things have a mind of their own. And I still don't know why you didn't go with the locals for your desk. Buying goods from humans, it was the scandal of the year."

Moloch waved his hands. "I ate the guy who made it and didn't spend a cent. Besides, I hate those lava rock desks, always leaving black streaks on the paperwork. I swear by the time I get your memos, they look like soot."

Baal pointed to the television. "It's back. Holy shit, it's the barkeep!"

The newscaster played shaky amateur footage of the Scottish barkeep blowing the head off the demon. "A valiant and brave bar owner in this Scottish seaside town managed to kill one of the demons before being attacked. Unfortunately, the rest of the footage is too graphic to play here. He will be remembered as a hero. Keep him and his family in your prayers. As for the attacks themselves, eyewitnesses described them as sudden, full-force, and then over before they even knew what hit them. From the

MICHAEL TODD

looks of it, the demons were not out for total destruction. Some say it's a way for them to make a statement, and others think they're toying with the mercs, most notably, Katie of Katie's Killers. Katie has been known to tussle with these giants more often than not. Katie was not immediately available for an interview, but we're sure she won't let this go without a fight."

Moloch swished his hand through the air, turning off the television. He balled his fist and narrowed his eyes. "That's exactly what we're hoping for."

Katie let the wind blow her hair back wildly as she flew faster and faster through the air. She took a chopper to the local airport but fancied a flight of her own from there to meet with the general at his base. The air was beautiful, and she could feel fall starting to creep in. It was her favorite season.

Pandora couldn't agree more. *Call me basic, but I love those pumpkin donuts they have every year at Krispy Kreme. And Halloween is pretty much my favorite holiday ever. Everyone feels justified in being bad, slutty, and free of inhibitions. It's like my Christmas.*

Katie smiled. *Even as a Damned in a completely new life, I always get excited the first time the weather starts to cool. The smell of cinnamon, the change of the leaves, the hot chocolate. I'm a sucker for it.*

Pandora sighed as they spotted the base ahead. *I remember the first fall in the mountains I ever experienced. I was with a hot naked man in the woods. He had a small cabin and*

124

would chop wood, do me, make fires, and then do me next to the fire. That's what you need in your life.

Katie lifted an eyebrow. *A lumberjack and log cabin? I think I've roughed it enough lately. I'll take my New York City condo, thanks. Besides, before we get all fall crazy, we have some hot days ahead of us.*

Pandora grimaced. *Ugh. I don't know how I let you talk me into these things.*

Katie circled around the base, waving at those on guard duty. They all watched in awe as she flew over, then gracefully landed in front of the general's main building. They weren't really sure what to do. They knew who she was, but they were also supposed to check her in. Katie just laughed as they stood there arguing. She waved her hand and entered in through the front doors.

Before she could walk through the security gate, a guard stepped in front of her. He was a big man with no fear in his eyes. He crossed his arms over his chest. "I'm sorry, but you're going to have to check all of your weapons before you can enter."

Katie shrugged it off, trying to walk forward. "I'm here to see the general. I don't check my weapons."

He stood firm, blocking her path. "Everyone checks their weapons."

Katie narrowed her eyes and pushed her finger into his chest. "I don't think you fully understand who I am. I don't check my weapons for anyone. I've been through this before with you fools."

The security guard just stared at her. "I know full well who you are, Katie. But the rules are the rules, even for you. I know you think you're above the law, but in this building, you follow my rules."

Katie backed up and laughed. "Look, big guy, if you didn't notice, I'm not exactly normal. One swipe from me, and I can send you through the wall. I don't want it to come to that, so I'm asking you to move aside."

The guard stood taller. "Are you threatening me?"

Pandora laughed. *I like this guy. Reminds me of Calvin but with bigger muscles. He gives no fucks who you are.*

"Not a threat, just letting you know how it is. I keep my weapons with me all the time."

As they argued, the general stepped out of his office and walked down the hall. He glanced up from the papers in his hand and sighed, shaking his head. He walked over and tapped the guard on the shoulder, who immediately jumped to attention.

"What's going on here?"

"Sir, your visitor is refusing to comply with the rules of the base. She will not remove her weapons," the guard reported nervously.

The general looked at Katie, who grinned. "What? You know I don't disarm for anyone."

The general gave her a disapproving look and turned to the guard. "She's fine. Let her through."

The guard looked at him, shocked. "But sir!"

The general folded his papers and put them behind his back. He fixed the guard with a cold stare. "Son, are any of you demons here?"

The guard looked at the other men and back at the general. "No, sir, none of us are infected."

The general put his hand out for Katie. "Then I don't

think the woman with the angel wings is going to shoot you."

The guard stepped aside, but he scowled down at Katie as she passed through. She gave him a huge condescending smile and bounced along next to the general. He shook his head at her. "Come on, we can talk in one of the clean meeting rooms. I still don't understand why you bring all that here. You know I'm not going to take you down."

Katie shrugged. "I have to always be ready for trouble, especially these days."

The general opened the door to the meeting room and waved her in. "I suppose you're right. Still, we need to find a better place to meet."

"Whatever you need, boss," Katie agreed as she took a seat across the table from him.

The general opened up a file and ran his finger down it. "I figured while you're here, I'll update you on the six incursions across Europe."

Katie leaned back and folded her hands in her lap. "Sounds perfect. It's been on my mind."

The general pulled out the paper. "Okay. Manarola, Italy sustained damage to thirty percent of their town, sixty percent of their small port, and the body count is up to fifty-three, but that doesn't account for those fully swallowed, sent out to sea, or ripped into pieces. Portree, Scotland sustained fifty percent damage, and a casualty count of a hundred and fifty so far. Bled, Slovenia reports their castle is completely demolished, and the town had a seventy percent destruction rate. The casualties there are climbing by the second due to the wreckage, but the last report was over six hundred, mostly tourists."

Katie shook her head. "This is out of control."

The general put up one finger. "Not done yet, that's only halfway. Bibury, England sustained a sixty percent damage to its historic buildings, which is basically the whole town. They reported twenty-three casualties. Fewer people there, but priceless pieces of history. These last two are the big hitters. Sintra, Portugal had a festival for the moon goddess going on, and there were thousands of people there. Destruction of the castle and the outlying city is at thirty percent, but the body count is nearing two thousand.

"And last but not least, Giethoorn, Netherlands. This place got their ass kicked. Fifty percent of the town is just gone, and their death toll is five hundred and rising. There are pictures of the canals they use to get around. The water is red with blood."

Pandora growled. *Those places were chosen specifically to piss me off. They were important places to me, at least two of them. Moloch is just being a straight-up dickhead now.*

Katie sat quietly for a moment before speaking. "I'm sorry we weren't there for that."

The general shook his head. "No, Katie. The places were so far off the map that no one picked them up. The portals opened, demons poured out, and then *bam*, they were gone. There didn't seem to be any planning. We couldn't have gotten there fast enough, even on your wings."

Katie sighed and tapped her finger on the table. "It's a tragedy, and I'm afraid it will continue."

The general shut his folder. "I know. That's why getting

you set up as quickly as possible is imperative. How is the move coming?"

"Last I heard from Calvin, they were getting settled in and waiting on the big trucks to deliver equipment. Of course, they will make their changes to the property, but knowing them, it won't take long at all."

The general nodded. "Good."

Katie sat forward. "Look, it's obvious here, they are eating us a little bit at a time. If we don't do something to force them on the defensive, we might be done."

"What are your thoughts? Do you have an idea?"

Katie smiled. "Why don't we attack hell?"

The general's eyes grew wide. "As in going down there and going nuts on the bastards?"

Katie tilted her head back and forth. "I think it will have to be a little more structured than that, but in the end, we unleash Earth on hell, angel style."

The general chuckled, wiping the sweat from the back of his neck. "The idea makes me nervous, but we're at a point where I don't see many other ways than to take the fight to them. How will our soldiers fare down there?"

Pandora scoffed. *Shish kebobs.*

Katie grimaced. "Well, they can't go down there unprotected. Humans will roast, so we'll have to come up with a solution for that. We'll also have to get a deeper understanding of the terrain and climate."

"Yes, well I think this will be a good time to bring in Research and Development. Those guys are constantly tinkering down in their labs. They're working up with all kinds of new technology based on studies of the infected that we've procured."

Katie agreed. "I think you're right. Being an infected, I've never been too hot on R&D, but their usefulness may be what we need right now. This isn't a mystery to Pandora, but she doesn't know any of the nuts and bolts science of it. To the rest of us, it's foreign territory and not on this planet."

"Other realms aren't exactly something we've taken the time to really study. In fact, until recently, other realms were some urban fiction shit. Then again, my whole life seems to be that way. I definitely think this is doable. I just want to make sure I'm not sending these men in on a suicide mission."

Katie shook her head. "No, I won't let anyone else go if that's the case. There's no point in me taking men out there if I know they'll come back in an urn. We'll make sure everyone is safe, and I want this to be volunteer-based. I don't want anyone down there who doesn't want to be there."

The general understood. "That's not completely out of our realm. I'm sure we'll have ample brave volunteers."

Katie slapped her hands on the desk. "You get a team together, and I'll lead them. We get in, we get information, and we get out. Then we plan our attack."

The general ran his finger over his lips and then grinned. "I've got a team for you."

"Son of a bitch," one of Brock's team members muttered, squashing a bug against the tattoos on the back of his neck.

Brock chuckled. "You okay, Turner? You got one of those bloodsucking birds on your back?"

Turner rolled his eyes, slashing his machete through the thick brush. "This is fucking stupid. If I'd thought I'd be spending my time humping through the jungle, I would have skipped out and been drinking mai tais on a beach somewhere."

One of the other guys pulled out his gun and pointed it at a huge snake. "Stop bitching. I got snakes on a plane over here."

Brock took his knife and threw it hard, pinning the snake to the tree. "You know these demons aren't going to make it easy for us. This time they had to open up portals right over ancient voodoo sites of mass sacrifice. You aren't going to find those right in the center of New York."

One of the other guys snorted. "You might. Have you been to New York lately? It's a wild town."

Turner groaned. "We've all been there, asshat, remember? Or are you still drunk from our trip there?"

They all laughed as they humped through. Suddenly, the sound of cracking branches stopped Brock in his tracks, and he put up his fist. His finger came to his lips, and he signaled for the guys to get low and look around. They all followed orders. They crouched down and began reaching into their holsters and pulling out their guns.

Suddenly, a large monkey leaped straight at Turner. Its eyes were an inflamed red, and its fangs dripped yellow foam. Turner spun and pulled the trigger, hitting the monkey between the eyes. It shrieked and turned to dust, and Turner freaked. "What the fuck? Demon-infected animals? You've got to be fucking kidding me!"

Without warning, other animals appeared in the dense brush surrounding them. Monkeys and gorillas, panthers and snakes. Huge lizards and small, quick foxes. All of them had burning red eyes.

Brock roared at his team, "It's showtime, boys!"

The guys moved fast and hard. They quickly fanned out, forming a loose perimeter and blasting the beasts with everything they had. The monkeys and smaller animals went down fast, but the panthers lurking in the bushes took some group effort. By the time they were finished, piles of dust were everywhere, and all the guys were panting.

Brock knew they were close to their target. Someone was attempting to keep them away.

He pulled his M16 around in front of him and checked the magazine. "I bet you the all-you-can-eat buffet at Mr. Fung's that we find a nice big demon right over that ridge. Who wants in on this?"

"I got you." Turner chuckled.

The guys moved through the bushes carefully, trying to make as little noise as possible. As they reached a small clearing in the brush, they heard a huge cracking sound. Brock raised a fist, and the team halted.

A large uprooted tree flew straight for them, trailing creepers and dirt. They all dropped to the ground as it soared over their heads and came crashing down somewhere behind them.

In front of them was a monstrous beast, all cracked black scales and bulging fangs. He huffed and snorted, daring them to come into his territory.

Brock swirled his arms. "Line up, and let's send this bad boy back to hell!"

The men fell into formation and leveled their automatic weapons. Brock gripped his pistol so tightly his knuckles went white. The demon was hideous. "Steady."

As soon as the beast took one step, they started to blast him. He wailed as he charged them, swinging his arms at the guys even as bullets tore into his chest and shoulders. The team scattered as he broke their ranks. Turner and a few men broke off to try and flank the beast. Brock wasn't so lucky. He backpedaled away from the demon, but the beast's fist caught his ankles and flipped him to the ground.

Brock's weapon went flying into the bush, and he was suddenly alone with a snarling nightmare.

Bullets slammed into the beast and knocked him back. Turner grabbed Brock and pulled him to his feet, then shoved a Desert Eagle pistol into his hand.

Brock leveled the hand cannon at the demon and shook his head. "Okay, one more time. And this time, aim for his fucking head."

Brock and Turner blasted the beast from the front while the rest of the team flanked him. Every time Brock pulled the trigger, a huge hole opened up in the demon's hide. The beast growled and tried to leap at Brock again, but Brock's gunfire took the top of his scaly head off. He fought the special bullets valiantly, stumbling first at Brock and then at the flanking team, but he finally fell to the ground. Turner saluted. "Timmmbeerrrr!"

As soon as the beast hit the ground, it exploded into dust that blew all over Turner. Brock and the others laughed as he spat the ash from his mouth. The radio on Brock's shoulder crackled, and their commander's voice came over loud. "Hey! Stop playing in the jungle and come back to base. It's urgent."

Brock lifted an eyebrow and clicked the button. "Yes, sir, on our way."

Brock found his pistol in the bushes and they all turned to walk back, Turner kicking the dirt. "Fucking playing in the jungle. Let's see him take on a panther and a giant ass demon."

One of the other guys chuckled. "And a fucking demon monkey. That shit was wild."

12

Joshua, Timothy, and Calvin stood at the gate to the base. Behind them was a barren desert, before them was a cold structure they had once called home. All of the lights in the armory were off, no cars parked in the garage, and the defenses had been disabled.

Calvin put his arm around Joshua. "Well, this was a nice place to lay my head, at least for a while."

Joshua nodded with a half-smile. "It was. Next time we move, though, it would be nice if it wasn't because we were attacked by demons.

Calvin chuckled. "Amen, brother. How about you, Timothy? You happy to be moving on to our next place of residence?"

Timothy shrugged. "I guess. Doesn't make much difference to me as long as it's comfortable. I spend a lot of time on my own at these spots."

"You got Stephanie and Korbin now," Calvin replied.

"Oh, yeah. Still, it is what it is, I suppose," Timothy lamented.

Calvin slapped him on the back. "Why do you look so sad then?"

Timothy glanced at Calvin and back at the ground. "They had to shut down my servers for the trip."

Calvin laughed loudly. "Yeah, man, that's usually how it works. It'll be even better at the new spot. Korbin says you're getting twice the room."

Timothy perked up a bit. "Hell, yeah, and it better be more impressive. They promised me godlike internet speed. I better not get over there and find out it moves at a glacial pace."

Calvin smirked. "Look, the big rig is on its way there now."

The three guys stared into the distance as the rig turned down the road. Timothy held his keys up and smiled. "At least I got a fun ride to get there in."

The guys piled into Timothy's Jeep, no top, no sides. They headed out of the base for the last time and made a quick right turn onto the main two-lane highway. Timothy looked in his rearview mirror and sighed. "Why do we always have to live so far away from everything? Now I'm even farther from good shopping."

The guys chuckled and shook their head. A loud roar blasted over them, and they watched as fighter planes flew overhead. Timothy rolled his eyes. "They better cap that noise near our new place, sister. Girl needs her beauty sleep."

The mountain sat looming high into the clouds. Jagged rocks covered in ice and snow glistened in the late evening light. The wind blew hard, shifting the powder back and forth, but no one was there to see it. The mountain was far too dangerous for even the most avid of climbers, and only saw action once or twice a year. The rest of the time, avalanches sat perched at the ready, waiting for a shift in the ground.

The only sounds piercing the air were the shudder of the trees in the wind and the random chirp of a bird flying through on its way somewhere else. The ground was untouched, white and sparkling, but the quiet was a dangerous façade. At any moment, that silence could be filled.

As the breeze began to dull a bit, the snow began to shift. Small balls rolled down over the ledges, plunging to the deeper swells at the base of the mountain. The sound of ice cracking echoed across the valley and into the distance. From above, the falling snow began to compound, growing larger and larger as the avalanche began to slide.

Brock's team saluted the guard at the base and presented their ID to the guards. They were covered in dirt and sweat, and a plume of ashes floated along behind Turner. They took their weapons back to their barrack tents and dusted Turner off outside. The guys laughed as he coughed and choked.

Brock leaned forward and whispered in Turner's ear. "You owe me Mr. Fung's buffet."

Turner groaned. "Can't this be payment enough? My cinder-covered embarrassment?"

Brock shook his head. "Nope. That's just an added bonus. A karmic cycle completed because you, my friend, are just too cocky."

Turner bucked playfully at Brock. "I'll show you cocky."

The team stowed their gear and straightened up as much as possible, then headed to the main building where their commander was waiting for them. Brock stepped to the door with the others behind him and glanced back. "Remember, let me do the damned talking. You morons always seem to get us in some sort of trouble."

They all chuckled quietly as Brock straightened his jacket and knocked on the door. The commander opened the door immediately, and all of the soldiers came to attention. "At ease, boys. Follow me. We're going to get comfortable in one of the meeting rooms. Too many of you assholes for one small office."

They all followed him down the hall and to the third door on the right. They sat down around the table and waited for the commander to close the door and begin. He dropped a large file folder on the desk in front of him and stared from man to man, getting a feeling for where they were.

After a few less than comfortable moments, he cleared his throat. "Boys, you're my best men. Fuck, you're probably the military's best men. You've been through hell and back and come out in one piece on the other side. I'd venture to say you're as good if not better than our mercenary squads out there. The Damned can be tricky if they don't get the right demon, no offense to whoever is infected on this team."

Brock glanced back and forth down the line. "We're all Damned, sir."

The commander lifted an eyebrow. "I forget that. You act so damned normal. Either way, you're the best of the best. I have an operation being offered to your team and only your team. You were requested specifically, and I can tell they're really hoping you take the job."

The guys waited for more information. The commander shook his head and chuckled. "The thing is so stupid. I'm sure you're going to die doing it. So knowing how much you do for the rest of the teams, you need to think long and hard. It's a volunteer mission only. No one will be looked negatively upon if they decide not to go. You'll simply stand by and wait for word your teammates haven't returned and then join another command."

Brock narrowed his eyes. "What is the assignment? I can't imagine it being that much worse than anything we've done before. Is it another incursion?"

The commander scoffed. "When you find out, you'll wish it was an incursion. After those six locations in Europe were hit by the demons, the government and their consorts decided we're living on borrowed time. We're getting beaten up little by little, and before we know it, we'll be hanging out on a limb. We don't want to get to the place where we're stuck between a rock and a hard place. We don't want to have to surrender to the demons to keep some of humanity intact. Now, I'm not saying that's gonna happen right now, but we're getting closer every day. The government thinks we need to be more aggressive with our approach."

Turner looked at the others to make sure he wasn't the only one who didn't understand. "What does that mean, sir? What's the mission?"

The commander shook his head. "Boys, your end goal is to go to hell."

Several of the guys chuckled. Turner chimed in. "If it's all the same to you, I think we'd rather end up in heaven, sir."

The commander smiled. "I'm sorry, boys, but no."

They all fell quiet, and a sense of unease permeated the room. Brock broke the silence. "What exactly are you saying?"

The commander slid the file across to Brock. "I've read the operation every which way you can read it. I didn't believe it at first, but then I remembered what kind of war we were in. The file says that your goal is literally to storm the gates of hell."

No one said a word. They all sat there absolutely stunned. Sure, many of them had joked about it before, but no one had actually thought it would be a reality.

Brock's demon laughed loudly in his ear. *Oh, this just takes the cake, sweetie pie. There is no way in hell, literally, no way I am marching back into that place.*

Brock ignored his demon and narrowed his eyes. "With whom would we be storming these gates, sir?"

The commander pulled the file back from Brock and shook his head. "This is top level secret, but I don't expect you boys to go marching into hell without knowing who you'll be working with and for. It's not a military member,

I know that for sure. It's actually a woman, let me see. Her name is here somewhere."

Brock and Turner exchanged a glance. Turner mouthed, "You think?"

They looked back at the commander and asked in unison, "Katie?"

The commander flipped through several pages and then found the name. He looked up, surprised. "Yes. How did you know that?"

Turner snorted laughter. Two of the guys high-fived each other. Brock took a moment to look at each team member. One by one, they nodded. Brock swallowed and looked at the commander. "Hell, sign us up!"

The guys all cheered and stood up, talking loudly to each other. The commander was dumbfounded, but pulled out a stack of forms and plopped them on the table. "Okay. Just fill out one of these forms each. It's liability waivers, next of kin, that sort of thing. I'll put my John Hancock on it and send it off to the general."

The guys rushed the stack, pushing each other out of the way to get to the forms. The commander just shook his head. He had never seen any soldier excitedly signing up for certain death. He looked at Brock, who was calmly sitting in his seat waiting for the others to finish up. Brock couldn't hide his smile. He shrugged his shoulders at the commander.

The commander threw his hands up. "You men are some of the most ballsy idiots I've ever met. Either you've finally lost your minds, or you really think you have a chance at this ridiculous assignment. Whichever one it is, this Katie lady must be one hell of a leader to get you guys to jump on it like this."

Turner handed Brock a form and winked at the commander. "Sir, when you find a badass like Katie, you want to be part of whatever she's working on. She wouldn't take us to hell if she thought we wouldn't come back."

The commander scowled. "Hey, it's your flesh that's gonna melt off, not mine. Just know if you don't come back, I'm going to be damned pissed. You're my finest men, and it's gonna be hard to replace you."

Brock handed the commander his paper and shook his hand. "Sir, I can almost promise you we will be coming back. We may be beaten up, a little sunburned, and possibly even grumpier than normal, but we'll be back. Besides, we can't let these other idiots fight the demons. You won't have any teams left."

The commander collected the rest of the forms and sighed, resigned. "Hell, you're probably damn right."

13

One of the lead Research and Development doctors stood in the center of his messy lab, his bright red hair sticking out in all directions. He turned, hitting his head on one of the lamps and grabbing it to stop it from swinging. At six feet tall when all the other doctors were short, he was at a bit of an architectural disadvantage in the building. He cursed and rubbed the bump on his head.

His assistant stopped in the middle of picking a gadget out of a box and lifted her eyebrow at Doctor Thorough. "What's wrong? You look more pale than usual."

"Just trying to run through the list of things I know we'll need to take with us to hell. This is a bit more confusing than I expected it to be when they tasked me with it."

Doctor Thorough was a genius, one of the top researchers in the program. His mannerisms, though, weren't quite up to the neat standards of everyone else. He was very focused on the technical side of things, which was

143

a good thing, but it left him little brainpower to deal with cleaning, people, or anything else that wasn't research.

His assistant, Alice was all about the work the doctor did on a regular basis but was finding herself a bit out of her element on this latest assignment. "You better get your head straight, and for the tenth time, do not forget the sunscreen. There may not be sun per se, but you burn close to an oven, so hell might crisp you. I don't want to bring you back here in an urn."

The doctor was too busy mumbling to himself to pay attention. Alice sighed as she went through one of the boxes. "Sign up for research in the military, they told me. It'll be a huge bonus on your resumé. Right. See new places and meet new people. New places like, I don't know, hell. And new people like, I presume, the Devil himself."

She tossed an empty toolbox into the large metal trash can and picked up a small box with all kinds of wires sticking out from it. There was a dial on top, but she knew better than to mess with one of the doctor's gadgets without knowing what it was. She put it down in the "I don't know" pile and grumbled. "Those recruiters were as bad as my friends said they would be."

The doctor glanced up. "Oh, yeah? How so?"

"Well, I heard the stories about recruiters lying to the low-level bullet sponges. Tell them it'll be easy, they won't get deployed, they will have great opportunities outside of the military, and so forth. I thought sitting down with the head of the department for a job-style interview would make me an exception. Nope. They said, 'Oh, Alice, you don't have to worry about being on the front line in R&D.' Pfft. Yeah, right. They should have said,

'Unless you work for a nutso doctor with just a tad bit too much enthusiasm for science and adventure.' Then I might have stopped for a minute and really thought about it."

At that point, Alice was on a rant, and the doctor knew it was no use trying to stop her. She was in one of those moods and had been since the doctor volunteered them to go straight to hell, literally.

She continued. "I mean, what am I supposed to say? The military owns me now. I know it was a volunteer situation, but what kind of pussy would I be if I backed down? A live pussy. That's right. I should have just said, 'Nope,' and turned and walked gracefully from the room. I couldn't send you in there by yourself, though. You would get mesmerized by some type of lava rocks you've never seen before and turn to a cinder in five seconds. You're brilliant, don't get me wrong, but you have the curiosity of a cat."

The doctor chuckled under his breath. Alice clanged a box closed. "Spend my days studying in a library or looking into a microscope in some lab somewhere? Oh, no. How about we take a little field trip to *hell*?" To emphasize her point, she dropped a large book on her desk, causing several stacks of paper to blow to the floor.

Dr. Thorough pushed his glasses higher on his nose. He sighed and gave her a comforting smile. "If you had looked a little further into the notes of what the other R&D teams have been doing, you would see that some of them are on the front lines all the time. They don't have a nice office with a perfect set of tools and air conditioning. They fight for their lives every day. Instead of microscopes, their lab techs carry M16's. The only reason you aren't there all the time with them is that our theoretical work doesn't require it. In fact, it's almost the opposite."

He picked up some of the papers from the floor and tried not to smile at her pout. "Alice, all these tools and analyzers we've been theorizing with should tell us more about the other dimension. All the work we've been sweating and pouring our lives into is actually going to get a chance to be tested. That's more than most theoretical scientists ever get to say. Most of their work is numbers-based and usually isn't even tested until long after they've died. We get to see everything in action live and in person. It's historic. Really."

Alice nodded her head with slumped shoulders. "But why *us*?"

He looked at her strangely. "Who else is going to know if the tools and inventions are working correctly? It's only the ones who designed them, isn't it?"

"I can't argue with you on that one. You had to go and teach me the dark arts of theoretical dimensional data acquisition. Now I'm finding a nice vacation to hell as my reward."

The doctor put down the stack of papers in his hand and walked to Alice. He took her hands in his and looked at her seriously. "I know this is scary stuff, Alice. I do. But think about the reason you began studying all of this in the first place. You've dedicated yourself to science. You're not looking at the stars, but instead, you are focused on saving the entire human race from annihilation by the demons. Be proud that you're going on this adventure. Be honored, and be brave. If this works, your name will be known around the world, right alongside mine. We will be the most revered scientists in history. We are going to be the first humans to set foot on this new world. Don't think about it in a biblical sense, think about it in a scientific sense."

Alice narrowed her eyes. "I suppose you're right. It would be pretty sweet to end up coming back a hero. When the world is saved, I can move on to any research institute I want to. They'll let me head up teams. And on top of it, if you eliminate the fear constant, which I have to say is hard to do because the fear is pretty constant right now, it's pretty exciting. I suspect this is how an astronaut feels before going into space. Only without the visions of demons ripping their limbs off and eating their entrails as an afternoon snack."

The doctor chuckled and shook his head. "Focus on sorting through the pile of gear over there. Just call things out, and I'll say 'Yes,' or 'No.' If you know already, then put them in the right spots."

Alice grimaced and dug into the pile. "You know, if I lose a limb, you are totally inventing some incredible replacement for me. I want to be fucking Cable or something."

Doctor Thorough nodded as he got lost in his own pile of gear. "You got it. Best superhero robot arm ever."

Alice mumbled to herself as she tossed one of the gadgets in the "go to hell" pile. "Better be the best arm ever."

She reached into the pile and pulled out a long rod with several wires flopping at the top. She squinted one eye and then nodded, reaching down and pulling up a large orb that attached. "Low-sensor-radioactive-charging-synthe-sizer. Yep, that's going with us."

She reached down again, coming up with a flat plastic rectangle. Alice looked around for the doctor, but she didn't see him. "Dr. Thorough, do we need the high-molec-ular-bandwidth-distribution-and-atom—fuck, what was the last word?"

The doctor's voice echoed from somewhere in the room. "Don't remember, and no!" There was a moment of silence, then quick footsteps from the back room. The doctor stuck his head out of the back corner and narrowed his eyes. "Wait. That project weighs nine thou-sand pounds and is bigger than this room. How would we bring that?"

She looked down at the item in her hand and turned it over, slapping her forehead. "Oh, this is the remote control. How was I supposed to know? That was Trent's project!"

The doctor's face fell. "For a top-of-your-class Ph.D., you sure have your share of blonde moments. Let's try to keep those at a minimum in hell. And if you had tried a little harder to get along with Trent, then maybe you would have remembered that."

Alice stomped her foot, throwing the remote over her shoulder. "Hey! I can't help it if he wasn't the brightest crayon in the box. I tried to be nice to him, but he always thought he was right, even when I proved he wasn't. He nearly melted down the entire core of the R-27 Hadron project that we worked nine months on. I don't control stupid, doctor."

Doctor Thorough chuckled and picked up a black case, opening it to reveal three glass cylinders of bright green liquid. "There you are, my babies. Alice! I found the demon blood we were experimenting on."

"Perfect! Don't drop it. You know what happened last time. They had to rebuild the entire south wing. Thank God, it was closed at the time. It was genius, though, absolutely genius to combine their blood with the molten special metal and hydrochloric acid. You can literally kill them with themselves."

The doctor shrugged. "Yeah and melt a hole in the Earth to the core."

Alice waved her hand dismissively. "Meh, that won't matter in hell. If we get attacked, just have the merc chuck one of those at the demons and throw us through a portal. Bye bye, hell. Hello, Tahiti."

Thorough closed the case and carefully set it on his desk. "I think I'll ask them about it for next time. Don't really want to test the stability on our first trip to hell. Don't need it blowing up in my hand from the heat, either."

"Probably a good idea. Save it for the big finale. Make a huge fireworks show out of melting demons."

"Maybe you should have written movie scripts for a living."

Alice stood up quickly with excitement. "Look! The atomizer I built when I first started working with you. We got the results for that first specimen that was brought to us. That woman who had the nasty demon that tried to chomp fingers off."

"Oh, yeah. I forget what happened to that specimen."

Alice laughed. "She nearly took Trent's nose off, and he put a bullet in her head."

Thorough shook his head. "That's right. I came in to

find a pile of dust on the examination table and Trent whistling in the back."

Alice smiled. "Hey, the best kind of demon is a vaporized one."

The avalanche skidded down the side of the mountain, taking droves of trees with it. It finally came to a stop at the base, pushing dunes of snow for about two miles. The cracking of the ice didn't stop, and before long, large chunks were toppling down the mountainside. The echo of the snapping could even be heard two towns away from the mountain and all over the military base.

Hundreds of feet up the side of the rocky terrain, a crack formed in the ice, splintering across to the other side of the large block. It sat for a moment, slowing to a stop until suddenly, a huge fist slammed through it from underneath. The large, long talons stretched wide before slowly receding back down below the surface.

Again, the hand blasted through the ice, sending chunks flying every which way. The balled fist swung from side to side, pushing the ice out and over the edges of the mountain. The beast rumbled angrily inside, working as hard as he could to get himself free of his icy coffin. What was stirring below had awoken, and his bright red eyes beamed up through the shattered ice.

"Everyone got everything they're going to need?" Brock asked, pulling the straps to his rucksack tighter.

One of the guys looked up, holding a picture in his hand. "They're going to store the rest of this, right? And if something happens to us, they'll send it to our families?"

Brock shrugged. "I'm assuming so, but I don't know what the deal with this assignment is. It might be a disavow kind of assignment if we don't come back. Most likely, it'll be one of those 'Died in a training accident,' things. Yes, I think your family will get your stuff."

Turner tossed a magazine into the trash. "Just in case. I don't need my mom seeing my wrinkled-ass 1983 copy of Playboy. Might make her upset."

The other guys laughed, and Brock shook his head. "Listen, guys, this is no different than before. We get to work alongside Katie, and you know she's going to watch out for us. Now come on, we got to get out to the pads so when the choppers arrive, we can get the hell out of this jungle."

They all finished packing up their things and headed outside, carrying only what they would need for the mission. They lined up near the helipads to wait, the choppers not quite there yet. Several of the guys in their unit walked to shake their hands.

"Good luck, guys," one of them volunteered.

"Seriously, let's end this bullshit. And if you see Lucifer, tell him I'll see his ass soon, and I'm gonna have words." Brock chuckled and slapped the guy's hand.

The last guy in their unit nodded his head. "Give them hell…in hell. Shit, that's redundant."

Katie tapped her fingers against the arm of her seat. She looked out the window at the base approaching in the distance. She was in the middle of Colorado, the mountains looming in the background. It was gorgeous and definitely looked a lot colder than it was in New York.

Pandora was excited to get on the ground. *I'm freaking starving. Let's get this over with, so I can dive into some donuts.*

Katie smiled. *We have a lot of work on our hands, so just chill out, okay? You'll get your food, I promise.*

Better. Oh, look, an old ass base. Great.

Katie leaned forward for a better look. Coming up beneath them were two massive hangars. They were large enough to hold old blimps and had concrete buildings on each side. Katie knew those buildings led to the underground area of the base. Katie had gotten very used to underground bases and had come to like them better than most.

In the distance, dozens of heavy large electrical lines swooped down from tall poles about half a mile away all the way to the base. She wondered what all of them were for since her last base hadn't had anything quite that extensive. At the same time, they didn't have military money to work with, either.

Pandora was not at all in the mood for what they were planning. *You know, this is a decent idea. I'm not going to say it's not.*

But?

But what I really want right now is an Italian dinner, a tight dress by an Italian designer, and an evening in a nightclub with a bunch of Italian men.

Katie rolled her eyes. *Work and then play, Pandora.*

You were all about play a few days ago.

I was all about sleep. That's different.

They both involve lots of time in bed. Katie could almost hear Pandora's grin.

Work now. Bedroom activities later.

Ugh, I feel like I've done enough work in my life.

The plane began making its descent, hitting the runway gently and quickly coming to a stop near one of the large hangar bays. She grabbed her bags and exited the plane. The place was quite a bit louder than she'd thought it would be. Shirtless men were maneuvering all around her, cleaning and prepping the base again. Katie lifted an eyebrow as two of them walked by. *I think I found you the hot men you wanted.*

That one kind of looks Italian. Do you think he can make me lasagna?

I'll just grab a radio and bam! Club on the go.

Pandora sniffed. *Although I prefer the ones who wear cologne and buy me drinks, these specimens will do.*

One of them walked up to Katie, wiping his forehead on his T-shirt—that was in his hand. Steam rose off his skin, and Katie just stood there staring. He nodded toward the plane, oblivious. "We'll get you unloaded and put your stuff in the secure hangar bay. If you head to the main building, they're waiting to take you to your room."

"Thanks. And nice uniform, by the way."

Katie left him grinning on the tarmac. Pandora whistled loudly. *Look at you getting all sassy pants hours before you voluntarily roll into hell. I guess you are feeling yourself today, sister.*

Katie laughed. *I guess I am.*

They headed across the base and to the main building. One of the staff, a woman this time, was waiting to show Katie to her bunk. Pandora didn't like the sound of "bunk." *It better be nicer than a fucking cot. I'm a queen.*

Katie rolled her eyes. *You used to be a queen. Now you're a demon living inside a volleyball player. Plus, you're on our side.*

Don't say that too loud. You'll ruin my reputation.

The soldier led them into the underground base. They walked behind her hurrying to keep up. The base seemed to be all empty rooms and dimly lit halls. Wires snaked along the walls. Some were attached, and others just dangled from the ceiling. They passed by a large room full of computers and monitors, but none of the lights were on inside. A thick coating of dust covered almost everything in the room. Katie wrinkled her nose. *This was probably mothballed decades ago.*

I wonder if any of it works anymore. Hell, I'm wondering if we're even breathing clean air. Pandora coughed dramatically.

Katie ran her hand over a small, broken screen on the outside of one of the rooms. *It's kind of like a ghost town. It's weird.*

Pandora grumped. *Yeah, well, all I know is the general better come through with his promise of donut delivery every three days or Momma is going to be so pissed off. If it wasn't a ghost town already, it would be when I got through with it. I'll work from fucking New York City. It's a civilized place. There are comfortable living arrangements, donuts down the street, and it doesn't look like a sunken ghost ship.*

"Here's your room, but feel free to explore. The general left instructions that you had free reign. Please let us know if you need anything." The soldier offered her a smile as she handed her a key.

"Thank you," Katie replied, and the soldier left them alone.

She turned and stared at the door, almost too afraid to go inside. *How about we explore first, and then maybe our room won't seem so terrifying?*

Pandora sighed. *Yeah, probably a good idea. I don't smell donuts in there anyway.*

They took a tour back through the hallways. The hallways led to rooms mostly filled with empty bunks and abandoned equipment. They traveled back to the top of the base. Katie took in a lungful of fresh air.

No donuts up here, but no ghosts, either.

Katie froze a moment, startled. *Ghosts? Can you really smell ghosts?*

Not yet.

But if they were here?

They'd probably pay us to exorcise them from the spooky old base. This place sucks.

Katie snorted laughter and walked to the other hangar bay. Inside, there were people everywhere wearing welding helmets. They were working on creating steel walls for more protection against anything that might follow them out of hell.

Pandora looked around the room, impressed by the work they'd done so quickly. *Guess this is the transfer room. We'll work from here.*

Katie scoffed, staring at the high ceilings and expansive space around her. *More like the transfer hall.*

"Katie." The deep voice came from a tall man with a bushy mustache and perfectly pressed uniform as he walked over.

Katie smiled and shook his hand. "That's me."

"I'm Commander Ellison. I'm one of the men in charge here. I'm sorry I didn't greet you as you got off the plane. As you can see, we're working around the clock to prepare everything for you and your team."

Katie looked around with him. "I see that. It looks like it's really coming along."

The commander looked proud. "It's an old place, but it's perfect for the cause. Have you been to your quarters yet?"

"Yes. Well, kind of. We decided to do some exploring first."

He smiled. "Of course. I hope you find everything comfortable. We didn't have a lot to work with. It's not quite up to par with the base you just moved from, but it's getting there."

"I'm sure it will be fine."

Commander Ellison put his hands behind his back. "I can make sure we get you whatever you need. You will tell me if anything's missing?"

Do it. Do it. Do it.

Katie bit the inside of her lip and shrugged. "Donuts?"

Yesssss.

———

Timothy smiled at Stephanie and tapped her on the butt as he walked by. She was putting a fresh coat of paint on the walls of the new barracks.

"Lookin' good, sister."

Stephanie gave him a huge smile. "Thanks, girl, just trying to make it feel less Top Gun and more Vogue Homes."

Timothy's room was on the third floor, and the comms room was in the basement. He'd spent several hours down there already, testing equipment, getting everything moved around, and getting caught up on what he'd missed.

"Mm-hmm, I know that's right. Hey, where's Calvin?"

Stephanie pointed down the hall. "Third door on your right."

"Thank you," he replied, blowing her a kiss.

Timothy sauntered down to the room and peeked his head inside. "Yoo-hoo, Calvin."

Calvin groaned as he finished hanging a shelf and climbed down off a ladder. "Is that straight?"

Timothy tilted his head to the side. "Straight enough."

Calvin lifted an eyebrow at him. "That's not really what

I was hoping for, but all right. What's up? Did you get everything set up? It's been on my mind, but I didn't really want to come down there and harass you about it."

Timothy nodded. "That's appreciated. I don't work well with big black men standing over my shoulder."

"It's a race thing?"

"It's a concentration thing. I need my private time. Trust me, whatever anxiety you've been feeling about the new digs, triple that, and you have me. I went right down to my home away from home and set up the system first. We're working for people, here. Then I got down to the real work. I added all my antivirus stuff, encrypted a bunch of text, and made sure all the cables were neatly stowed. The last thing I need is for you or Korbin to come stumbling in there like the oafs you are and trip over some crucial wiring. It could crash the whole damned system."

Calvin sighed with relief. "Good, and we're not oafs. I was really worried about the security and IT stuff. I know it's the basis of almost everything we do. I was afraid we would be shut off from the world out here. The move was risky. We don't know who could have been watching. It would have been the perfect time for an attack. Do you need anything extra out here since we're even farther from the main strip?"

"Nope. I have all the computers running, and everything is humming along perfectly. I even got to see the different sectors. There were small portals but nothing too big. The backup system I placed at the station in New York kept everything going for them while we were down. I have to say, I'm pretty proud of it." Timothy lowered his voice conspiratorially. "Between you and me, I didn't have a chance to test that thing after installing it." Timothy put his hands behind his back and followed Calvin around the room.

Calvin stopped, and Timothy nearly ran into him. Calvin stared at him a moment. "Is there something else?"

Timothy wrinkled his nose. "Actually, yeah. Do you have a minute?"

"Sure. What's going on?"

Timothy had already sat downstairs for over an hour, trying to decide whether to tell Calvin about what he'd heard. He felt like a spy in the midst of his own people. It wasn't a good feeling. However, after giving it a lot of thought, he realized Calvin would be pissed if he weren't told what Katie may or may not be up to.

"Well, I was doing some system tests and running a few different search programs, and I came across some chatter."

Calvin raised an eyebrow. "Is chatter a euphemism for shit you aren't supposed to know?"

"If you haven't noticed, while you're up here punching and hammering and being a big manly man, I'm down there keeping my little ears to the ground. If it comes through my system, then I'm supposed to know it. Just like I told you with the radio thing, if you don't want people to know, you better not be broadcasting that shit on open channels."

"And this chatter was on an open channel?"

Timothy grinned sheepishly. "Well, not exactly. I mean, it wasn't hard to get to, if that's what you're asking. Anyone with a smidgen of talent would have been able to tap right into the chatter. They weren't going by their little military book protocol, so it's not my fault that I heard it."

Calvin pinched the bridge of his nose. "Can we move through this and get to what you heard? I've got about six more shelves to hang, furniture to move in, and then we need to have a comfortable place to sleep."

Timothy put up his hands. "Right. Right, sorry. So there's a rumor that a strike team is going down into hell. And by rumor, I mean the military personnel at the staging area were talking about it on a very lightly secured channel."

Calvin turned quickly to Timothy. "Katie?"

Timothy pursed his lips. "Please, like they're admitting that. They may have been dumb with their security measures, but they aren't that ridiculous. However, if you really think about what's about to go down, can you think of anyone else who might be involved? Storming the gates of hell does not sound like something anyone of sound mind would do. Which leaves Katie and her wild child demon queen."

"I don't think…" Calvin pointed his finger at Timothy but didn't finish his sentence. Instead, he dropped his hand and pulled his phone out of his pocket. "I'll make a call."

Timothy gave him a sassy look and tapped him on the shoulder. "You do that."

Calvin tapped the phone against his lips. He knew full well that this had to be one of Katie's plans. She was the only one on Earth who could open a portal and get through to hell. Things must be as bad as he'd feared, or worse. He knew she wouldn't attempt something this dangerous unless there were no other way. Things must have gone beyond some breaking point.

He sat down on the foldout chair in the middle of the floor. He chose his words carefully, figuring out exactly what it was he wanted to say to her. If invading hell was in the cards, he was damn sure going to be a part of it. He had fought too hard and too long to back down now. He was going to kick some demon ass right there on the steps of hell.

If this was the only way he could get the revenge he sought for the lives of the friends and family he had lost, then so be it.

Brock and the team buckled their seat belts as the large military plane began to make its descent to the base in Colorado. The cargo area didn't have any windows and it damn sure didn't have luxury seating. They had no idea what they were flying into. Brock looked around at his team. "You guys ready for this?"

"Hell, yeah," several of them screamed out.

Turner laughed, tilting his head against the seat and shutting his eyes. "Send me to hell, but fuck, don't make me ride in one of these tin cans again."

The turbulence hit them, rattling their teeth. Everyone laughed as they gripped the bottoms of their seats and tried to settle themselves. The landing gear folded down, and the plane hit the runway, bouncing for a second before slowing down to a stop. The guys unbuckled their harnesses and began gathering their stuff as the back hatch opened.

"All right, let's unload, and then we'll go from there. Just don't get too comfortable," Brock shouted as they headed off the plane.

They unloaded onto the runway and stopped as a group, looking around them at the old base. Turner lifted his eyebrows. "Uh. Don't think I could get too comfortable here even if I tried."

One of the other guys chuckled. "This shit is moth-balled as fuck."

Brock pointed a finger at him. "Hey, we're only here for a little while. Make the best of it. I'm sure they're putting all of this together at the last minute. If it's good enough for Katie, it's good enough for us. Now, put your rucks down, and let's unload. Weapons and ammo check."

The guys piled their sacks against a wall and started carrying crates off the plane. One of the guys lifted a huge crate of weapons, his muscles bulging under a dense network of tattoos. He side-glanced at the other soldiers walking around without shirts. He set the crate of weapons down and elbowed Turner. "So shirts are optional in this military?"

Turner's head flew up. "Does that mean for the women too? I'm all about that rule if that's what that means."

Brock slammed a crate down in front of him. "I'm sure you'll have time to figure out that you're completely ridicu-lous, but for now, can you stay focused? The plane has a schedule to keep, and we need to get these crates off."

Turner wrinkled his nose. "Sure, act like it didn't cross your mind."

The tattooed soldier laughed and walked back toward the plane. Brock was about to follow him when a hand landed on his shoulder. He stopped and turned. A staff sergeant stood in front of him. "Yes, staff sergeant?"

"I've come to take you and your men to your quarters."

Brock nodded. "We have these last five boxes, then we'll grab our rucksacks. Are we meeting with anyone tonight?"

The staff sergeant stood perfectly tall and straight, and Brock held back a smile, realizing he was new to the unit. "No. Your orientation is at eighteen hundred. You and your men are to come in desert BDUs, and everything else will be explained from there. We'll also be handing out gear and specialty uniforms for the action."

Brock slapped him on the shoulder. "Perfect. And where can we get some chow? We're starving."

The staff sergeant nodded. "Of course. I'll wait and escort you from your rooms to the chow hall. It starts in thirty minutes."

Brock turned to the guys and cupped his mouth. "If you boys want chow tonight, then you have exactly five seconds to get those crates over here so they can shut that plane up."

The guys looked at each other and scrambled to grab more crates. Turner jostled his tattooed teammate. "I got this one. I got it."

"You're slow. I haven't eaten in a week."

"More like six hours."

Tattoos groaned and leaped up the plane to grab another crate. He slammed the last crate down, and Brock laughed as he grabbed rucksacks and started tossing them to their respective owners. "Dummy One, Dummy Two,

Dummy Turner, get your gear. Come on, get your shit together, we're having steak tonight."

The staff sergeant muttered, "I don't think chow is steak tonight."

Brock glanced at the sergeant. "You're in for a treat tonight, sergeant. These boys are a mess."

Calvin put the phone to his ear and waited for Katie to answer. It rang several times, then he heard loud noises in the background. "Katie?"

"Yeah, hold on. Let me get somewhere a little quieter," she yelled over the noise.

She made her way to the other side of the hangar bay and put her finger in her other ear. "Calvin, you there?"

"I'm here. Where are you? A construction zone?"

Pandora scoffed. *He has no idea.*

Katie ignored her. She knew if he was calling, he probably had some idea of what was going on. "Kind of. It's quieter now. How's everything going over there? Is Timothy up and running?"

Calvin smirked. "We're getting there. Timothy has everything set up and is monitoring everything as we speak. Stephanie is making the place pretty, and Korbin is working on defensive measures. I just got done hanging some shelves and getting everything unpacked. It's a lot, and it's a mess, but nowhere near what the other base was when we moved in."

Katie sighed with relief. "Good. I know the general is

worried about you guys. He wants to know the armory is up and running as soon as possible."

"It's all headed in that direction," he replied.

"So, what's up?"

"Well, I heard a rumor. It's a pretty good one too. The rumor has it you're going to hell."

Katie laughed. "Wow, but Daddy, I didn't diddle that guy."

Calvin chuckled. "Not for sex before marriage or I already have a reservation. I'm talking about a real operation."

Katie shook her head. "Oh, I wonder what birdy told you that?"

Calvin tried not to snort, but he couldn't hold back. "I bet you can figure that one out pretty quickly."

"Hmm, was it one that really likes clothes and refers to everyone as 'girlfriend?'"

"No comment, so the guilty can remain blameless."

Katie tilted her head toward the ceiling. "There is definitely truth in that rumor. We decided to do a low-risk R&D operation. We're going to gather a bunch of information on hell. The climate, the terrain, mineral information —that sort of thing. In and out very quickly. Ultimately, sure, it will be used to storm hell, but right now it's just reconnaissance. We're trying to make sure we can sustain human life down there, or out there, wherever it is. The place almost killed me, and we know what kind of tolerance I have. I can't send humans or lightly infected in just to have them melt into the lava pits. We need a test run so when I do decide to take the war to them, we know exactly what we're facing."

Calvin listened. He understood the need for the mission, but he felt like he was being left out. "Here's the thing. You're missing a very important part of this project."

Katie smiled. "Oh, yeah? What's that?"

"Me. I should be there."

Katie sighed. "Look, Calvin, I understand you want to be part of this, but it's really unnecessary at this point. It's not worth the risk right now. You need to be at that base. They need you, and we need it up and running."

Calvin tried to keep his emotions in check. "If I stay here much longer, Korbin is going to have me filling sandbags and digging embankments myself."

Katie grinned. "Oh, I see how this is going to go. This is a sympathy play, is it?"

"Hell, yes. Whatever it takes, so I'm not digging dirt out in the desert. It's hot out here, Katie. Hell would be a relief."

Pandora cackled loudly. *Dude has a point.*

Katie grumped. *I don't want to take the chance of losing him. He's too important to me right now.*

Oh, get off it. Let him come. I can have fun with all twelve inches of him.

Calvin bit the inside of his lip, waiting for her to say something. "What does Pandora think?"

Here, let me drive. I'll describe my thoughts in great detail. First, he's dressed up like a Roman Centurion, and I'm me.

Katie rubbed her face. "It's too complicated to go into right now. She says something about letting all twelve inches of you come. And I mean come here, not the dirty version."

Calvin chuckled. "You know *she* means the dirty one."

Pandora scoffed. *Damn right. When do I ever* not *mean the dirty version?*

Katie growled. "I don't want to do this and have something happen to you. I know Korbin can take care of the base, but we need you long-term. This is just research."

"Come on, Katie, when is it ever just research?" Calvin could feel her wearing down.

"You have a point. Every time I've been to hell I've either had to fight something terrible or I've been chased out."

"Wait. You've been to hell more than once?" Calvin was confused.

Katie looked around to make sure no one had heard her. "Yeah, but that's not important. That's secret agent stuff, top secret shit."

You're a terrible secret agent.

Calvin squared his shoulders and stiffened his voice. "Look, this is important, and I feel like I need to be there. The base will get taken care of without me, and you know that."

He'd be great for the team.

I'm thinking.

And he'd look great in a toga, or one of those leather skirts they wore back in the day.

Katie was silent for several moments before finally giving in. "Fine. Good lord. But you have to do what I tell you, and if I tell you to get out, you get out. Understand?"

"Yes!"

Yes! Toga! Toga! Toga! Cross my Rubicon! Invade my Gaul!

Katie rolled her eyes, but she was secretly feeling better now that her partner was going to be there with her. "Get ahold of Angie and have her handle the plane. She's the only one outside of this base who knows where you're going. If she questions it, tell her she can call me, but she might not get a signal. I can't believe you talked me into this."

Calvin chortled. "I told you from the beginning, Katie. We're a team, and that means if you go to hell, then I am going to be right there beside you, no questions asked."

Katie nodded. "All the way to hell, huh? That's a big thing to do for a friend."

"Please, you know you're my family. You jump, I jump, Rose."

Pandora growled. *That's my line.*

Katie shook her head. *Yeah, except only one person made it to the end of that movie.*

15

The screeching sound of a gate opening in the forest echoed through the tree line. Gentle waves of snow trickled down as Moloch poked his head out and looked around, ruining the peaceful scene. He shivered and wrapped his arms around his big body before he climbed through the gate and let it shut behind him.

He stood there for a moment, steam rising from his body. "Great. I'm in a fucking winter wonderland." He glanced down at his horrible nether regions "All right. Let's get this over with before the boys freeze the fuck off."

He tiptoed across the ground, jumping with each step as if the ground were hot to the touch. Anybody watching would have thought he was in burning pain. He found a large log on the edge of the mountain cliff and brushed the snow off. Moloch took a seat and rubbed his hands together, his knees shaking.

Moloch had been watching the frost giant from the warmth of his office in hell, but he decided this particular creature needed a personal touch. It was necessary for him to come here and wait for the giant to emerge the rest of the way. The vibrations in the ground beneath Moloch's taloned feet let him know that the giant was close. It was freezing cold outside, and he bounced his legs up and down, listening to the pounding and cracking of the ice below.

Moloch rolled his eyes. His horns were already accumulating snow, giving him a white crown. He was so over the cold wind whipping across the mountain and the constant dusting of ice crystals falling from the tree branches over his head. "Come on, you big frozen bitch, get up and get moving. I don't have all day. I'm going to fucking freeze to death out here."

Moloch thought he was talking to himself, which made him jump even harder when a booming voice came from over the edge of the mountain. "It would take a thick-skinned demon like yourself a very long time to actually freeze to death, Moloch."

Moloch jumped to his feet and grinned a sharp-toothed grin. "Old friend, good to see you're up and moving around! I've been keeping tabs on you from my office and figured I'd come and welcome you back to the land of the living." Moloch spoke in demon, a language of guttural utterances and wet, snotty growls. English wasn't really in the frost giant's vocabulary.

A large hand pushed through the snow and slammed onto the ground in front of Moloch. He watched as a twelve-foot Leviathan pulled himself from the snow and onto his feet. His large, scaled body was blue with enormous icicles hanging from his chin like ornaments. His bright red eyes narrowed as he looked at Moloch.

Moloch backed up a bit as steam blew from the beast's nose. The frost giant bent down on one knee and glared at Moloch. "So basically, you've known I've been struggling to get free for days, but instead of coming to help me, you watched from afar? Please, Moloch, tell me what was so important that you weren't able to come here and help me out of that frozen tundra?"

Moloch laughed nervously. "World domination? No? Really, I thought I would get in the way. I didn't want to mess up your efforts. It helps warm the blood, and you've been sleeping a very long time... in a freezer, no less. Don't you feel better, now that you were able to stretch it all out like that?"

The frost giant growled, and the mountain shook. Snow rained on Moloch's head. The frost giant poked Moloch with a frozen finger. "Why does it not surprise me that you haven't changed? You're still the arrogant asshole I've known for centuries."

"At least I'm reliable."

The frost giant pulled a tree from the ground and began stripping branches off. "So what is this all about? You've woken me, and I've discovered I don't like the waking world. Speak."

Moloch shivered on his stump. "Well, Baal and I are working on taking over the world. We're tired of the cramped space below, and we want to branch out. We haven't been doing that bad, actually. We're causing some decent chaos, using strategy and everything. The angels haven't really interfered with us at all. I thought by now they would have put together some sort of huge attack, but they have pretty much stayed out of it. So we're free to fight the battle with the humans."

The frost giant sneered. "They always did wait until the last second to make their grand entrance. Very dramatic." He finished clearing branches from his tree and began stripping the dark bark off, revealing white wood underneath.

"There is one angel, though. She's actually not even a full angel, but she's been giving us hell, pardon the pun. I guess she's technically half-angel and half-demon. Well, that's not entirely accurate either. She is half-angel and Pandora."

"Pandora?"

"Lilith. The bitch is fighting for the humans." Moloch lowered his head as the frost giant's eyes grew wide. He roared and swung his newly fashioned club over Moloch's head. Moloch ducked quickly, avoiding the club, and it slammed into a row of trees. The trees cracked and fell, sending clouds of snow into the air. Moloch shuddered as it slid down his neck.

The frost giant breathed heavily and angrily, staring at Moloch. "Why is that bitch always a problem? I hate her. I always have. She's always in the way of every good plan."

Moloch scoffed. "Tell me about it. She killed her brother T'Chezz. Oh yeah, chopped his head right off with a sword she got from the angels. Yeah. An angel sword. No shit. She came to hell and saved a human. It's fucking crazy, right? Now she's fighting for the humans with her meat sack angel body. She's always been a needy bitch."

The frost giant let out a deep sigh. He used his claws to

shave the tip of his club down, giving it a crude point. "What is this new world like? Is it different than the last time I was here?"

Moloch looked at him like he was crazy. "Dude, it's been centuries."

He shrugged. "The humans weren't very bright last time I was here."

Moloch snorted. "Things have changed, my friend. They built huge cities, polluted the Earth, invented all kinds of technology. It's nuts."

The frost giant looked at him, unimpressed. "And women? Are there still lots of women?"

Moloch looked around them atop a huge mountain. "Well, there are none up here, but down in the cities, they're everywhere."

"Are these cities crowded?"

Moloch nodded, blowing warm air into his hands. He cupped his warm hands over his crotch. "Shit yeah. The cities are so crowded they can barely walk next to each other. Easy targets for a big demon, but they come in numbers. That can suck for us sometimes."

"What about weapons? Still shooting with arrows and bows?"

Moloch furled his brow and blinked. "No, dude. They not only have missiles, guns, bombs, and grenades, but they have nuclear and hydrogen bombs. Crazy shit. I wish I'd thought of it. They held nothing back when it came to weapons. They were at war with each other, and now they've turned their attention to us. They also have special metal that severely injures demons." Moloch pointed to the frost giant's crude spear. "I don't think that's going to cut it."

"Really?"

"Yeah. Special metal. It's a bitch."

The frost giant considered his spear, then snapped it in two. "What about language? Icelandic? Slavic?" He started to shave the other end of the spear into a point.

"Uh, no. Almost everyone speaks English where we're going, but there are a plethora of other languages out there. Hundreds of different languages, really, but English is definitely high on the list. They still haven't deciphered our language, except for when the bitch, Lilith, is involved." Moloch snarled, feeling the anger inside the Leviathan filling him too.

The frost giant held up his two new spears. "There! Two!"

Moloch sighed. "I really didn't sell the special metal like I should have. Spears are old-school. You're going to need to think a bit more like a human, here."

The giant tossed his spears to the ground. "Well, I guess I can't go walking around like this then."

Moloch looked at him with sorrow. "No, friend, that would be a dead giveaway."

The frost giant stood up and cracked his knuckles. His eyes sparkled and glimmered, blue energy crackling around him. The frost giant's body began to shrink smaller and smaller until he was the same size as an average human male. Moloch nodded, impressed, until his eyes landed on the man's naked lower half.

The frost giant rolled his shoulders and neck, getting

comfortable. "Now I am ready to conquer these pissant humans."

Moloch put his fingers to his lips and then pointed. He stopped himself and pressed his fingers to his lips again. The frost giant rolled his eyes and put his hands out. "What is it now?"

Moloch gestured to the frost giant's dong.

"What? Have men lost their dicks now?"

"No. I just think it might be a good idea if you got some clothes before you try and conquer anything. They value a bit of modesty now." Moloch tried to hide a smirk.

The giant waved his hands in disgust. "These humans and their issues. If it's not one thing, it's another. We started with no clothes, went to fully dressed, back to barely any clothes, and now it's suddenly rude to walk around as nature intended. Whatever. I will get these clothes, but then I'm building my army again. I'm going to take over Europe."

Moloch put his hands on his hips. "I hate to tell you this, but you can't have all of Europe. I've put in work. I want to be a Lord."

"But I'm a lord, or at least I was," the giant grumbled angrily.

Moloch narrowed his eyes. "What's in a name? Lord? Frost giant? Leviathan? Just names. Now things have changed. You have to fucking share. You were never any good at that."

The giant looked at him like he was going to explode. "Fine, whatever, we share. *But* I get Schwyz, Uri, and Unterwalden."

Moloch nodded and smiled appraisingly. "Good choice,

Switzerland. That's what they call it now. I understand the women are particularly attractive."

The giant eyed him and laughed. "You not like?"

Moloch shrugged. "Can't live with them, can't eat them when they piss you off. They give you indigestion, alive or dead."

The giant curled his lip. "You never did like the human women much. Except of course when you were in the human body here on Earth. Then you didn't mind them so much. Of course, you would kill them anytime they got on your nerves."

Moloch sighed. "They can be so damn needy. No, I don't want to give you children. No, I don't want to hold your damn human hand. Yes, I absolutely expect to be fed small live animals and human heads whenever I snap my fingers. That's the one that always got them."

The giant chuckled. "I remember that one girl, long ago. You walked into the house and poured out your sack full of human heads and announced, 'Dinner is served!' The sounds of her screams could be heard for miles."

Moloch and the giant both laughed, shutting it down quickly, remembering they really didn't like each other too much. The giant's eyes flashed for a moment. "I remember you tried to take my countries. You were always jealous of me."

Moloch choked on his own spit. "Jealous? Come now. You know I'm never jealous. It may be a demon thing, but it never got me. I'm sorry you were weak."

The giant stood up angrily, clenching his fists. Moloch slapped his shoulder like they were old friends. "Just busting your balls. Things will be different this time. We'll share, and everything will work out for the best."

The giant gave him a sideways glance. "We will see. For now, I'm going down to start on building my country. It takes a lot of work, and I have slept far too long."

Moloch looked over the edge. "You're just going to walk down the mountain buck ass naked?"

The giant growled. "Why not? Who fucking cares?"

Moloch shrugged. "Just sayin'. It's a different world now."

The giant smiled slowly. He pointed to Moloch's crotch. "Have demons lost their dicks, too?"

Moloch balked. "It's very cold out here."

Without warning, the frost giant punched Moloch hard in the chest. He flew up off the ground and back into the trees. The giant could hear the echo of crunching limbs as the demon crashed through the forest and tumbled over the side of the mountain. Moloch's voice rang out with every roll and every smash into a rock. "Fucking Leviathan... Ow! Icy prick... Fuck! Son of a bitch... Ouch."

The giant grabbed his stomach and started laughing hysterically. With every curse and every crunch, the Leviathan lost it just a little more. He cupped his hands and shouted to Moloch, "That's for tricking me in Norseland!"

He shook his head happily and headed down the mountain. The cold did not bother him, and he was quick on his feet. Over the curves and cliffs, around the trees, he moved with ease. He paused as he reached a hiking thoroughfare. He waited, crouching in the snow until he saw two hikers coming down the trail. It was a man and a woman. They didn't see him coming at all. He ran through the woods and leaped high into the air. He grinned as he landed right in front of them.

"Woah, dude, put some clothes on," the guy blurted out, putting his hand up to cover his eyes.

The frost giant shook his head from side to side. "The thing is, I don't have any. So. I will kill you and take yours. Thank you."

The guy looked shocked. "What the fuck? Who the hell are you?"

The frost giant jumped forward and grabbed the guy's head and twisted hard. There was a wet snap as his neck broke. The frost giant dropped him to the snow. "I am Juntto, your future ruler."

The woman screamed loudly and dropped her pack. She ran through the snow, falling and sliding as she tried to get away. Juntto sighed and walked quickly forward, moving faster than any human possibly could. He grabbed the woman by the arm. She turned and slugged him hard in the face, breaking her hand on his ice-chiseled chin. She screamed at her ruined hand and began to cry. She brought a knee up into his groin and broke her leg on his frosty junk. She struggled, and he attempted to wrap his arms around her. They fought back and forth for several moments.

Finally, Juntto simply grabbed her arm and tossed her over the side of the mountain. "Too much trouble."

He turned and walked to the hiker. He realized he didn't know how these new clothes were fastened or hooked or whatever. He snarled and waved his hand, transferring the hiker's clothes to his own body. Juntto was now dressed in a plaid shirt, snow pants, and a heavy jacket. It wasn't at all like the last time he was there. He changed his body to fit the clothes, a bit more in the belly, a bit less in the shoulders. His face melted and twisted to look more like the hiker. He swirled his hand around his head, shortening his hair. It became black except for one prominent strand of silver.

The strand fell in his face, and he pushed the lock of hair back. "Damn rules. Always just one strand of silver."

———

Back in hell, a large gate opened back in Moloch's castle. The demon stepped through with an irritated look on his face. The snow on his shoulders and horns instantly steamed off of him from the heat of hell. He stood there for a moment, reveling in the scalding air.

Moloch raised a hand, and the gate slammed shut behind him. "Motherfucker. He had to be an asshole, not that I didn't fucking deserve it."

He continued to mumble and curse as he walked toward the fireplace. He brushed his arms, pulling branches free and yanking twigs from between his scales. He grumbled angrily as he snapped the branches in half and tossed them into the fire. The flames sparked and grew, the souls in the pit of the fire screaming out in agony.

Moloch looked down at the souls as the last bit of snow evaporated from the top of his head. "Oh, you think you're upset. You didn't fall straight down a goddamn mountain."

He shook his whole body and growled, stomping his foot and shaking the furniture in the room. He put both of his large, taloned hands on the fireplace mantle and leaned his head down, letting the heat of the fire warm him. Moloch hated the cold more than almost everything, except for Juntto and maybe Lilith.

A few moments later, Baal walked through the door, whistling gleefully. He stopped dead in his tracks and sniffed, snarling his lip. "It smells like fucking Christmas in here. That's disgusting."

"Tell me about it," Moloch growled from across the room.

Baal looked at him, and his eyes grew wide. There were scratches down Moloch's legs and several twigs he'd missed still stuck in his scaly back. "What the hell happened to you?"

Moloch waved the question away and plopped down in a chair by the fire. "I spoke to Juntto about our problem. I told him I needed him to start assembling his armies again."

Baal's mouth fell open, and he carefully sat down in the chair across from Moloch. "You woke that ass up? I thought you said you'd never deal with him again after the last debacle?"

Moloch groaned and leaned his head back. "I know, dammit. I don't have a lot of choice at this point. I need his armies. You know how good he is at taking over countries. He's already set his sights on Europe, especially Switzerland. He can move among the humans without being noticed. No red eyes, no scales. He looks like one of them and can fit in if he really wants to."

Baal scoffed. "That's the key—if he really wants to."

Moloch looked at Baal. "Don't underestimate him.

Remember, he's taken over countries before. He has led great armies. He may be an idiot with a temper, but he gets shit done when it needs to happen."

"What if his armies get too big?"

Moloch shook his head. "You know Lucifer won't let that happen. If he gets too big for his britches, then we'll have to take him down a peg or two. He may have powerful armies, but we will always be able to keep him in check."

Baal wasn't completely convinced. He stared at the souls writhing in the fireplace. "I don't know about this. It seems so risky."

Moloch stood up and waved his hands at Baal. "Trust me. We'll just have to figure out a way to kill him when we no longer need him."

Baal sighed and tilted his head to the side. "That will be two hundred years from now. Perhaps the humans will do it anyway. They got Tiamat."

Moloch cut him off before he could finish, turning quickly toward him. "Only because she was leaving hell. On top of that, she was beaten to shit. If she had left here healthy, they would all be dead by now. We were done with her, and that's the point. She needed to be exterminated, and we made sure to let that happen. We kept our promise and released her and took care of loose ends at the same time."

Baal took a step back and decided not to mention Tiamat again. "What's Juntto doing now?"

Moloch poured himself a pint of Scotsman's blood and took a long sip. "He's out doing what he does, conquering.

He's going to build a new country for himself, starting with Switzerland."

"He always did like those blondes."

Moloch snorted and finished his drink, holding a glass up to Baal as an offer. Baal shook his head, and Moloch poured himself another glass, taking his seat again. He stretched his feet toward the fire, getting rid of any last feelings of cold. "Have you seen Pandora lately?"

Baal waved his head back and forth. "No, thank Lucifer."

Moloch sneered slightly, smelling the aroma of his drink and staring into the flames in front of him. "I wonder what that bitch is up to. She's been quiet for too long. That only means one thing, she's planning something evil and twisted. Normally, I would applaud it, but considering she's on the other team, it doesn't bode well for me."

Baal cleared his throat, trying to hide his worry. "Nah. She's probably nursing her wounds. Her little pet was hurting pretty badly."

Both Baal and Moloch turned their heads when one of the servants came through the door. "I have your dinner, most terrible Moloch."

Moloch stood and motioned to Baal. "Excellent. What are we eating tonight?"

The staff came in after the servant, setting a large platter down in the center of the table and two small ones at both the seats. The staff grunted as they lifted the lid off the large platter. The head servant bowed. "The main course is baby elephant, plucked from its mother just two days before. It's not sedated or anything."

The baby elephant tried to scramble off the table, but its

legs were tied. The servant pulled the covers off the other two platters. "On the side is a young dove medley and a fried pear stuffed with hamsters."

Both of the demons clapped excitedly. Moloch looked at the servant and he snapped his fingers, sending a younger demon scrambling to set another platter down at the end of the table. The head servant pulled the lid off. "For dessert, you will have Jell-O-encased human brains with spinal fluid and fresh blood sauce, flambéed in a sugar crust."

Moloch nodded his head. "Very good. No servants will be tortured tonight."

Everyone scrambled quickly from the room, hoping he didn't change his mind. Moloch and Baal sat down at the table and stared across at each other as they began dinner. Moloch lifted his glass into the air. "To us, Baal. I think Juntto will play perfectly into our hands. We're geniuses, and we deserve every bit of terror we can have on our new planet. Here's to the future of Earth!"

16

The helicopter's whir echoed through the mountain. The pilot was trying to keep a safe distance from the slope, wanting to scope out the area while avoiding an avalanche. The chopper was an unmarked military unit with three men inside. First Lieutenant Andrews curved the chopper toward the mountain and hovered over the slope.

He pulled his microphone down. "That's where the portal appeared. It happened long after the avalanche."

Second Lieutenant Troughtman craned his neck to look at the slope. "I don't get it. Why in the hell would a portal open way up here? No one is ever out here, and it's colder than Alaskan poontang. As far as I know, demons like warm weather."

First Lieutenant Andrews yelled into his microphone, "That's not all. The first portal opened here, and the second was way down the mountain. One after the other, too. The intervening time wasn't long enough to take the hiking trails down."

The staff sergeant in the plane piped up, "What, like he fell?"

First Lieutenant Andrews grinned. "That would be the quickest way down."

"A big ass demon tumbling head over foot down the mountain would be funny as hell to watch."

"Fall makes sense. I don't really see these things having the stamina or desire to go on a climb like this. Patience doesn't seem to be their strong suit."

Lieutenant Troughtman waved a hand to get their attention. "Are those footprints I see walking down to the left?"

Everyone shifted their focus, trying to see what he was talking about. Andrews clicked his headset as a call came in. "Give me a second." He spoke quickly, but none of the others could hear his conversation.

The sergeant narrowed his eyes. "So there were two? One went tumbling down the mountain, and the other took a walk...barefoot through the snow? What kind of shit is this? You would think there would be no survivors. I don't know demon anatomy that well, though."

Lieutenant Andrews clicked on his mic. "Uh-oh, boys, I've got an alert. We have two dead bodies."

Lieutenant Troughtman searched the tree line. "Where? On the mountain?"

The pilot turned the chopper and started following the path that led down the mountain. "In the direction of those footsteps."

The chopper swooped down the mountain, following

the path. It didn't take long before they saw the flashing lights of emergency rescue vehicles. Another chopper was hovering over the group of vehicles as two bodies were being airlifted up.

The sergeant's face went white. "How likely is it this is all connected?"

Lieutenant Troughtman shot the sergeant a look. "Well, two portals, two dead bodies, and no demons. I would have to say if it isn't connected, it's the biggest coincidence I've ever seen. Looks like these hikers picked the wrong day to go for the summit."

Lieutenant Andrews clicked his mic back on. "Come on, let's head back to base. We don't want to get in their way. There's something seriously strange going on here, and I don't think it has anything to do with the avalanche."

The sergeant looked out his window at the mass of fallen ice below. "How much you want to bet that avalanche was just a side effect of demon activity? We need to report this ASAP. Things are getting worse as the minutes pass."

Brock sat back in one of the empty rooms, holding court. He put his feet up on the old desk. "A monkey tried to kill me." Turner chuckled as he said it. Brock's entire team was there, listening to him relate their adventures to Katie.

"All the animals were infected?" Katie asked. She sounded skeptical.

Brock nodded his head. "Sure as hell, they were. Every

now and then we'd come up on some big-ass demon and have to blow his nuts off, but usually, it was the animals."

Katie shook her head. "I've only seen that once. It was an animal near the old base. I think it was a coyote. Had to put her out of her misery. I know they don't have as much control of animals. They must have been desperate out there."

Brock nodded thoughtfully. Suddenly he started laughing and sat forward. "So one time, we all went out, and Turner and I were in the front."

Turner groaned and rolled his eyes. "Do you always have to tell this story? Doesn't it get old?"

Brock pointed at him. "No, dude, it will never get old. Anyway, we were humping along. Turner had my flank. We were bullshitting, and he turns to check his six. I nearly shit myself. On his back was this huge, hairy tarantula. I'm talking big as my head. So I stopped the team and told Turner to stay really still, but I don't tell him why. I've got my M16 on him, sort of pointed sideways at the spider. I didn't want to shoot him, but this motherfucker had red eyes and fangs."

The tattooed soldier giggled uncontrollably. "I told him to let loose. Fuck it. Maybe he takes out Turner, but at least he gets the spider.

Brock chuckled. "So he's standing really still, no idea what is going on. And this thing puts two hairy legs on his shoulder, climbs up and looks him right in the face. You could hear his scream for miles."

Turner slapped his hands on the desk. "It was the biggest spider on Earth. No lie."

"Our commander called in and asked if we had encountered any civilians because they had heard a little girl screaming from miles away."

Turner shook his head. "Thing came close enough to kiss me."

Brock looked wistfully into the distance. "I killed it, but it was beautiful."

The soldiers laughed. Katie wiped tears from the corners of her eyes and held up her hand. "Okay, no more. No more."

The loudspeaker over their heads crackled and shrieked, grabbing their attention. "All hands, R&D arriving on the tarmac."

Katie sniffed once and got herself together. "That's our cue. Gotta go meet the brains of this operation."

The team headed out of the building. Once outside, they saw workers reinforcing the walls yet again. Metal armor was bolted over metal armor. Brock frowned. "How many layers do we need?"

Katie shrugged. "That's the thing—we don't know. They want to make sure the walls will hold in any demons that get out of the portal. That way, they can be killed easier and don't go rampaging through the base. It's just precautionary, but we have a feeling there are beasts in hell we haven't seen yet. Who knows what they're like?"

Brock huffed. "Great."

As Katie and Brock walked out to the runway, the military prop plane came to a stop. The crew hurried around, readying the staircase and the door. When the doors opened, a tall red-headed scientist came tripping out, followed by a young female assistant. He looked like he was surprised to be back on the ground, while she was trying to keep up with him. Her hands were full of bags and a box of strange-looking equipment. She struggled under the weight of it all and barely made it to the ground without taking a tumble.

Katie put her hand out to Dr. Thorough. "I'm Katie. So good to meet my R&D team."

Thorough shook his head and looked around wildly. "Yes, yes. Who is unloading? Because they need to be very careful with these instruments."

Alice juggled her load and reached out to shake Katie's hand. "Sorry. I'm Alice, the doctor's assistant. Don't worry about him. He doesn't watch television."

Just then, the doctor snapped his fingers and pointed at Katie with excited eyes. "Oh, yes. Specimen 182!"

Katie's eyes instantly narrowed. They glowed red, and the doctor took a step backward. He pushed up his glasses and looked her over. "Did I say something wrong?"

Alice sighed and rolled her eyes. Brock clenched his teeth and stepped into the doctor's personal space, staring him blankly in the eyes. The doctor leaned back a bit and looked him up and down nervously. Brock cleared his throat. "Katie is not a specimen."

Dr. Thorough stepped back, looking from Katie to Brock and back. He shook his head, realizing how rude he had just been. "Oh, I'm so sorry! They never provided a name for you in the reports, only the…uh…182 designation. It's done that way on purpose."

He reached out, and Katie eyed him for a moment before shaking his hand. "Try 'Katie' on for size before I'm tempted to leave you behind in hell."

Dr. Thorough grimaced at her grip and pulled his hand

back, shaking it out. "No need to be ugly. I'm not the one making the rules."

Alice slapped her hand to her forehead. "Sometimes he numbers me too. He really is harmless. I guess he can be a bit clueless as well."

The doctor looked from Alice to Katie. He seemed to understand something then. He cleared his throat and stood up straight. "Shall I try that again? My name is Doctor Cleary Thorough, Research and Development and a ready participant in your mission. I have brought the best instruments that I could bring. I've also brought my assistant, Alice here, who is almost as knowledgeable as I am."

"Sometimes more," Alice whispered, making Katie smile. Katie took a bag from Alice to lighten her load.

The whole group loosened up except Brock. He made it his mission to stare the doctor down. Dr. Thorough tried to ignore him, but he was pretty good at making his point.

Katie chuckled and patted Brock on the chest. "Down, boy. He's harmless."

"Rude," Brock grumbled, but stepped back.

Turner put his hand on Brock's shoulder and whispered to him. "I think Katie can protect herself against a nerdy fire-headed scientist like that guy. She's faced demons bigger than him before. He doesn't seem too interested in dragging her back for experimentation at the moment."

Brock glanced over his shoulder. "You've got to be kidding me. Those freaks at R&D have been dying to run tests on Katie. They all know they'll never get close enough to even take a vial of her blood, much less chain her down for research. She's half angel and half demon, the strongest weapon we have against the demon race. They would pull some crazy cloning shit on her in a heartbeat if they could."

Turner squeezed his shoulder. "Yeah, but can you imagine it? Not a single one of them would have their balls left. They would be hooking up probes and shit to her and then walking around with stitches, emasculated. You know Pandora would be wearing that shit around her neck like a tribal warrior."

Pandora snickered inside Katie's head, hearing the whole conversation even if Katie was focused elsewhere. *Damn, I like that idea.*

Katie put a smile on the outside, confused on the inside. *Huh? What idea?*

Wearing my enemies' balls on a rope around my neck. I could eventually make a suit out of it. People would think it's all cool until they realized my jacket was made of foreskin.

That's freaking disgusting, Pandora. Get your head back in the game.

Pandora mumbled to herself. *I'll get someone's head back in the game.*

Katie looked at the doctor. "They will carefully unload your gear. You don't have to worry. They're professionals. Why don't we go into one of the meeting rooms and we can talk about the mission?"

The doctor looked at her for a moment and then nodded. He clutched his bag to his chest and followed her across the landing strip to the main building. He stared around at the old building as they descended into the underground section, leaving the construction noise behind.

Alice glanced into one of the empty rooms. "Dang. This place is old."

Katie chuckled. "It's seen its day, that's for sure, but we're preparing the main hanger for the mission. Trust me, it will hold up under scrutiny."

She showed them to the meeting area, and everyone took a seat. Katie leaned back in one of the creaky chairs. "Do you think you brought everything necessary to successfully take the readings you'll need?"

The doctor muttered to himself and examined the equipment Alice had been carrying. "Everything that we have invented so far. We'll have to assemble some of it, but my question is, what can we bring? What sort of secondary team will I have? Can we transfer larger equipment?"

Katie glanced at Alice and back to the doctor before leaning forward. "I want you to fully understand what we're doing here. We're walking into hell. There are no reinforcements on the other side, no one who's cleared the area beforehand. We walk into whatever is waiting over there. You want my opinion? You bring whatever you can carry and no more. Understand that we might have to move fast and work under combat type scenarios."

The doctor pulled out a notebook and began writing feverishly in it. "All right, anything we can carry. Got it. That rules out quite a bit of the equipment, but I suppose in the future, we may be able to go back with more time. Has anyone taken any temperature readings in there?"

Katie chortled. "Not that I know of. I can promise you, it's fucking hot. The unprotected human body alone won't be able to survive for more than a few minutes. I've been told, though, that's one of the problems that you've been working on."

The doctor nodded, still writing. "Mm-hmm, yes. Thermal gear has been taken care of. We don't want internal combustion. It doesn't bode well for the study."

Alice swallowed hard, trying not to show her nerves. "And how will we be entering into this brave new world?"

Katie smiled. "Come on. I'll show you."

They trekked back to the hangar bay. As they walked through the doors, Katie put up her arms in a grand gesture. "This beauty is our transfer chamber, or at least it will be by the time we're ready to go."

Alice was too busy staring at the men without shirts to even hear what she was saying.

The doctor turned in circles, a shocked look on his face. "Where's the machine? Where is the big circle? Isn't there a big gate or something that we will switch on and walk through? You know, like the movies."

Pandora began cackling loudly. *He's looking for the fucking Stargate.*

Katie hid her smirk and reached out to touch the doctor's shoulder. He jumped slightly and pushed his glasses up.

Katie cleared her throat. "This isn't a sci-fi story, doctor. We don't do it like that. I'm afraid you might have to adjust your expectations accordingly."

Katie left the doctor and Alice to the staff on the base and headed back to her room. She walked in and sneered at the place. A bunk with a military issued bluish-gray scratchy blanket barely fit between a tall locker and a tiny bathroom. Everything was clean, but it wasn't exactly luxurious.

Pandora grumbled. *Great. We're risking our asses, and we're given a room that looks like a cell at Leavenworth.*

Katie ran her finger across the desk. *I'm pretty sure they don't have private bathrooms there. It's just for a little while, and it'll make the comforts of home feel all the better when we get back.*

We could go back now and enjoy those comforts tonight.

You could quit your bitching.

Katie walked to the bed and sat down on the edge of it, listening to the springs creak and whine.

Pandora appreciated the sound. *Oh, what beautiful music I could make with you.*

Katie ignored her. She leaned her back against the wall and put her hands behind her. It wasn't home, but it would do until they got everything finished and back on track.

Pandora sniffed around. *Seriously, the general and I are going to go to war. Where are my fucking donuts? How does he expect me to go rolling up into hell on an empty stomach? I saw the chow. It's not as bad as prison food, but I can promise you, I am not eating it.*

Katie shrugged. *I kind of like it. It's like we're really part of the military. I always wondered what it would be like. I bet the guys are loving their individual quarters after sleeping on a cot for the last who knows how long. That's what's wrong with you. I spoil you rotten.*

And I should be. And so should you, for that matter.

No, I'm talking about sacrifice. Sacrificing creature comforts is the least you could do.

Nope. You've got it all wrong. If you're going to put your pretty little ass on the line, you should be rewarded with a nice mattress and maybe an area rug or something.

The light next to her door flashed, and an intercom went off over the bed. "Katie, please report to Hangar Bay One. Your team is arriving."

Pandora whistled. *Big-Dick Calvin has arrived. Bet the plane gives a huge sigh of relief, not having to lug that around anymore.*

Katie giggled but groaned as she pulled herself to her feet. She tried to look at herself in the mirror on the wall, but it was too foggy to see anything. She grabbed her ID and put it around her neck before heading out and down the hall. As she exited the building, she could see her private jet coming to a stop in front of the hanger.

Pandora sniffed the air. *Can we just go chill inside for like five minutes? I can't get the smell of gray paint and mold out of my nose.*

You said it smelled like a sunken ghost ship inside.

You're right. It's all bad. New York City, here we come!

No. We have work to do here.

The doors to the jet opened, and Calvin stepped out. He spotted Katie instantly. She hurried over as he walked down the steps, his arms wide. "I can't wait to go straight to hell. Don't pass Go, and don't collect two hundred dollars."

Katie hugged him tightly. "Well, we *do* get to collect a fee, but that's neither here nor there."

Calvin walked Katie back to the luggage storage

compartment. "Don't tell them, but I would do this for free."

Katie smirked and leaned in. "They probably can hear you."

Calvin popped the door open and waved his hand. "Ta-da. Joshua has provided us with a shit-ton of new toys and ammo so our pretty little asses, or big asses for Pandora, can come back in one piece."

Swoon. I'm swooning. Tell him I'm swooning.

17

The general tapped his pen on his desk. He was staring at the large television screen in his office, willing the newscaster to break into a grin and tell his audience it was all some sort of prank. He knew it wasn't. The news program was replaying scenes from the six incursions that had recently occurred. The death tolls seemed to rise by the second as they began piecing bodies back together and clearing out the debris. The general shook his head in frustration. "It's a goddamned shame."

The buzzer on his speaker phone went off, and his secretary came over the com. "General, you have a call from a Lieutenant Andrews on line one. They're one of the teams in Europe. They have some news for you, sir."

The general clicked off the television and picked up the phone. "This is General Brushwood."

Lieutenant Andrews was exhausted by that point. "General, Lieutenant Andrews. I am a pilot for one of the teams in the Alps. I know I don't report to you, but the higher-ups told me I should give you a call and keep you informed of what's going on in the area."

"Yes, Lieutenant. Have we found something new?"

He cleared his throat and spoke quietly. "Actually, sir, yes. It started about two hours ago. There was an avalanche on one of the peaks, followed by two portals appearing in our system. We took a chopper out to see them. We haven't come to any definitive conclusions, but it looks almost like a demon entered Earth at the top and then somehow, in a short amount of time, exited halfway down the mountain."

The general lifted an eyebrow. "The demons are snowboarding now?"

"It looks like… Well, we think that…"

"Spit it out, Lieutenant," the general demanded.

The lieutenant paused for a moment to gather himself. "It looks like he fell down the mountain."

General Brushwood choked a little and sat up. "So we have a cold-weather clumsy demon on our hands. Interesting."

"That's not all. There were a set of footprints leading in the other direction down the side of the mountain. They were human-sized, but whoever it was, he was barefoot. There were two bodies discovered where the footprints led, one completely naked and the other tossed over the side. She was impaled on a tree before she hit the rocks below."

The general narrowed his eyes. "You're saying a human did that? A barefoot human on the side of a mountain?"

The lieutenant nervously swallowed. "It appears that way. Shortly after that, three more bodies were discovered in a small town right outside the base of the mountain.

Two of them were inside a small restaurant. They found the bodies shoved in the freezer. The third was a delivery boy. His car was stolen and his head bashed in."

"And we think they are connected?"

"Yes, sir. We tracked the prints and then the tire tracks through the snow, but we lost him not far from there in a medium-sized town to the west. There's a lot of traffic there, so he blended right in." The lieutenant shuffled some papers around, waiting for the general's response.

The general thought about it for a moment, remembering the footage from the most recent attacks. "Surely someone there got a video of this, either purposefully or by accident. Did either of the dead on the Alps have a camera or anything on them?"

"No, but we are searching for video footage as we speak. So far, nothing has come up, but I'm sure it will."

The general sighed. "All right, keep me informed. This shit gets weirder every day."

"So wait, this doohickey is a what, now?" Calvin asked, holding up a piece of equipment.

Alice stared at him for a moment and took it out of his hand. "A heat-sensing molecular model simulator. It's just a piece of the puzzle. We take our readings in hell, then come back. This doohickey will help us build a computer simulation of the hellscape. That way, we'll be able to better analyze the data and understand the environment."

Calvin nodded. "Right. And when you do that, we'll be able to plan for a war that we take to them."

Alice looked at him and blinked. "That will be one of the uses, yes. We will also be able to make uncountable and previously inconceivable scientific discoveries about another dimension. Alien life. It's huge, very huge."

Calvin looked at her, unimpressed. "I wouldn't call them alien. I think more supernatural. They are demons, fallen angels, the soulless."

Alice sighed. She did not want to have that discussion again. "Okay, let's suppose you're right. Everything in the bible is true, and we are fighting Lucifer and his army. Then where is God in all of this? Shouldn't we be as interested in exploring that side as we are this? Shouldn't we be sitting down with God and creating an alliance so he can send in troops and give a sister a hand?"

Calvin stared at her, seeing she obviously was not on the same page as him. "I don't think it works that way. Besides, they did send an angel down."

Both Alice and Calvin looked at Katie. She was in a corner talking to herself. They watched as she cursed loudly. "Look, bitch, you'll get your goddamned donuts. Just shut the fuck up so we can get this done."

Alice gestured to Katie. "I can see that her angelic qualities lead the way."

Calvin knew when he was beaten. He left Alice to her doohickey and walked to where the teams were divvying up the gear. Brock held up one of the vests. "We need to put some gear aside for Katie."

Katie waved her hand. "No, just worry about you right now. I'm going to need the least amount of gear in the beginning."

Brock nodded. "I think that goes for Calvin and me,

too. The three of us have pretty strong demons, that should help keep us together. I want the rest of you guys protected, though. We've never been in this environment."

The doctor tapped Katie on the shoulder. "Excuse me? There is plenty of gear, but how about the instruments? Most of this stuff is vital. Tactically, I mean. It's going to give you the information you need to make informed decisions in the future."

Katie looked at Brock. "You guys got this part?"

Brock and Calvin gave a thumbs-up. "Got it, fearless leader."

Katie put her hand on the doctor's back and led him to his area. "Okay, show me how it works."

He looked at her, startled, and began. "By measuring subatomic—"

"No, no. Not the technical. Just show me the gear you need to bring and how it transmits its findings. Keep explanations to on and off switches, please."

The doctor pointed to a pile of gadgets in boxes. "Those are the machines that will take all the readings. We will need to adjust some of them once we are on the ground. Those readings are then instantly sent to the receiver packs on my and Alice's side. All the readings are stored in there and backed up into the system if the connection allows it. Otherwise, the data sits in these until we get back."

"Oh, okay. So the machines take the readings, the readings go to your fanny packs, and everything is sent to your backup. That makes it a little simpler." Katie mumbled to herself.

She walked to the pile and put her hand on her chin,

looking at the amount of equipment. She ran some ideas through her head, trying to figure out the best way to handle all that gear. "We can't have the guys carry the equipment. I need them for protection. It's too much to Ghostbuster strap to your backs, that's for damn sure. Let me think…wait. I have an idea."

The doctor watched as Katie ran from the main room into the hall and came back, pulling a large rolling cart behind her. She stopped it in front of the doctor and put her hands out. "This is specially made to withstand the heat. It's made of an alloy–based metal…"

The doctor looked at her with a straight face. "Yes, it can withstand up to twelve hundred degrees Fahrenheit. I am familiar. What does this have to do with me?"

Katie snarled and pointed at the equipment. "We take your equipment and rig it onto this cart. We'll be able to make it so you can remove it if necessary, but the cart will keep it secure on the unknown terrain and allow for quick movement."

The doctor's face turned beet-red. "You're telling me you want to destroy one-of-a-kind inventions that will change the course of science as we know it by drilling into them and bolting them to a luggage cart?"

Katie lifted an eyebrow. "Don't you have the plans for these inventions?"

The doctor nodded. "Well, yes."

Katie waved a few of the soldiers over. "Then stop whining. They can be remade, but you can't. We do every-thing smarter not harder. In and out as fast as possible."

The guys walked over, staring at the cart and the equip-ment. Katie smiled and batted her eyelashes. "All right, gentleman. The doctor here needs this equipment mounted on these rolling carts. They need to be removable, and they need to function on the cart. If there needs to be insulation, fine; whatever the doctor says. We want our hands to be as free as possible."

Brock stared at all the equipment. "They make phones that fit in your pocket with apps that can turn your sprinkler on from another country, but you can't condense this?"

The doctor snapped his head toward Brock. "I'm sorry. We have made ungodly technical advances in the few brief years of this war. We didn't know we would be leisurely strolling into the depths of hell in my lifetime. We weren't really worried about condensing it down yet."

Katie laughed, patting Brock on the shoulder. "Just help him figure out how to load all this shit in. This is why we're going, after all. When we're done, let's all get some rest. We'll leave right after."

Katie pushed her barracks door open and closed it behind her. She yawned loudly and took off her holster, tossing it onto the dusty table. She was exhausted and hungry, but it was too late for chow at this point. She undressed and sat down on the bed, running her hands over her sore scalp.

Pandora grumbled loudly. *How am I supposed to make sure you're at your best under these conditions?*

Lord, you act as if we're sleeping outside on the ground.

Katie laid down on the bed, pulling the scratchy blanket up over her. She could feel the coils beneath her body expanding and contracting as she moved. Pandora scoffed and started to laugh. *Oh, this is fucking rich. While I'm supposed to be setting you up to be tough and strong tomorrow, you're going to get a rib punctured by a fucking mattress coil. They could have at least brought in the decent ones or given you the same privileges as the officers.*

Katie groaned and attempted to roll over. The bed squeaked loudly under her. *We all have the same conditions. Just relax and try to get some rest. The more you bitch about something we can't change, the less time we have to power up for tomorrow's trip.*

Pandora grumbled but quieted down. Katie closed her eyes. Just as she began to drift off, her phone rang loudly. She growled at the phone. Pandora growled along with her.

How do you even get a signal down here?

Bargain-bin mattress technology, state-of-the-art phone technology.

She clicked on the phone and pulled herself from bed. "General Brushwood. I was wondering when I would hear from you."

"Sorry to call you so late. I was wondering if I could speak to Pandora about a possible problem."

Katie began pacing the floor. "That sounds interesting. Sure, hold on one second."

She pulled the phone from her ear. *Oh, darling, it's for you.*

Thanks, boo. Don't wait up.

Pandora took over Katie's body with every intention of letting the general have it over her distinct lack of donuts. "General, you have some explaining to do."

The general cut in, "Before you say it, the donuts will be there in the morning, bright and early. I had to go with a civilian because everyone else was busy preparing the base. I had a delivery guy, but he was some burnout kid who couldn't get the security clearance to pass through the gates. I've got my best on it, though."

Pandora shook her head. "Leave it to the military to hurry up and wait on hot and ready."

The general laughed. "In the meantime, something has gone down. I had a call from an officer this afternoon telling me there was an avalanche on a mountain. After the avalanche, there were two portals, one on top of the mountain near the summit and another farther down the mountainside. There were also footprints, apparently human, leading down the side of the mountain to a location where two hikers were discovered dead. One was naked, the other, the woman, tossed over the edge and impaled on a tree. A little later, they discovered three more bodies in a small town at the base, a stolen truck, and tracks that led to a city about sixty miles away."

Pandora froze as she thought about the events. "That sounds like a full days' work. Where exactly is this mountain?"

"The Alps, near Switzerland."

Pandora resumed Katie's pacing. "Interesting. It maybe sounds like Juntto, one of the seven."

The general was taken aback by that. "A Leviathan? But I thought they were all sea creatures?"

Pandora shook her head. "That was Tiamat. Well, maybe Baylahn as well. But no, we demons tend to call the Seven Monsters of Time Leviathans because their ability to destroy is legendary. It's not based on their size. They come in all sizes and shapes, just like you humans. Tiamat was one thing, but Juntto is something else."

General Brushwood started writing the information down. "Okay, Juntto. Do you have any information on this character? What is he? What does he want?"

Pandora pointed her finger. "Yes, he's a giant."

The general huffed in frustration. "I thought you said they weren't all large?"

"I did, but Juntto isn't Tiamat-large. He's just a few stories tall, I think. And he isn't always large. He can shapeshift his body. He can change into just about anything he wants to, at least anything living. He isn't originally from Earth, like Tiamat."

The general stopped, slightly stumped. "So, wait, there are aliens? We have demons, and now we have aliens? Hell has aliens as allies?"

Pandora rolled her eyes. "General, what would you call me? Indigenous?"

General Brushwood face-palmed. "Right. You aren't from Earth, are you?"

Pandora smirked. "Not even close. Anyway, his kind are about fighting, fucking, and food. The three premier Fs that your planet is always willing to provide. Pretty much in that order, too."

The general cracked up. "Sounds like the rest of the men on this planet. Food is important, but not as important as the other two."

"Yeah, except he's extremely powerful. Don't underestimate him because he can appear in human form. He can morph at any moment, and his strength is godlike."

The general sighed. "Any idea what he is up to?"

"He will likely try to find a base of operations and then start building an army. He's kind of obsessed with building himself an empire. He did all kinds of fucking with humanity a few millennia ago, then he just disappeared. We never had to mess with him."

"Interesting," the general mumbled.

"I suppose it is if you're into that kind of thing. He's like a bad Thor, only his fists are his hammers, his hair isn't as nice, and he gives zero fucks," Pandora replied.

The general looked up, thinking about superheroes. "Any idea what his weaknesses are? Every villain has a weakness, just like every superhero."

Pandora leaned her head back and rubbed her eyes. "Women, for about ten seconds, and even then he might just kill them. I'm assuming that's what happened to your hiker. She probably tried to fight him off, and he got tired of it. He's like a big, scary Viking. He starts out as a Frost King and can withstand any temperature. Coming down the mountain barefoot and naked was probably like a spring afternoon stroll for the big guy. He didn't even feel the wind against his frozen balls. Most likely, he put on the naked hikers' clothes so he could blend into the town he entered. He's resourceful, as are most of his kind. He is capable of adapting to any time and place pretty fast. It won't be long until he is swiping right and left on a dating app."

The general cursed. "So we have an alien who shapeshifts, is incredibly strong, and likes to kill, and he's wandering around Europe right now. Oh, and he's planning on building an empire. Did I get that all correct?"

Pandora gave him a thumbs-up. "Pretty much."

The general put down his pen and scanned the information in front of him. "Am I looking at two separate problems here? I thought the demons wanted Earth. Now I have aliens with superpowers who want it too?"

"It's all connected, General. Moloch is probably the one who roused him from whatever corner he'd slunk into. I know they have a history and aren't exactly the best of friends. Juntto is good at building armies so Moloch will try to use him. They'll probably figure either you'll kill him after losing a whole shitload of your own men, or they will have to kill him in a hundred years or something. You aren't thinking like a demon. We don't think short-term, we think long-term. If your Earth politicians are thinking you'll have this wrapped up by next year, they have a big turd of a surprise coming around the corner. The elections are going to suck for the incumbents."

The general smiled. "Politicians have no concept of time. Half of them don't even know how long the World Wars took. You mention a time period any longer than four years and their eyes haze over. Not in their term? Not their problem."

"Humans are so small-minded sometimes. Unfortunately, this is everyone's problem. The purpose of us going to hell is to see if we can take the pain to them. Otherwise, the attrition percentages aren't going to stack up in humanity's favor."

The general closed his notes and leaned back, putting the pen in the corner of his mouth. "Okay, so tell me this. What happens if we kill a demon in hell?"

Pandora shrugged. "Not sure. Normally when you kill a

demon, they're tossed into the depths of hell, and it takes them a shit-ton of time to get back."

The general snarled his lip. "I was hoping for something more like, 'They die for all eternity.' I don't think we want to parade that information around. People are looking for a quick fix, and they tend to put things off if they don't think it will personally affect them. Thus the whole global warming problem. The demons might win, but they're going to inherit a bunch of shit, just like the president did."

Pandora cackled. "Such is the circle of life. We all inherit some kind of past shit. Hell, I'm rolling around in this human-angel body fighting a war my predecessors started, and I didn't even want to do anything but fuck, eat, and get away from my ex-husband."

"Sounds like my ex-wife. I'm starting to think she was a demon, but then I remember that, no, she was just a bitch. She started out like a firecracker but became a mean old woman running around in short skirts, going on cougar cruises, and getting tattoos. The midlife crisis never left that one. Anyway, I would appreciate it if you kept that information about demon regeneration to you and Katie."

Pandora giggled. "Yeah, no shit, General Holmes."

The general snickered. "Thanks."

Pandora yawned loudly. "No need to say thanks. Just bring me the donuts with sprinkles on them, and I'll call it even."

"I think I can handle that. Now, can I talk with the human hybrid? I have a couple of things to go over with her."

Pandora put her hand to her forehead and saluted.

"Sure thing, boss. I'll just be here waiting for that donut guy."

The general smiled, waiting for the changeover. He was glad that even in dire times like these, his colleagues and allies were still capable of making him laugh. Pandora might be a demon, but her spirit helped the general never give up.

Katie cleared her throat, coming back to the front. "I'm here, General. That was an interesting story about your ex-wife. She sounds like a winner."

The general hunched his shoulders. "You heard that, did you? Well, not every woman can see the beauty before them. She was a wild thing from the beginning. Young love —it'll kill you."

Katie laughed. "I'll remember that, although love is the last thing on my mind right now. I don't really see the settling-down thing in my future."

The general tilted his head, thinking about that for the first time. "Never say never, Katie. We don't know where all this will lead us. How do you feel about your trip to hell?"

Even now, hearing that out loud made Katie cringe. "You mean my trip *back* to hell? I don't know. I think it sounds easy from the outside. It sounds like a quick in and out, but if I know anything about this war, nothing is ever that quick. The demons are going to be highly defensive this time around. They saw the destruction we caused last time, and now they have Pandora and me on their radar. They will be keeping their eyes open to make sure we don't come knocking on the door."

The general was starting to be concerned. "Do you have a contingency plan?"

Katie crowed. "Do I ever? It usually involves fighting like hell, breaking some necks, shooting some guns, and then getting the hell out of Dodge."

"Will that work in this situation?"

Katie sat down. The bed squeaked like a metal mouse being squashed. "Sure. They fight there just like they do here. Poorly. But it will be their home turf. Even I struggle with the climate and atmosphere there, but that doesn't mean I can't fight. Hopefully, for everyone's sake, before the demons even know we're there."

The general took a long pause and lowered his tone. "And what happens if they find you? Or if they accidentally stumble upon you? You're going to be completely exposed. Not to mention the fact that you're bringing enough equipment, armor, and men that you would be hard-pressed to find cover."

Pandora laughed. *I'll tell you this much. If demons just happen upon us, they are going to be confused as fuck. Who comes to hell for a vacation? Timeshares don't work down there. No one but the goths and freaks wants to rent them out.*

Katie choked and covered her mouth. "According to Pandora, we would surprise the hell out of them. She says the real estate business in hell really isn't booming, and the last attempt at pulling in tourists ended in a ball of fire."

It's hell. Everything ends in a ball of fire.

The alarm went off bright and early, but Katie opened her

eyes feeling more refreshed than she ever had sleeping on her expensive mattress in New York City. She pulled her outfit on and brushed her hair back into a ponytail. Pandora yawned loudly. *Where are my GD donuts!?*

A knock sounded on the door. *Ask, and I shall provide.*

She opened the door to a tall soldier with a handsome smile. "Donuts, ma'am."

Aw, the general sent breakfast and dessert. Come on in, soldier boy.

Katie cackled. The soldier stood there confused until Katie shut the door on him.

18

"If you look to the right, you can see where they're finishing up the mounts for the .50 calibers. Those will have to be manned, but it's a good line of defense. I'm thinking of some sort of armor for them. Make the shooter safe inside. Something like a tank." Korbin was explaining to everyone what he'd been working on.

Timothy whistled. "Those are some mighty scary guns, sir."

Korbin smiled. "That's what the demons will say. The rest of everything out here Timothy can control from either the IT room or the security guard shack, or if it comes down to it, from devices inside of the armory. I wanted to make sure we were live in all areas. You never know where you'll be when an attack happens."

Stephanie rubbed Korbin's back with her hand. "Good, now you can come inside and finish hanging shelves. Calvin didn't get done. He had to jet out for his nice warm vacation in hell with Katie."

Korbin grimaced. "I hate hanging shelves, but I'll take that over a vacation in hell."

Joshua smirked. "That doesn't sound like the Korbin we used to know."

Korbin patted his belly and put his arm around Stephanie. "I'm an old married man now. I like to garden, fish, and live in the country. My shows are a priority, that and fixin' whatever the little lady needs."

Timothy put his hands to his cheeks. "Aw, you guys are like Little House on the Prairie, only without all those kids. Good night, Pa. Good night, Mary Lou Retton."

Korbin crinkled his forehead. "Mary Lou Retton was a gymnast in the eighties."

Timothy waved his hands. "Oh yeah, the one with the haircut that made bus drivers famous all over the world. I love it. She was sassy."

Korbin was about to respond when the roar of massive engines came over the hill. Everyone turned to watch as several big eighteen-wheelers pulling three M109A6 Paladins on trailers emerged. Korbin whistled loudly. "Well, that's about four point eight million dollars of 'Go back to hell' coming in right there."

He turned toward Joshua, who was eyeing the big guns. "Think you can whip up a few shells for those bad boys?"

Katie and Calvin were the first to arrive at the transfer chamber. Brock and his team members showed up shortly after and began checking their gear. Dr. Thorough and Alice were the last to arrive. The doctor mumbled something, and Alice wrote it all down furiously. The doctor stopped talking when he saw the grim faces of the soldiers. They resumed preparing in silence. The whole crew was oddly quiet. No one really knew what to expect. Twenty regular soldiers lined the outside of the chamber.

Doctor Thorough saw them and brightened. "Oh, fantastic. We'll have backup?"

The tattooed soldier shook his head. "They're staying here. Their mission is to keep whatever is on the other side of the portal out."

The plan was simple, in theory. They would open a portal and enter hell. Any demons that crossed over and escaped into the chamber would be held at bay. Then the army would exit, and the chamber would be filled with silver gas to kill the escapees. There was also backup on the outside of the hangar, just in case something managed to survive the gas.

They had been through enough to know that you needed backup for your backup.

The doctor looked forlornly at the soldiers. "Backup for backup, but no backup for us?"

Tattoos grinned. "I'm your backup, and you're mine. It's going to be great."

Doctor Thorough didn't return his enthusiasm.

Katie rolled her shoulders and glanced at Calvin. "You ready for this whole thing?"

Calvin smiled big and cracked his knuckles. "Fuck yeah, I'm ready. I've been ready for years. I've been holding back on this one. I just wish this was our time to attack. I'm itching to show them who's boss in their own territory."

Katie giggled. "All right, black Rambo. Keep your head.

We don't want any unnecessary battles in here. Don't go running into the inner circle and turning to ash. I can't save you once you're no longer in a body."

"I can't make any promises." He chuckled, knowing he was going to play it safe.

Three extra six-wheeled units carrying tools and equipment were lined up behind them. Calvin was pushing one, Brock and his team the next, and Alice was in charge of the last one. They would hopefully get them into hell and back out without incident. The whole crew was equipped with state of the art fireproof suits and special gloves to touch the metal once it had absorbed the hellish heat. They all wore helmets with glass visors.

Brock looked at his suit and then at Katie. "Are you sure these wetsuits are going to keep us safe?"

Katie looked at the doctor, who nodded. "In theory, these suits should repel the heat for the amount of time we need to collect the data. I made them as thin as I could, without interrupting the flow of the suit. I knew you would need dexterity."

Turner looked at the doctor. "Hold up, let's rewind three spaces. Did you say, 'In theory?'"

Alice rolled her eyes. "Yes, dumbass. We haven't actually been to hell, remember?"

Turner wrinkled his nose. "Sheesh. Rude."

"Sorry, I get sarcastic and snippy when I'm stressed. I'll tone it back a notch," Alice replied abashedly.

Katie clapped her hands and stepped forward. "Okay, guys. We're going in, setting up defenses, and waiting for the tools to work. Let's do this safe and fast so we can all get a beer afterward."

Pandora cleared her throat dramatically. *Let me just say one thing before we get to it. I suggest, no I adamantly request, that you steer clear of any angel antics while we're in hell. Angels set off a whole mess of alarms in hell, and they'll be on us faster than flies on shit. Keep it to yourself unless it is absolutely necessary. Even then, check with me first. No waves, just in and out.*

Katie nodded astutely. *Got it. Let's get this show on the road before these guys start chickening out.*

Pandora pushed herself forward. She focused and dug her fingers into empty air. As she pulled her claws apart, they tore a wide gate open in the space in front of her. Everyone closed their eyes as a wall of hot air blew into the chamber. It was hotter than Katie remembered.

"Holy hell," Tattoos muttered.

Turner's eyes went huge. "Are those rivers of lava?"

The tattooed soldier checked his weapon nervously. "And volcanoes in the background, just rocking and rolling. I feel like I'm in Mordor."

Katie waved her arm forward and led the crew into hell.

Brock kept a straight face as he stepped through the portal. "There can be only one."

Pandora laughed. *My precious.*

Outside, the soldiers standing around the building put their arms up to block the heat. One terrified private couldn't help himself. He lowered his arm and looked at the panoramic view of hell through the portal. Fear grabbed him, and he doubled over, vomiting. The rest of the guard stood perfectly still, watching as the team stepped through the gate onto the shimmering black rocks.

The carts bumped along the black rock, waves of heat rolling over their conductive surfaces.

Doctor Thorough suddenly stopped. "Here. Here's good."

Brock waved to his team and they fanned out, forming a perimeter around the three carts. Katie and Calvin took the front and the rear, their eyes peeled for trouble.

Alice shook her head. "This is going to be hell on my hair. This is a curly-haired girl's fucking nightmare."

The doctor pulled a cart to him and went straight to work, flipping switches and readying the equipment. "I don't want to waste any time. Get every reading we can."

Alice started turning devices on as well. "Join the military, see the world."

Turner glanced at her. "Stressed?"

Alice just stared at the volcanoes in the distance. "You think? Let's get this done and over with."

Brock started helping wherever he could, standing next to Alice. "Is this going to be worth it?"

Alice looked at him and blinked, almost as if she was coming to a realization. "Doctor Thorough is a fantastic scientist. He's probably one of the most brilliant minds in the whole world. If this doesn't work for him, it won't work for anyone. I can promise you that."

Brock understood. "Then we'll hold off everything we can for as long as we can. Move fast, get as much data as you can." They watched the doctor mumble to himself as he stood over a cart. "And keep him on task."

Alice cracked a smile. "I think I can handle that. It was

kind of in my job description. Though I have to say, hell was not mentioned once."

Brock chuckled. "No, I suppose it wasn't really in any of our contracts. We may find out why in the next few minutes."

Katie looked over her team, making sure they were all through. She gave the soldiers on the inside of the hanger a wave. One of them waved back.

Let's get this shit-show on the road.

With a wave of her claws, Pandora released her hold on the gate. It fizzled shut behind them. Alice jumped, startled by the sound, and looked at where the portal was. In its place was nothing but a landscape of darkness and pain.

Turner slapped the tattooed soldier on the chest. "I'm rethinking the whole idea of going to hell as being a fun thing. I don't want to spend my eternity with the lava people."

Tattoos just looked at him straight-faced. "Please don't go getting all crazy religious on me right now. I am not a pastor or a priest. I cannot help you at this moment. You better be looking at Katie as God right now, because she's the one who will get us out of this."

Katie walked farther away from the group. She could feel her angelic energy boiling. She had to hold back her angel powers as if they were an automatic reaction to being in hell. She wanted to go to angel turbo. *Home again, home again.*

Pandora sneered. *You know when you were little, and you would be gone a long time and then come back home, and the scent would make you feel all warm inside?*

Katie nodded. *Yeah. Though the smell was less sulfur and more warm apple pie.*

Yeah, well, I don't get that feeling when I come home. In fact, all I feel is rage and your angel powers tingling.

Katie stared at the volcanoes erupting in the distance. *I have to say I'm relieved that you think that way. I don't really want you to come here and have warm feelings about the place. No pun intended. This is no place for hugs and sweet dreams.*

You got that right, sister.

Alice peered at Katie, took in the hellish scenery, then turned back to her machines. "That's just fucking unsettling. I always wanted a landscape of death and sin in my view. Maybe I should take a selfie and post it. Hashtag kicking it with my demon homies in the pits of hell."

"Hashtag Damned good time."

"Hashtag hell of a weekend!"

"Hashtag doing it demon style," Tattoos finished with a grin. Then he realized where he was and spun around, his weapon at the ready.

Doctor Thorough held his information screen in front of him, excitement blooming on his face. "The readings are just pouring in. This is insane. The ambient temperature is 205 degrees, oxygen levels are holding steady at ninety-three percent, and the heat index is nearing twelve. What level of hell is this?"

Pandora giggled. *One step down from the outer ring. We are seeing readings that will triple in the final rings of hell.*

Katie walked back to the group. "We're not that far in, doctor."

Brock walked up to Katie, breathing heavily. "We need to have a better vantage point to see anything that's coming. I feel like something could come around the corner at any second. I think we should move a hundred and fifty yards in that direction toward that outcropping. We'll find a good defensible location."

"I agree. Give them space to continue their findings, but pull your men back. We can see them 150 yards away," Katie replied.

Brock walked back to his men and explained the maneuver. They were trying to conserve as much energy as possible, so they moved with caution and precision. If they were going to have enough energy to fight anything, they were going to have to be extremely cautious. Even with the suits, they could overheat very quickly. Their M16's would be the most effective form of combat for them.

"Keep your eyes peeled. Watch your six. Your first reaction to any contact should be to call out the threat. You can pull your weapon, but no one fires until I give the word. We don't want to alert anything to our presence if we don't have to." Brock slapped Turner on the shoulder, and led them down to a craggy black outcropping.

Katie and Calvin followed behind, staring in awe around them. The place was insane, with rivers of flaming lava and shores of black stone. It all seemed like a dream to Calvin. "This is pretty cool. I mean, when I was a boy, I was in awe of the first man on the moon. Now I get to be one of the first humans in hell."

"Well, not exactly."

"True. We're the first ones not purposely sent here for our crimes."

Katie smiled. "I don't know if I've been the first anything before. At least not until I ended up Damned."

Calvin pointed to her back. "And an angel."

Pandora cut in. *I hate to break it to you two explorers, but technically you're not the first humans. However, if you make it out of here alive, you'll be the first to leave hell in one piece.*

Katie didn't like how that sounded. *Who were the first humans? How come no one knows anything about that?*

It was kind of a bust. Let's just say the last time, it didn't go so well for the humans or the Ta'lgherk.

Calvin looked at Katie's face. "What? What's Pandora saying?"

Katie tried to wipe the worry from her face. "We aren't the first humans, but they never made it out alive. And Ta'lgherk didn't fare so well either."

Calvin sneered. "Who the hell is Ta'lgherk?"

Katie looked up, realizing she had no idea. "Yeah, Pandora who is that? Or what is that?"

Pandora pushed through Katie's voice. "This really isn't the time to go down that path. Very long story and makes little sense until you've seen what hell can be like for real."

Katie put out her arms. "Uh, we're living it right now. Here we are, lava rock and all. Flowing streams of death as far as the eye can see. Sulfur clouds hanging low in the sky and no source of specific light, but it's not pitch black."

"Alloy interlaces," the doctor called out excitedly.

Calvin and Katie looked back at the doctor. He was laughing wildly, and Katie and Calvin just looked at each other, unsure of what that even meant. Calvin ventured a guess. "I have alloy rims on my car."

Katie pursed her lips and patted Calvin on the back. "I don't think he's referring to rims, but good try."

Calvin nodded. "Yeah, I have no idea. Failed freshman science. Was never very good at that stuff."

"It's all right. You tried."

They moved to the outcropping. A black stone wall was behind them, to their right was a stack of fallen boulders. To their left, the stone ended in a jagged cliff. A hundred feet below the cliff was flowing molten rock.

Katie watched the team set up a new perimeter. *A good place for a fallback position.*

Or a last stand.

Calvin squinted at the river of lava, then stepped back. "What do you think would happen to this place if all the demons were killed?"

Pandora pushed forward and laughed. "Honey, hell will always be here. You gotta have a place for lost souls. It's not about destroying hell. It's about controlling it and putting the fear of God back in these bastards. Believe it or not, they used to have it."

Katie rubbed her chest and grimaced, looking quickly at Calvin.

He saw her face. "You okay? Look like you have heartburn."

Katie came forward, wincing. "My heart does feel like it's on fire.

That's not what it is. It's a warning.

"Shit. Get ready. Something's coming."

19

Katie groaned, her legs wobbled, and Calvin had to catch her before she fell. She could feel the strength of the approaching demons permeating the air like a bad smell. Calvin stood her up and looked concerned.

Brock ran up and took Katie's hand, waiting for her orders. She looked at him, her eyes changing from red to ice-blue and back. "Three demons are coming from the east. They're...big. Tell your men." Calvin and Katie ran to protect the doctor.

Brock sprinted back to his team. "We're gonna have contact! You see those boulders? We're going to set up there and keep watch through the cracks. As soon as the demons approach, Turner and I take point. Cover us. I mean, shower them with bullets. We don't want them to slip past the rock and get between the doctor and us, so our shots have to be precise."

The guys listened carefully and got low, making their way to the boulders. Their guns were at the ready. Brock carefully peered through the crack in the rock. Just as Katie had sensed, three large demons were lumbering toward them, obviously on their trail.

Brock put his hand up to the others with a closed fist, waiting for the perfect moment. Turner crouched near one of the boulders, ready to move. Tattoos got low, lying on the ground and tracking the demons. The other team member steadied his rifle on a boulder.

The demons snorted as they approached. One seemed to sense something, and all three of them dashed toward the boulders.

Brock shouted, "Go!"

He jumped out from behind the boulders as Turner jumped on top of one. The entire team opened fire, sights aimed directly at the beasts' heads.

The demons roared with anger and raised their hands. Bits of demon flesh flew in the air as bullets bit into their arms and hands. One snarled and leaped straight for the boulders. Tattoos aimed carefully from his spot on the ground.

He gulped in hot air, then slowly let the breath out of his lungs. His finger eased around the trigger. The shot snapped the demon's head back. The beast fell to the ground, hissing and gurgling before he disintegrated into ash.

Another demon was quicker, he dodged around the boulders and managed to get behind the team. Brock moved fast, firing intensely. The last team member spun around and fired wildly. The demon seemed confused; he was suddenly under a barrage of bullets. He tried to escape, but he tripped over his own feet. He yelped as he fell backward over the ledge and into the lava pits below.

Brock looked at his teammate and grinned. "That's two! One last scaly sonofabitch, boys!"

Turner was blasting the last demon with his weapon, but he couldn't manage a headshot. The demon got close enough to grab the barrel of Turner's weapon and push it away. Suddenly the beast was hissing in Turner's face.

Tattoos flew out of nowhere, landing on the demon's back. He pressed the barrel of his sidearm to the beast's head and pulled the trigger before it could react. "Nightnight, fucker."

The demon whimpered and blew apart into a cloud of dust, dropping the tattooed soldier to the ground. Turner put out his arms and caught him, backpedaled, and landed hard on the boulders.

Turner stood and helped Tattoos up. "That was badass. And now you know how it feels to be covered in ash. Not fun."

Back up on top of the ledge, the doctor and Alice were working really hard, trying to get everything they needed. Alice was shocked at all the information coming in. "I've gotten so much data. This place is more like Mars than Earth, except we can breathe."

The doctor laughed. "And there's no vacuum. Look at the soil toxicity levels. In reality, there should be liquid under these rocks. A sea of just radioactive materials."

Alice walked to the cart and looked down at one of the machines. The lights were blinking rapidly, and no readings were coming out. "The spectro-sensor for hydration atmosphere levels isn't working. I'll open it and see if I can't figure out what is wrong."

She grabbed one of the screwdrivers and lifted off the lid. A plume of steam rose from under the cover. Everything was coated in steam and water. She grabbed a rag off the cart and began pulling pieces off and wiping them down. They needed that machine to tell them about the weather patterns in hell throughout the year, whatever a year was in hell.

"Fuck, fuck, fuck. If we don't get this right, we could send the troops in on a day when acid rain falls. We could have a bunch of humans fucking melting on their way to a major battle." Alice was slightly panicked, but she was working hard on getting the machine fixed.

The doctor continued to scan the data, adjusting dials as they went. Katie jogged up to him, clapped her hands to get his attention. "Doctor, things are starting to heat up. How much time do you need?"

He flipped through the findings. "Uh...uh, we need at least twenty-five more minutes. We are running very important tests, here. Can't rush good information."

Katie wasn't expecting so long. "Shit. Okay."

"This information will help us armor troops in the future. It's crucial."

"We'll do our best, but move your asses. Demons are coming, and it won't be long until they know exactly where we are."

Katie turned to tell the others and stopped as Brock and his team jogged up to her. Katie could see the redness of his teammate's eyes, not their normal demon pupils. "All right, guys, the doctor is running a vital test that will help our troops come back here and fight. We need to buy him twenty-five minutes if we can. I know you're tired and your bodies are rejecting this, but we can do this."

Calvin tapped Katie's glass helmet. "You okay?"

She laughed. "I'm fine. It's like a vacation in here compared to the last time. We need to come up with a defensive network right now. We can probably turn all this information into battle tactics when we come back."

Brock put up his hand. "The guys and I were talking. The suits are keeping us alive, but they're not great for fighting. Dexterity is terrible. They stick to your skin like rubber when you move and inhibit your range of motion, and we all know one moment of hesitation against these bastards can mean the difference between life and death."

Katie pointed at the guys. "The right button on your helmet is to change comm channels. The one below that records a diary of sorts. I want you all to individually start recording your private thoughts on how to change these suits into something you would feel comfortable going into combat with. Give me everything you can think of. Need to pee but can't? Tell me. Everything. If there's a situation where we need to live in these suits for days, what is that going to do to us? You might technically be able to breathe out there, but you won't last thirty seconds. You need to think of this the same way the astronauts do their suits. It's our lifeline. Only assume we're fighting aliens on their home planet."

Pandora thought about it for a second. *I'm going to communicate with their demons.*

Is that a good idea?

Sure. They can help you. They keep their humans alive by

fixing problems from the inside out. Want people to stay cool or function better? Their demons are the ones to ask.

Okay, give it a shot.

Hiedar ud gazaer, *assholes.* La raph qae qoht.

There was a flurry of demonic conversation, then Pandora spoke using Katie's voice. "We are doing what we can to amp up your metabolisms, lower your hydration needs, and recycle your waste more efficiently. We'll try to keep you going, and keep you from having to deal with things like taking a shit in the suit. It's imperative we keep the inner workings tip-top so you can function without struggling."

Calvin whispered to Katie, "What does she mean by that?"

Katie shrugged, "As long as they keep us all alive, I'm good with it. We can figure out the details later."

The demon inside the tattooed soldier spoke to Pandora. *I remember something from the old days that may be useful.*

Pandora was a bit nervous, considering they all remembered her horrible past, but listened anyway. The demon actually had a good idea. *So, there is a modification of an early spell that will basically amp up all the inner workings of the human body and allow it to work with minimal fuel, minimal hydration, and minimal sleep. It's like steroids for them. They're jacked—stronger, faster, and more in tune with everything around them.*

Pandora nodded excitedly. *Yes, yes, I remember that spell. But it takes a lot of focus by the demon. They have to pretty much do it while simultaneously healing from battle. Here, hold that thought. I'm going to try it on Katie. She's indestructible.*

Katie perked up, hearing her name. *You're gonna try what on who?*

Pandora laughed. *Just chill. This will be a good thing. I hope.*

Shit. Just be careful.

Why don't we move away from the team for a second?

What? Why?

Just a precaution.

Katie walked over to the boulders, away from the rest of the team. *Don't make me explode or something. Please.*

No promises.

Pandora centered herself inside Katie and pulled on the energy of hell. *Zhael ya mhael oth xuihg ya ednardhy. Duzz ya chords oth yeild ya banks. Yiz suzor's xaeges lizz laent aer siks, minimal needs oz ya qiza goes xes. Aerja zes zdazz lizz xnaot ya cycle, sending ya xaeges xoyt qae cycle.*

An electric shock zipped around inside Katie, moving from one part of her body to the others. Katie's hair stood up straight on her arms, and her legs went weak. She grunted and dropped to her knees. Calvin ran up and grabbed her under the arm. "Are you all right?"

Katie shook her head and slowly stood back up, feeling refreshed, awake, and stronger than ever. She looked at Calvin with wild eyes. "Holy shit. Pandora just did some sort of crazy spell on me, and now I feel like Neo at the end of the first *Matrix*. The part where he flexes space and time." Katie dashed up the boulders, flipped off them, and ran back to the rest of the crew.

Shit, yeah. I'm a fuckin' ninja.

Pandora laughed. *YES! All right, demon friends. It worked.*

Get to work on your guys, and don't fuck up the words. I don't want to have to explain that mess.

Katie opened and closed her fists, feeling the power in her. *Why have you not done this from the beginning? I feel like I could fight for days.*

Pandora cleared her throat uncomfortably. *Well, we don't really know what will happen when we take you off the juice after prolonged use.*

Are we talking hangover or something worse?

Let's say hangover for now. I figured it was the only thing that would keep the team going in this climate. The guys were already about to drop. The only thing I can't do is help the humans.

Hopefully, this is the last time we'll bring any normal humans to hell. Once the R&D is done, they'll be Earth-side.

They glanced at the doctor and Alice, who were moving quickly around the space. The machines were ticking and spitting out reports. The doctor was organizing the data as Alice started to pack up all the tools and pieces they no longer needed. It was obvious that she was done with the place, and as soon as the experiment was complete, she wanted to rock and roll right out of there. Her time in hell was just about over. She was sure of that.

Katie ran around the crew and flipped over the carts like she was superhuman. She stopped with a skid in front of the doctor. "How's it going?"

He glanced at her, and she saw he wasn't doing so well. The conditions starting to wear on him. His face was drawn, and his eyes were watery and bloodshot. "We have eight minutes left on the experiment. As soon as it's done, we unplug and run."

Katie nodded and started to turn away. "Good."

The doctor suddenly grabbed her arm. "The problem is, I've just acquired radar capability through one of my programs."

Katie didn't understand. "That's a good thing, right?"

He turned the screen toward her. "You see those large dots? I'm tracking a group of demons not that far over the mountain to the...uh...to the..."

Katie looked up and around. "Oh shit, you can't tell direction here because there's no sun."

Alice yelled, "And don't even think of a compass. The metal in these rocks will just make the needle spin. This is not a place you can easily tell direction in. It's more a maps kind of place."

Pandora pushed forward and cut in. "It's never totally dark here, but there's no light source like you're thinking. It's not like Earth, with that big star looming overhead warming up the place."

Katie shook her head, pressing the record button on her helmet. "We are going to need a way to figure out where things are. We need to map as much of the terrain as possible. We don't need to get lost out here. It's not really the place I want to wander around in for eternity. We need drones for surveillance and perimeter patrol. I'm not going to become a fucking cartographer in hell."

The doctor coughed dryly. "You're going to need sonar detectors, and heat screeners that can withstand these types of temperatures. You want to be able to see the demons coming at all times, and this is a really good way to do it. I'm not sure how your comms work between dimensions, but if we can figure that out, you can have an IT guy on the other side manning drone feeds and detecting dangerous heat levels."

Katie nodded and repeated the information into her recording device. She looked at Alice. "Do you have any idea how the metal on those carts is handling the heat?"

Alice looked at the metal cart simmering below her. "It's not touchable without thick gloves, but it's not melting either. I'm not sure it will keep its strength for more than a few more hours. The bullets you guys brought, whatever metal this is? They're not reacting to the heat at all."

Pandora rolled her eyes. "Great. The metal we need to keep things stable also happens to be the metal that can do damage to the mercs. We're going to need some damn good gloves to touch shit like that."

The doctor cleared his throat nervously. "Whatever direction is actually north or east, it doesn't really matter at this point. The demons seem to be coming toward us, and they're closing quickly. They look to be very large, and given their speed, they are either demonic gazelles or they take very long strides."

Katie took her conversation with Pandora inside. *Uh, you don't have demon gazelles, do you?*

Pandora chuckled. *No, just big-ass demons.*

That's what I thought.

Man your stations, chick. This shit is about to get real.

Katie and Brock exchanged glances. Without asking, he knew what was coming. He yelled, "All right boys, drop your cocks and grab your socks! Showtime!"

20

The general paced the floor. He was a bundle of nerves, and his chest was tight. He reached up and unbuttoned the top button of his shirt. He wanted to be on the base receiving firsthand knowledge of the mission, but he had to keep everything else on the up and up while Katie was in hell with her team.

"Fuck this. I need an update," he growled, heading to his desk.

He dialed his contact number to the commander in Research and Development. "Commander, it's General Brushwood. I'm anxiously awaiting any news right now. It's been a while, and I thought they would be back by now."

The commander sighed. "I did too, but I don't have anything to report."

Suddenly a flash of light blinded the commander for a moment. A portal opened just outside the building, in the open air. "Hold on, General. Someone is coming through."

The commander set the phone down and walked to the door. Doctor Thorough, Alice, and two of the carts came bursting through. The portal immediately shut hard behind them. They stumbled forward, pulling their masks off and bending over to take in great gulps of air. Steam rose off everything.

The doctor sat down hard on the floor. "Oh, my. It really is quite a bit cooler here than it is in hell."

Alice stumbled to the commander, and he grabbed her arm to support her. "Commander, Katie and the rest of the team aren't coming back, sir."

The commander brought Alice into his office and sat her down in one of his chairs. He handed her a bottle of water and a towel to mop the sweat pouring from her forehead.

He picked up the phone and put it to his ear, not wanting to relay the information he had just heard. "General, Katie and the others haven't returned yet. The doctor and his assistant are back."

The general slammed his fist on the table. His voice was cold. "Let me talk to whoever gave you that news."

"Yes, sir. Her name is Alice," the commander replied before handing the phone off and leaving the room.

Alice pushed a sweaty lock of hair back and put the phone to her ear. "This is Doctor Alice Cromwell."

The general could hear the exhaustion in her voice, and he calmed himself before he spoke. "Alice, I'm glad to know you returned safely. Did you get all the data you needed?"

Alice shook her head. "Not all of it. There's still one

very significant test running. It's almost done, but we picked up a large movement of demons heading right for us. Katie didn't want to risk human lives, but we didn't want to take the chance of not getting all the data we could. She told us to come back. From the looks of it, the comm system is working between the two dimensions. We still have data streaming into our programs through the portal."

The general was angry with Katie, but he was also thankful that she'd had the brains to get the humans out. "When will they be back?"

Alice did some calculations in her head. "It shouldn't be long. As soon as the timer counts down to zero, they can get out of there. Katie has her team, and she knows how to bring the equipment back. Even if it gets left behind, we have all the data, sir. She and her team are going to hold off as long as they possibly can. The doctor is pulling up the countdown clock right now."

The general began to pace the floor of his office. "Where is the commander now?"

Alice looked up. "He's in the chamber with Doctor Thorough. I'll take the phone to him."

"Thank you, Alice, and good work out there. That data is imperative to the success of future missions." The general was sincere, but he was still worried about the others.

Alice ran into the chamber and handed the commander the phone. "He wants to talk to you."

The commander set the phone down and put it on speaker. "General, you have the doctors here with you, too."

"Commander, I need you to get the noncombatants out of the chamber and prepare for a quick exit and fumigation. You need to be able to pull Katie and the others out of the chamber, hold back any demons coming through the portal, and then gas the motherfuckers. It is imperative that you do not hurt our people. I can't make that clear enough. Katie, Calvin, and the four special ops are vitally important to the future of these missions. We need all of them in one piece."

The commander motioned to his men, and they started moving quickly. "I'm on it, General. We're clearing the field now."

The doctor hadn't been paying much attention. He leaned over the speakerphone and spoke excitedly. "General Brushwood, this is Doctor Thorough. You will not believe what we've discovered. Acidity levels are way lower than we expected and the oxygen level is far higher, but the temperatures are crazy. It affects everything in the area. If you look at the raw data, you would think it was a planet like Mars. There's no source of light, yet it's never dark there. There was no detection of dark matter, which seems scientifically impossible since dark matter and matter go hand in hand. However, there is life there, as we know. There are geological formations and organic creations."

The general tilted his head. "I guess that doesn't shock me much. We are talking about demons and angels here. I expected there to be a scientific conundrum."

The doctor mopped sweat from his neck. "I haven't seen anything like this since we started trying to measure the forces at the event horizon. This is even more baffling than that."

Alice put her hand over the doctor's mouth. "Which part of 'Get out of the way' didn't you understand?"

The doctor realized he was no longer needed. "Goodbye, General."

The general laughed. "Goodbye, doctor. I promise we will talk soon. I want to know everything about this place."

"It's a fantastical dimension or world or whatever it is, and the data we collected will shine a lot of light on the future," the doctor replied.

The soldiers ushered the doctor and Alice out of the room and got them safely into the R&D main area. They signaled the commander, and he picked up the phone. "General, the area will be clear as soon as I leave. We will get your people out of there, and I'll give you an update as soon as anything happens. The IT guys are transferring the countdown clock to your office. As soon as that clock hits zero, we should be expecting action from the other side."

"I sure as hell hope so. Good work, Commander. Keep me up to date."

The general hung up the phone and clicked on his television. The screen flickered and shifted until a countdown clock came up. He sat down on the edge of his desk, watching the numbers as they ticked down. He had to admit, it was the first time he'd been this nervous in a very long time. Katie was important both tactically and personally, but the matter was completely out of his hands.

All he could do was sit and wait.

Calvin sat on a boulder and propped his rifle on one leg, surveying his surroundings. "Anyone got a deck of cards?"

Katie climbed on top of the boulders and peered out over hell. "No, but I have a rather large demon coming around the hill."

Calvin stepped up to look, and his mouth fell open. "That's one large sonofabitch."

"Yeah, but this time he doesn't have any fucking buildings to climb on. Maybe fighting on his turf will be to my advantage."

Calvin laughed. "You sure do see the bright side of every hopeless situation."

Katie waved to Brock and his team. Brock nodded and turned to his team. "All right, guys, I need two of you to stay here with the equipment. Protect that shit at all costs. I need you to be ready to launch that fucker through the portal when it opens. Watch the timer. That's when the experiment ends. Can you handle that?"

Tattoos pointed to the large display. "This hits zero, and we get the fuck back to Earth?"

"Fucking-A right."

"I love it, boss."

Brock waved Turner on, and they ran to meet Katie. She dropped from her boulder. "I need you two to prepare a perimeter to protect those machines. You are the first line of defense for this information. It is more important than our lives. This information will give us the capability to fight back on our terms. Without it, humanity faces a dire consequence."

Turner lifted an eyebrow. "Damn, that's some heavy shit."

Brock slapped him on the chest. "We got this, Katie. Just make sure that when the portal opens, you two get your asses back there. We don't want to leave anyone behind."

Katie nodded. "And *you* remember that information is more important than me."

Calvin and Katie walked back to the boulders. Katie turned to Calvin and grabbed him by the shoulders. "Here's the deal. This bad boy is going to need some personal attention. Weapons alone aren't going to do it. I have to take care of this. I'm going to be coming back and coming back hard. I need you to make sure you guys get out if Pandora throws a portal open for you. Then, get everyone out of the building. Who knows what will happen? That chamber won't contain a bitch like that."

Calvin understood but grabbed her arm. "If we go through the portal, what will *you* do?"

Katie looked at him for a moment and shrugged, averting her eyes. "I just need to know I can count on you to make the hard decisions. I need you to get that equipment and those guys out of here. I don't trust that Brock can make that choice alone. I'm afraid he'll stay behind if I can't go through with him."

Calvin pulled her into a one-armed bear hug. "I got you. I'll leave your ass behind in a heartbeat."

Katie laughed. "Good to know."

Calvin flashed her a wide smile and turned back to the guys.

Katie turned to face the demon, adrenaline rushing through her. She watched the beast stomping toward her with purpose. She was the only one who could give the team a chance to get out of there, but she had never faced a demon this huge. Not even T'Chezz was this big, but there was always a first time for everything.

Pandora cleared her throat. *So, uh…if they leave us behind, what do we do? I may not have the energy to open a portal.*

Katie didn't answer. She climbed to the top of the big boulder, getting out of the way of the guns. She looked back over her shoulder as Calvin situated himself with Brock and Turner. She nodded at him, and he returned it. Then he pointed at the demon charging full-speed toward them. She could see a swarm of lesser demons running alongside him, trying not to be trampled.

Calvin waited for a moment and then gave the order. "Light them up!"

The sound of gunfire filled the valleys of hell, and bullets flew wildly through the air. The monstrous demon didn't seem deterred. The lesser demons scattered and reformed, not faring quite so well. Katie lifted her foot and put it on a taller rock, resting her hand on her knee. She watched the demon shrug off gunfire and advance.

She was thinking about the kind of future this mission would give mankind.

Pandora whistled. *I don't think my cooch has ever been this sweaty, and I used to live here.*

Katie didn't answer.

Pandora poked at her. *Are you still in there, or have you finally succumbed to the heat? You are just on autopilot right now, right?*

Katie didn't move a muscle. *That is a giant son of a bitch.*

Yep. They grow em' big down here. We don't like to brag, but ours is always bigger than yours.

Katie laughed. *He's eighty feet tall at least. He's big, but you can have him.*

I may have had him once, way back when. I don't quite recognize him, though. Pugluzz? Shit, is that Pugluzz? I take it back; sometimes yours are bigger than ours. Pugluzz is not exactly well-endowed.

Whoever he is, he's striding fast, but maybe not fast enough. I don't know that he'll beat the clock here. Balls. I hate clocks. All movies end with a countdown for something. It's ridiculous.

Pandora narrowed her eyes. *What was that one movie you showed me where the guy blew up the asteroid, but he was still on it?*

Armageddon.

Pandora clicked her tongue. *That's it.* Armageddon. *Fuck that shit. I would have gotten in my spaceship and blasted the rock with a laser cannon. That's how it's done. Why be a hero? It's only cool until you, I don't know, fucking die.*

Katie smirked and shook her head. *Humans have this obsession with being heroes. That's why you will always find someone willing to volunteer for a suicide mission. They want a school or a library named after them. I don't know. I guess I can relate, but I want to save my people. I don't care about the school.*

One of the lesser demons charged ahead of the pack, roaring in his own language until he was hit in the forehead by a spray of bullets. He tripped, face-planted, and skidded over the black rock before coming to a stop. His body turned to ash.

Calvin lowered his smoking weapon and turned to the other guys. "That's right. Give the man a prize. I'll do this all day."

"The way it's going, you just might have to." Brock

switched magazines and focused on the huge demon still lumbering toward them at a crazy pace.

Turner tapped his foot. "Why does this shit always have to be last-second? Why can't it be, like, there's a count-down, and it reaches zero a good ten minutes before the demons get here? Why does life always have to have some crazy-ass clock on it? I hate this shit with the passion of a thousand suns."

Brock snorted. "Wow, Turner, that is some serious hate. Besides, what kind of hero story would that be to tell the girls? Oh yeah, this huge demon came lumbering toward us, and the clock was ticking down. We took our time, played some cards, and then leisurely walked the equipment back through the portal. Talk about a lackluster ending. If I'm going to go down, it's going to be fighting for the whole fucking world, and fighting against the clock. That's glory right there. I don't want to be the guy in the first three minutes of the movie who dies because he was smoking a cigarette in the wrong place."

Calvin raised his eyebrow. "If it's all the same to the two of you, I'm against the idea of dying out here altogether. I've had enough close calls during my lifetime. I think I want a nice, slow walk off. Easy score.

Brock nodded toward the demons. "Well, that bastard right there isn't going to let us out of this one with our hands intact. He's a fast fucker."

Calvin pulled his weapon up and fired. "Move forward and blow that motherfucker to pieces! Hold the line as long as you can, and for fuck's sake, aim at the fucking head."

The three of them moved forward several steps, their fingers steadily pressing the triggers of their guns. Bullets sprayed out as the fastest of the demons lunged forward, making it to them in a hurry. Calvin pulled the trigger on his weapon until it clicked empty. "Oh, shit." He dropped his weapon and crouched, pulling a knife from his belt. The demon launched itself at him and Calvin dove for his knees. He stuck the knife into scaly flesh and pulled it through, nearly severing the leg. The demon howled, then stumbled forward and knocked Calvin to the dirt.

Brock stood up and lifted his gun. "Motherfucker, you are *mine*."

He ran at the demon, taking his time and firing three quick shots. His bullets penetrated the demon's scales—one in its shoulder, one in its neck, and the last went right through the demon's eye. It fell in a cloud of ash at Brock's feet. He swung his gun around onto his back and grabbed a long rucksack. "Calvin's got a good idea. Close quarters, boys."

Brock opened the rucksack and yanked a sword out. The blade shimmered in the red light of hell.

Turner couldn't hide his surprise. "Where the fuck did he get that badass thing?"

"I brought it just in case." Brock turned as a small, lanky demon screamed and ran at him, leaping over their bullets.

He raised the sword high over his head and let it come down quickly, chopping the demon's head off his shoulders. It turned to dust at his feet. Brock pointed the sword at the crowd of onrushing demons. "You think you're tough, but look who's going to kick your ass right here on your own territory. *Me*, motherfuckers."

Turner ran up next to Brock and held his rifle ready. "That was some bad shit there, brother. I— Oh, shit."

Coming up over the hill were dozens of small demons, making haste to get to them before the big-ass demon in the back arrived.

Calvin holstered his knife and pulled up his rifle. He reloaded and fell in with the others. "Well, boys. It looks like we're gonna see some fucking action now."

Back by the equipment, Tattoos watched the timer tick down while his teammate focused his rifle on the huge demon coming toward them.

"Big fucker coming."

Tattoos shrugged. "We got a clock to watch."

"We shouldn't help?"

"It's pretty far out, and we're watching this clock. Helpful as a motherfucker."

"Right."

Tattoos peered into the distance, measuring the demon. "But if that big bastard gets close, we fuck it up, right?"

"Fuck, yeah."

The tattooed soldier gave him a thumbs-up and went back to watching the timer.

21

"For mankind," Turner said, staring at the demons rushing.

"For my brothers." Brock nodded, and they took off toward the hordes.

Calvin gripped his gun tightly, rushing with them and firing into the crowd of demons. He plowed right into them, firing right and left, taking down demon after demon.

Brock gripped his sword with both hands. "Come on, fuckers, show me what you got. I've been waiting for this."

A demon lunged for him and he swung his sword, taking its head off. Before it had even hit the ground, another jumped at him. Then another, and another, and another. They piled on top of Brock, scratching and snarling. One by one he threw them to the ground, slashing his sword again and again, separating heads from necks. He grabbed the last scrambling demon off his back and held it in front of him by the neck. His eyes were gleaming red.

Brock squeezed the demon's throat hard. "You think you're so tough, but you're nothing but disgust and sin."

He stabbed the demon through the body and pulled his sword back out, splashing black oozing blood across his helmet.

Calvin and Turner ran out together, blasting their M16s into the horde. One after another the demons went down, but more swarmed forward. They were tearing at the guys' suits, fucking them up and causing burns on their skin. Calvin shot the last of his bullets and flipped the gun over to swing at an oncoming demon, knocking his head back.

Turner laughed and quickly crouched and shot the beast in the throat, turning him to ash. "That was pretty badass, I won't lie."

A demon screamed and leaped at Calvin, and he pulled his knife and jammed it under the demon's chin. The thing howled and began to wither, but not before it raked its claws across the forearm of Calvin's suit. It scratched a long hole in the fabric, and Calvin winced, grabbing at it. His skin sizzled under the heat, and his eyes glowed even redder.

"You good?"

Calvin growled and launched into the horde of demons, taking his anger out on them.

Turner found Brock in the chaos. "That fucker's crazy."

"He's got the right idea, though." Brock pulled two small knives out of his belt and handed them to Turner. "Here. Go nuts, bro."

Turner smiled, looking at the sharp blades. "What will *you* fight with?"

Brock held his long sword in front of him with a mischievous grin. Turner rolled his eyes. "Oh yeah, the sword from *the Sword in the Stone*. I forgot."

The guys laughed and began to slash at the demons. Turner ran full speed at a medium-sized one, suddenly dropping to his knees and sliding right between its legs. He slashed the beast in its thighs and jumped, turning in mid-air and cutting it across the throat. The demon fell and turned to ash. Turner looked at the knives, impressed by his own skills. "Well, I'll be damned. I'm pretty good with these fucking things."

Just then, Brock screamed loudly as he flew through the air in front of Turner, slicing three demons' heads off with one swipe. He landed and held the sword up, kissing the blade and wagging his eyebrows at Turner. "I'm pretty damn good, too."

Turner just stared at him. "Always got to one-up someone."

Behind them, Tattoos cupped his hand and yelled, "Two minutes!" He turned to his teammate. "Right?"

"Yep. Two minutes. You're a great announcer, by the way."

"Thanks, bro." Tattoos pound his shoulder.

Turner ripped his knives free of a demonic corpse and watched the thing turn to ash. "I'd say 'See you in hell, boys,' but we're already here."

Brock chuckled and slapped him on the shoulder before running off to continue fighting.

Katie stayed perched on her boulder, watching the large

demon draw closer. A smaller demon scrambled up the boulder, and she shot it easily. It was ash before it hit the ground.

Katie squinted, looking at the big guy. *I don't think we have enough time before lard ass gets here.*

It's Pugluzz. I think. Maybe not, I don't remember Pugluzz being that tall.

Whoever it is, that asshole could fuck all of us with one swipe of his hand.

How about Fucknuts? That's a good name.

I like it. Let's go fuck up Fucknuts.

She looked at the guys fighting and holstered her gun. "*Stand tall!*" She leaped from the rock and landed in a roll, then took off toward Fucknuts at superhuman speed.

The giant demon made huge strides toward the group but paused, watching as the little human started coming his way. He wasn't used to them running toward him. They always ran *from* him.

Katie pumped her arms, breathing heavily. *You want in or out on this one?*

Pandora replied cautiously, *Why?*

Because I'm going to have to go all angel to beat this fucker. He's too big, and I am way too fragile in this environment to play around with his ass. I need to get everyone out of harm's way. I can't let Fucknuts over there make it through the portal when it opens. The guys on the inside wouldn't stand a chance, not even for a second.

Pandora growled, *Do I need to remind you that we're trying to stay inconspicuous?*

What's less conspicuous, an angel with wings and a sword or the queen of hell?

Pandora thought about it for a moment. *Considering the gossip, probably the angel but only by a hair. I still think this is a bad idea. We're basically calling for Moloch and the others to send all their troops.*

Katie pumped her arms faster. *I'm pretty sure they know we're here by now. Even if they don't, we'll be done and back home before they have a chance to send more demons. They're fast, but not that fast. Think about how long it took these to get here. Fucknuts may be closing in, but he moves at a glacial pace comparatively.*

You try carrying around a three-ton dick and balls and see how fast you *move.* Pandora started laughing before she even got the sentence out.

Katie grimaced, her eyes falling on the beast's swinging tackle. *Everyone thinks that demons eating people are what horror movie shit is about, but personally, I will spend the rest of my life trying to get the image of his dick out of my head.*

Pandora focused through Katie's vision. *Sheesh, Fucknuts is packing. Just think of it as a large swinging bell.*

A bell? Like a hot-dog-shaped bell or a snake ringing a bell? What are we talking about here?

Pandora sneered. *Okay, you just officially made me want to vomit all over your insides. I will never eat a hot dog again, and this is coming from someone who likes hot dogs of all shapes and sizes. But not that shape and size. If I ever come back here, I'm starting a business that sells enormous pants, and every demon is going to be required to wear a pair.*

Katie smiled. *I just made hell a little more civilized. I have done my duty in this world.*

You tricked me with your evil human-angel-demon-hybrid

ways. That's starting to get way too long to say. Don't add to that shit, or I'm going to start calling you Katie the Mutt.

Katie ignored the comment as she grew closer to Fucknuts. *It's you then, right?*

Pandora cracked her neck. *It's me.*

They both went silent and Katie slowed her pace, waiting on Pandora. After a couple of awkward moments and Pandora whistling, she cleared her throat loudly. *So are you going to pull me out or what?*

Katie smiled. *Well, I thought since you climbed back in on your own, you could get back out on your own.*

Pandora sniffed as Fucknuts and his scrambling horde came closer. *Thought you didn't see that.*

Katie stopped and crossed her arms. *Seriously? You crawled inside my body. I would have had to be dead not to notice that. It isn't the most covert thing. And you stepped on my liver when you came in. It felt bruised for a while. Still kind of stiff.*

Okay, okay, I get it. Pandora braced herself and stepped out of Katie's body. Katie felt like she was being turned inside out and ripped apart, and then it was over. Pandora stood before her, a sleek, demonic beauty. Katie examined her suit and found it undamaged.

Pandora shook her head, rattling away the fogginess that came with being very recently reborn. She reached her arms over her head and stretched, taking a deep breath and holding it while she cracked her back. She let out her breath and bounced on her heels, making sure all her jiggly parts still jiggled. "Fuck, yeah. Still got it." She grinned toothily and smacked her fist into her palm. "Okay, dickweeds, Momma's back."

Pandora took off into the crowd of demons between her and Fucknuts. Her claws were razor-sharp and cut right through the necks of the lesser demons. She grabbed a small demon's head and ripped it off his shoulders. She was quicker than them, and dozens of demons fell to her within a matter of seconds. She moved so fast that all the confused demons saw was a streak of color, and all they could hear was the crunching of bones and tearing of flesh.

Fucknuts stopped to watch the carnage. He narrowed his eyes and jumped back in surprise, realizing that the queen of hell was before him, and she wasn't on his side.

"This one's for you, you warty-dicked motherfucker!" Pandora locked eyes with Fucknuts as she grabbed a medium-sized demon by his head and ripped it clean from his shoulders, spraying blood everywhere.

Pandora rolled her eyes. "Come on, I've had my skin back for like ten minutes, and I get something on it."

Another demon walked up and hissed at Pandora, spraying spittle on her cheek. She wiped her face and stared back with bright red eyes. She pulled her hand back and let it fly, smacking the demon as hard as she could across the cheek. The demon's eyes bulged as she connected, there was a loud crack, and his head flew off his shoulders.

Pandora looked at her hand and the body falling to the ground in front of her. "Damn. My pimp hand is strong. I completely forgot what kind of power I have when I'm kicking ass in hell. That was fucking sweet!"

Katie felt a bit lighter, and her body picked up its amped effects. A demon charged at her, and in a smooth motion she holstered her gun and grabbed her knife. She flipped her arm up, bent at the elbow. The demon ran face-first into the blade and fell, turning to dust at her feet. She wiped the blade on her pants without even looking at the demon and put it back in its sheath.

Pandora called, "Katie, did you see that badass slap? I knocked his head at least three hundred yards."

Katie pulled Tom and fired a few quick rounds. A demon's head exploded into ash. "So you're a champion demon golfer?"

Pandora snapped her fingers. "You know what? That would be a badass sport. I would be really fucking good at it. I have good aim and everything. I mean, I could go on a tour all over hell and beat all the old misogynistic demons."

Katie cracked her neck and wiped the blood off her suit, the heat pulsating against her hand. It was hella hot down there, and without Pandora, she could feel the heat getting to her. She pulled out Harry and pointed it at a charging demon. The large bullet exploded from the chamber and flew through the air, going straight through the demon's head.

Katie looked at the barrel of the gun and smirked. "Huh, it's nice when I'm the one who's got *your* back and not the other way around. I can kind of sit back and relax back here, taking demons out right and left."

Pandora growled as she ripped a demon in half and then stared at Katie with her hands on her hips. "Moving a little faster might prolong life, though. You're backup, not second string. You can't just sit this one out."

Katie performed a double-take as Pandora flipped through the air to land on a demon's shoulders, snapping its neck. Her skin glistened as she dropped to the ground and leaped up and her huge breasts bounced around wildly, knocking a couple of demons in the face.

Katie rubbed her own breasts, wondering if that had hurt her. "Do you always run around naked here? I feel like too many flips, twists, and turns and you're going to end up with some serious chafing. I mean, with an ass like that I'd probably want to flaunt it too, but hell's bells, girl!"

Pandora laughed as she broke a demon's neck. "Aren't you the cute little angel, bringing your taboos to hell with you? It's hell, honey. We don't really have rules here. And what would you like me to do? Stop fighting demons and grab some clothes? By the time I got back, you would be dead and it would be all over."

Katie smashed the butt of her gun into the skull of a demon and kicked him hard. "It's not my delicate sensibilities. It's jealousy, bitch." She shot the demon in the face and watched his ashes blow away. "And I am a little tougher than you think."

Katie snapped her fingers as she had seen Timothy do a hundred times. Pandora threw her head back and bellowed. She was laughing so hard that she screwed up the spell she had been working on. Energy shimmered around her. Immediately, she jumped toward Katie and shielded her.

"Fuck!" Pandora yelled as a loud explosion of light blasted outward from behind her, taking down rows and rows of demons.

She slowly lifted her head and looked around. "Huh."

Katie was under Pandora, the demon's tit dangerously close to her face. "Huh, what?"

"I just fucked up that spell because you made me laugh,

and it turned out better than the original would have. I did not see that coming."

Katie smirked. "You're welcome?"

"No! Stop making me laugh. But seriously, that was funny as shit. Good joke."

Katie tried to move away from Pandora's encroaching boob, but she was pinned. "Uh, excuse me?"

Pandora looked down. "Yeah?"

Katie pointed at the boob almost rubbing her cheek. "Could you move your tits before you put my goddamned eye out?"

Pandora stood up. "Oh, sorry about that. They've got a mind of their own."

The radio on Katie's headset crackled, and Calvin's voice spoke to her. "Katie, the test is done. We gotta get out of here before we become toe jam to that huge-ass bastard."

Katie looked at Pandora. "Got to go, Pandora. We need an exit plan. As much as I'm enjoying your nude gymnastic display in front of the backdrop of a giant swinging dick, I want to get out of hell. The guys look pretty beat up back there and are going to need medical attention. What's the plan?"

Pandora looked over her shoulder at Katie and winked. "How about an ass the size of a car?" Pandora put her hands to her sides and grinned.

"Okay, really. We need a..." Katie closed her mouth. Something was wrong. Pandora was getting taller. Katie watched with wide eyes as Pandora grew larger and larger until she was face to face with Fucknuts. Katie had to crane her neck to look up at Pandora. Her huge ass cast a shadow over the entire valley.

Katie cupped her mouth and yelled up to her, "*Now* what's the plan? Ask him on a date? Because you are one huge bitch. Not many men will date a woman that size."

Pandora snapped her head around and glared down at Katie, her eyes bright red. "Can I save all of us or would you like to continue with your rude jokes?"

Katie stepped back, giving Pandora the floor. "No. Please, by all means. I want to see this. Just don't step on me."

Pandora nodded and turned back to Fucknuts, who was genuinely confused.

He growled and slowly put his paws up in a fighting stance.

Pandora laughed loudly. "Isn't that cute? He thinks we're going to fight."

Both Katie and Fucknuts tilted their heads to the side, trying to guess Pandora's plan.

Fucknuts decided to go the other direction. He gestured to his grotesque groin and gave her a questioning glance.

Pandora gave him a disgusted look and reared her leg back, then delivered the biggest kick to the 'nads hell had ever seen. Fucknuts growled and grabbed his balls, shaking the ground when he fell to his knees in agony. The guys near the gear grimaced, and even Katie could feel his pain.

Pandora spat on the demon. "Size doesn't mean anything to me, Fucknuts." She shot him in the head for good measure.

She quickly shrank to normal size and ran over to pull Katie away from the howling demon. Katie couldn't help but turn and watch the demon writhe in pain, drool coming out of the corner of his mouth and black blood from his head. "He really went down like a sack of potatoes. A whole hell of a lot of potatoes. I think his dick crushed like a dozen smaller demons when he hit the ground."

Pandora rolled her eyes, grabbed Katie, and threw her over her shoulder. "Hey!"

"Can't talk, saving a mouthy bitch right now."

Pandora ran across the field so fast that she was just a dark naked blur. Katie bobbed up and down, trying to clear her head of what she had just seen. "I never, by the way, want to be that close to a house-sized coochie again. I mean, never. I thought it was going to swallow me and I would be lost forever."

Pandora snickered. "I don't call it my hellmouth for nothing."

Tattoos and his teammate were anxiously awaiting Katie's arrival. Brock, Turner, and Calvin were spread around them in formation, picking off stray demons one by one. Suddenly a blur passed Tattoos and stopped in front of the cart.

Katie said, "What are we waiting for?" Her eyes were bright red; Pandora was clearly in control. "I'm ready to get the holy hell out of here. You guys okay?"

Brock nodded and gestured to his shredded suit. "Still alive, but we'd really like to get out of here." Calvin and Turner had equally torn suits.

Pandora patted him on the shoulder, and Brock winced. "The open spots are a little tender."

"Sorry. We'll get that taken care of real soon. Promise."

She rubbed her hands together, and tingling energy flowed through her. Inside her body, Katie began to get drowsy; the spell Pandora had cast was quickly diminishing. She spread her arms out wide and closed her eyes, tearing a gate through thin air.

Pandora turned and whipped her arm in a circle. "*Go, go, go!*"

22

The soldiers outside the hangar bay stood waiting for something—anything—to happen. The timer had run out, and it was now negative five minutes. They hadn't heard a peep, but the commander and the general held firm. They were determined to wait, knowing the team would come through at any moment.

"I don't know if they're going to make this," one of the soldiers whispered.

His friend shrugged and then stepped back as thunder sounded inside the building. A portal opened wide in the hangar bay. Hot gases and the smell of sulfur blew out, knocking the soldiers back a few feet. They all got their footing and raised their guns, waiting for someone to come out. If it was a demon, they would blast it to pieces.

Suddenly, the tattooed soldier and his teammate rushed from the portal. They groaned as they pulled the equipment into the hangar. The metal cart was warped and steaming, and the tires were flat. Both men fell to the ground and took their masks off, gasping for air. Tattoos raised a shaking fist and gave his teammate a pound on the back. "Clock-watchers. Fucking right."

Brock and Turner emerged next. They faced back toward hell, still firing their weapons at the demons attempting to come through after them.

"You can't come in, assholes. We don't like your kind here," Brock screamed, blasting two demons in the face and sending them back to hell.

Brock and Turner collapsed, and medics rushed to them. The portal stayed open, but only hellishly hot air came out.

The commander turned to a staff sergeant. "I want you ready for whatever the fuck comes out of there."

A low yell came from the portal. It was Calvin. He lumbered out of the portal with Katie in his arms. He set her down, and they walked away from the portal together. She was struggling a bit, trying to get her feet under her. Calvin helped her out into the open air. "Take it easy there, lady. That last little bit of magic took a lot out of you."

Pandora nodded. Katie was panting in the background. She raised her hand and waved it, closing the gate behind her. "It's like exercise. Don't do it for a while and you get tired easily."

Calvin chuckled. "Or sex. Guys will be out like a light if they haven't done it in a while."

Pandora patted Calvin on the arm. "I lasted longer, though, black Rambo."

Calvin narrowed his eyes, looking at Katie's face. He knew then it was Pandora who had the wheel, not Katie. She took off her helmet, the wind from the open hangar bay door blowing the smell of sulfur toward the mountains.

Calvin laughed. "See? Go to hell and fight demons. No sweat."

Pandora scoffed. "Speak for yourself."

Calvin looked down at his suit. "No, really, I think I stopped sweating like three seconds into it. I'm bound to heatstroke out any second."

Pandora considered his torn clothing. "You'll be fine. If we can survive it, you got this in the bag. Besides, your demon is working double-time to keep you going. He was just reminded of how good they have it out here. He doesn't want to end up back in hell for anything. You're sure to be kept in working order from now on, no matter what crazy shit you pull."

Calvin shook his head. "Was that all it took? I would have strolled through hell a long time ago if I thought it would light a fire under my demon's ass...literally."

The commander walked over and stood in front of Calvin and Pandora. "I'm sorry. We need to get you guys out. We have to set up the trap in case anything follows you."

Pandora groaned as she got to her feet. "I don't think anything is going to follow. The portal is closed, but it's definitely better if you're sure."

As they hobbled out of the hangar, the doctor was yelling commands to various soldiers. The soldiers were carefully pushing the machines out of the way, terrified they were going to break something. Dr. Thorough pointed to one man and muttered darkly, "Please be careful. Not all the data came through. It's on that machine. If you break it, we are screwed."

Pandora laughed and stepped outside to where the rest of the crew was sitting in chairs or on gurneys. It was a makeshift MASH unit. *I wonder how much it's costing them— or me—to pump special metal gas into a chamber that may not get a demon in it.*

Pandora shrugged. *Meh, it's okay. It'll save a hell of a lot of headaches. Besides, not a single one of us is in any shape to take on more demons. You should be passed out, and I feel like I could sleep for six years. These guys look like they might lie down and let the demon take them.*

Katie giggled. *I haven't seen them this worn out since the morning after getting wasted in New York City.*

Is that what Brock looks like after fucking? I don't know. He looks half-dead.

Katie stopped laughing and got serious. *That's not even... I didn't mean... Damn it!*

Pandora cackled inwardly. *It's okay, I know what you meant. Don't get your panties in a knot.*

"Stand back. Doors closing," one of the soldiers yelled as he closed the hangar bay doors.

Brock sat up on his gurney and took a water bottle from one of the soldiers. He took a long, deep drink. "You guys kicked some major ass down there."

Turner nodded. "You too, brother. You were like a kung fu master with your flips and shit."

Tattoos shook his head. "I saw Brock flip through the air and cut off three demons' heads with one swipe of that crazy sword. Chop! I *swear* he looked like he was about to rip the others' heads off with his teeth. It was the most vicious I've ever seen you, dude."

Brock stood up carefully, wincing. "Yeah, and in hell."

Turner gingerly touched one of the blisters on his arm. "I went to hell, and all I got was this lousy second-degree burn."

Tattoos leaned forward and showed Katie his hands. They were bright red and blistered from fingertip to wrist. "Hey, just so you know, you might want to get tougher gloves next time."

Pandora grimaced and nodded. "Noted. Thicker gloves."

"I can take care of that," a medic offered, bending down in front of the guy.

She was young, blonde, and pretty, and smiled sweetly at him. The tattooed soldier glanced at Turner and put on a wicked smile. "This might have been worth it."

Turner put up his finger for help, but she was already helping Tattoos to the sick bay.

"I got you," a deep voice rumbled behind of him.

Turner looked at one of the big male medics. He sighed and stood up. "Why is my luck in the shitter?"

Moloch leaned back in his dimly lit office inside his mansion and flipped through the channels on the television. He made it to CNN and put the remote down. He grabbed a glass of whiskey, cut it with Scotsman's blood, and took a sip. He muttered, "Where are you, you bastard?

I know you're building an army, but why haven't you made any waves yet?"

Moloch didn't know how to keep track of Juntto without specifically reaching out to him. After being knocked off the mountain, he wasn't interested in having any more personal contact with the frost giant. Still, he needed him to pick up the pace. He had come this far, and he wasn't about to put everything on hold just because one jackass wanted to take a century to conquer a few lousy European countries.

"In other news, there has been no new information about the two dead hikers found in the Alps. Sources say it was definitely a demon attack, but the details are still fuzzy. In the world of sports today…" The newscaster didn't linger on the story at all.

"Ah, fuck it," Moloch growled. He flipped off the television.

He took a big swig of his drink as a loud knock echoed through the office. "Come in!"

The door slowly creaked open, and Moloch's main servant along with five others scurried into the room and stood to the side with their heads down. Moloch waved his hand, not looking at them. "What is it? Is dinner ready already? I'm used to eating later than this."

The servant stepped a little closer and nervously put up his hand. "No, sir. We've gotten word that there has been a Lilith sighting in hell."

Moloch sat up quickly. "Do they know for sure that it was her?"

The demon nodded. "Invrrrnus is still bitching about his crushed nuts. Apparently, she grew to his size and kicked him in the balls. She then shrank back down and ran off with her human."

Moloch flinched. "Yeah, that's her. She was always a bit too quick to hurt the boys. I told her over and over that it wasn't fair play for her to kick a man in the balls. She never listened. I told her that one day it would get her head snapped off. I guess Invrrrnus wasn't fast enough."

He swallowed the last gulp of his blood and whiskey and walked to his desk, checking his schedule. He rubbed his chin and glanced at the servants standing nervously by the bookshelf.

He pointed at them. "You three in the front, you're coming with me. We have a bitch to track. If I'm going to be sure it was her, I need to do it myself. I can't seem to find reliable help anywhere in hell these days."

The head servant bowed and shooed them forward. He kicked one in the ass for good measure. Moloch grabbed his walking stick and nodded at the servant. "You and the rest can get dinner prepared. It's a long walk out of the inner ring. I'll be hungry by the time I get back."

The servant bowed and pushed the remaining servants out the door. "Absolutely. And let me know if any of them give you trouble. They should be on their best behavior."

Moloch closed the door behind him. It wasn't the news he'd expected.

Juntto downed the glass of whiskey and yawned, looking at the big-breasted blonde next to him. He gave her a fake smile as she continued to chatter.

She ran her hand over his knee and smiled. "It's just all this bullshit in the media today about men. I am so tired of society wanting everything to be equal between men and women. I mean, respect is respect, right? Everyone wants it. Seriously, there isn't a woman out there who doesn't want a man who knows what he wants and takes it. You know? I don't understand how these women can be content with men who tiptoe around their natural instincts."

Juntto smiled. "Yes, I like taking what I want. So why don't I take you?"

Juntto slammed his glass down and grabbed her. He tossed her over his shoulders. She squealed. "Oh, that—*oh!*"

He walked toward the door, and the whole bar quieted to watch the scene. The woman slapped him on the arms, trying to wiggle away. "Look, just because you have a nice ass doesn't mean you can grab me and take me wherever you want. You do have to be respectful about it. Maybe ask me if I want to go with you."

Juntto kept walking. "I'm confused. You're getting what you want—a man to take you and do what he likes."

"A man as in, a man I'm seeing, not some stranger in a bar," she scolded.

A drunk old man stood from his barstool. "We should help that damsel in distress!"

His drunk pal pulled him back down. "It's none of our business. Bartender, another round!" The drunk old man quickly forgot about the strange pair leaving the bar.

"You women need to learn your place. Don't speak, just do what I want done." Juntto grunted and shifted her weight as he carried her out to the street.

"I'm not playing around, asshole. You need to put me down!" she squealed, but Juntto ignored the cries.

He sighed as he walked along. "I don't understand. The women in this century don't tell the truth. You said you wanted this, so I give it to you, and you cry. Do you want me or not?"

She shouted, "You didn't hear what I was saying at all. I *do* want it, but not like this!"

Juntto rolled his eyes and tossed the woman to the ground in front of a large crowd of people. "Who knows what that means? I'm done with your attitude."

He wiped his hands off and went back into the bar for another drink.

He sat down at the bar, thankful that he no longer had to listen to the woman's chatter. The bartender poured him a double and walked away.

Juntto watched the news talk about the dead hikers and tucked the bloodstain on his sleeve up under his jacket. He took a big swig of his whiskey. The bartender saw him watching and gestured to the television. "That's some sad shit, huh? It's crazy, because those two came by here a few days before. They were stoked about climbing to the summit. I heard the guy was found butt-naked, and the woman was stuck in a tree or something. What kind of crazy shit is that?"

Juntto nodded. "Bigfoot."

The bartender chuckled uncomfortably, then turned and walked away. Juntto shrugged and continued watching, panning his head slowly as he heard the woman from before bitching to the bouncer. She was pointing at him. He smirked and turned back, finishing his drink and setting the glass carefully down. He folded his napkin neatly and wiped his lips before standing up and pulling some cash from his pocket. He tossed it on the bar. "For the damages."

The bartender puzzled over the cash. "Damages?"

The bouncer walked up to Juntto and patted him hard on the shoulder. "Hey. This woman says you accosted her and then threw her to the ground. Hey, I'm fucking *talking* to you."

Juntto turned and stared at the large bouncer. The bouncer narrowed his eyes and pointed his finger at Juntto's face. "You fucking out-of-towners think you can come in here and do whatever the fuck you want. Think again, asshole. That is *not* how this works. You and your half-assed Viking accent."

Juntto yawned and grabbed the bouncer's finger with one hand. He pulled back his other fist and punched the bouncer with everything he had. The bouncer was unconscious before he hit the floor. One of the old guys at the bar leaped up, knocking over his stool. "*Fight!*"

It was like someone had flipped a switch. The entire bar broke out in an all-out brawl. They were throwing fists, chairs, and anything else they could get their hands on. Juntto ducked as a beer glass flew over his head. He watched one guy pick up a smaller man and slam him down on a table. The table's legs snapped, and the whole thing collapsed beneath them.

Juntto cracked his knuckles, ready to go along for the ride. "This place is disgusting. No one says what they mean. How does one create a nation out of spineless drivel?"

A guy fell into him, and Juntto grabbed him by the shirt collar and punched him in the face. Teeth flew across the bar. Juntto tossed the guy into a wall and watched him slide down. The man didn't move. The frost giant was ready to fight, but he decided to pull his punches. He wasn't in the mood to kill someone and have to leave the town. Not yet, anyway.

Another guy walked up and stared at him angrily. "You're the fucker who started this whole thing. That was my friend you knocked out, asshole. I ought to—"

Juntto kept a calm expression and punched the guy in the face, knocking him to the floor. "I'm just warming up."

He swung at anyone who got near him. He knocked out four guys and then watched two huge men circle one another. They each had a broken beer bottle and were threatening each other with them. Juntto grabbed their heads and slammed them together. The big men dropped in a pile of the unconscious brutes surrounded by shattered glass. Juntto sighed and watched the brawl continue in smaller, more vicious groups. "This is boring. Good night."

He grabbed a bottle of tequila from behind the bar since the bartender was hiding and put it inside his jacket. He stepped over the unconscious men on the floor and pushed open the door. A young couple was about to come into the bar, but they stumbled back when they saw the chaos.

Juntto didn't have a scratch on him.

He whistled as he strode carefree down the street. He pulled the bottle of tequila out, popped off the top, and took a swig straight from the bottle. "Fuck me, that's something!" He laughed. "This place might have some serious pussies, but it is good to be free again."

Someone passing gave him a high five. "Right on, buddy. Freedom!"

Juntto put down his hand and sneered. "Idiot."

M oloch's walking stick clinked hard against the black stone rock. He grumbled to himself as he shuffled along, hating that his crew was too incompetent to do this on their own. He walked through a deep trench in the ground and looked around. One of the servants put his shaking hand up.

Moloch nodded and the demon swallowed hard, looking down at the ground. He was too afraid to make eye contact. "That is where the demon fell to his knees."

Moloch pursed his lips. "Mmm. She must have gotten him good. She definitely used her powers to grow to his size. That must have been a sight to see. An eighty-foot-tall Pandora with those big tits flopping everywhere."

He looked into the distance, seeing the remains of a gate that had burned the side of the mountain. He shuffled across the ground, kicking through piles of demon ashes as he went. "At least they put up a fight. It doesn't look like the demons won, though."

The servants zigzagged around the piles of their fallen
fellow demons, getting more frightened by the second.
Moloch moved up the side of the hill and looked around,
finding shreds of the team's climate suits simmering on the
hot ground. He picked one up and sniffed it. "She had reinforcements. Other Damned. But why?"

"Excuse me, Moloch, sir. There's something over here,"
one of the servants whimpered.

Moloch made his way over to the servant and went
down on one knee. He ran his large claw along the mark-
ings left by the equipment and sniffed the imprint thoughtfully. "Looks like they brought some sort of equipment
with them. Several carts full. The heated metal scorched
the ground along this ridge. What kind of machines would
they bring in here, only to take them back that quickly?"

Muttering rose from the group of servants, and Moloch
lifted his head to peer at them. "Well? If someone has
something to say, say it. Or I'll make a snack out of the lot
of you right now."

The group of servants tousled and grappled with one
another until they managed to force one fat demon
forward. His knees clanked hard together. Moloch
straightened, staring down the portly beast. "What's
your name?"

"Ricidiocalese, sir," the trembling demon replied.

"That's a fucking mouthful, isn't it? I'll just call you Fat
Rick. So, Fat Rick, what do you have to say? What
machines did they bring?" Moloch was teasing him but
hoped he would be more useful than the others. They were
cowering just out of his reach.

The demon pointed his small claws at the burn marks.

"I don't know for sure. I wasn't here. But I have seen machines before. So, maybe they were scientific machines? Maybe they were studying our land. Or something. I don't know."

Moloch growled. "Why would they do that?"

The demon flinched and put up his hand. "I don't know. To learn more about us, maybe? One of the demons who made it back said there were five soldiers and Lilith, obviously not enough to fight. There were two humans in special suits, too. They were the ones with the machines. The demons said they left first."

"Humans in special suits. I see." Moloch patted Fat Rick on the head. "Maybe you aren't useless after all, Rick."

Moloch squinted at the ground and tried to figure this new riddle out. "Who comes to hell on purpose? Especially when you have to wear a suit to keep you alive. And what about her angel bitch? She was obviously not in control when Pandora grew that tall. Just what the hell is our Queen of Kicking Demons in the Balls up to?"

Juntto finished the bottle of tequila and tossed it down an alley. As he turned a corner, he spotted another drinking establishment. Perfect. Inside, the lights were low, and the music was heavy. He didn't pay any attention to the people there, just went straight to the bar and ordered a drink. He threw some money down and turned around to view the crowd.

He sized up all the people drinking, dancing, and talking. Something was wrong. He looked at his clothes and then at the people again. He realized he wasn't dressed in the same style. Almost all of them were wearing black lace-up boots, jeans rolled at the bottom, suspenders, and either no shirts or a tight white t-shirt. Their heads were bald, with the exception of a couple of younger guys. They were sporting tall spiked mohawks.

He glanced at a girl who'd bounced up to the bar. She had jet black hair and was wearing a short plaid skirt and a black band T-shirt. Her arm was tattooed with a swastika. She looked at Juntto and smiled. "You don't look like you belong here."

Juntto chuckled. "I don't belong much of anywhere in this century."

She smirked. "Okay. I'm Mist."

Juntto shifted closer and looked down at her with a coy smile. "Mist, like the rain?"

She giggled. "Yeah, like that. You aren't from around here, are you?"

Juntto shook his head. "No, is it that obvious?"

"Your accent is hot." She smiled and ran her finger down Juntto's stomach and below his belt buckle.

A man with a bald head and a strap of a beard walked up and put one arm around Mist. He put his mouth on her ear. "What are you doing over here?"

She smacked her gum. "Getting a drink."

"Oh yeah? Is this lumberjack-looking motherfucker bothering you?" The guy looked Juntto up and down, but the frost giant wasn't looking at him. He was staring straight into the crowd, taking a nonchalant sip of his drink.

The guy grabbed Mist's ass and pushed her out of his

way. He stepped to Juntto. "Hey, fucker, I'm fucking talking to you. You come into our territory, and then you act rude to me?"

Juntto glanced at the guy and took another sip of his drink. He almost looked bored.

The guy's friend rolled up and slapped his friend on the chest. "What are you doing, dude?"

The guy stared angrily at Juntto. "This prick came into our club and is being rude to me. He won't even look me in the eye when I'm talking to him. He thinks this is some sort of fucking game."

His friend looked Juntto over, putting his thumbs through his suspenders. "Oh, yeah? Does he know how you carved up the last asshole who wandered in off the street?"

The guy chuckled, still staring at Juntto. "You know, I don't think so. I like to show rather than tell. Sometimes guys like this, with their plaid shirts and expensive fucking boots, come rolling in here and just need to get their fucking asses kicked. I mean they need a boot shoved so far up their ass that they walk funny for a little while."

The guys laughed, but Juntto just yawned, still not looking at them. The guy turned and pulled up his shirt sleeve, slapping his neo-Nazi tattoo. "You see this, prick? You're supposed to respect the supreme, and this means I am one of those."

Juntto finished his drink and set it on the bar, carefully wiping his lips. He turned to the guy and stared at him for a moment. "I like your attitude, but can you fuck with that big dick you're swinging around? When you say you have a twelve-inch dick, you should just whip it out."

Beside them, Mist giggled. The guy's face fell, then he

reared back and swung hard at Juntto. His hand contacted Juntto's face, and there it just stopped. It didn't even dent Juntto's skin.

Instead, the guy screeched and pulled his broken and bloodied fist back. Juntto lunged forward and punched the guy three times in the stomach as hard as he could. The guy fell to the floor, writhing in the fetal position.

Everyone stopped what they were doing and looked down at their friend. Instantly, the fight was on, with people lunging left and right for Juntto. He kept calm, swinging every chance he got. One guy came up behind him and jumped on Juntto's back, but he grabbed the man's arm and flipped him over the pool table. He grabbed the pool balls and grinned. He threw the balls, one after the other, at his attackers. Noses broke, teeth spun across the dance floor, and a few guys dropped to their knees clutching bruised nuts.

Juntto spun and caught a pool stick as someone swung at him. He snatched it from the guy and broke it in half.

He grinned deviously. "Two spears. I told that idiot Moloch. Two spears!" Juntto commenced beating the fuck out of everyone who was left. He was getting tired of the pricks, but he was pretty impressed with how hard they fought.

As he reached the center of the room, the guys pulled themselves together. They were bruised and bleeding, but now they were furious.

Juntto laughed and clacked his new spears together. "That's all you big guys got? Come on, challenge me!"

With that, five guys ran forward at once, jumping on top of Juntto and muscling him to the floor. They wrestled him down and pinned his hands to the ground. Mist's boyfriend with his chin-strap beard walked forward with an evil grin on his face. He was holding a knife in his hand and stood over Juntto.

Juntto smiled at him. "Is that for me?"

"It sure is, prick," the guy growled as he lifted the knife.

Juntto gritted his teeth and used his enormous strength to yank one arm free. He used the broken pool cue to slash at the men holding him, and suddenly both arms were free. The pool cues broke flesh and shattered teeth. Juntto rose with his spears and stared with wild eyes at the man holding the knife.

"I guess this just got serious."

The man lunged. He swung the knife right and left, but Juntto was faster. He thrust both broken pool cues into the man's chest and drove them deep. The man gurgled once, then died.

Juntto pulled his spears free of the dead man and walked to where Mist was cowering near the bar. The sounds of her cries were loud in the place. Juntto realized he'd managed to kill everyone in the place, minus a couple of guys with broken bones who were moaning and whimpering on the ground.

He decided to ignore the girl. Instead, he nodded at the bartender and placed both halves of the broken pool cue on the bar. "One shot of tequila."

Mist screamed and stood, and Juntto's hand shot out. He caught her in the back of the head, and she slid to the ground, unconscious.

The bartender shook as he poured the drink. Juntto

knocked it back. "Don't be nervous. I always respect those who give me free drinks."

The police sirens blared loudly outside.

Juntto sighed. He jumped over the bar, grabbed another bottle of tequila and left the bar by the back door. He found himself in an alley. "The *polizei* are getting faster, yes? Or maybe I am just getting slower. I will have to work on my technique a bit. It's been a couple thousand years."

He popped the top off the bottle and headed into the darkness of the alley, guzzling the tequila as he walked.

Inside, the police asked the bartender questions. "*Où est-il allé? A quoi ressemblait-il?*"

The bartender, stunned, shook his head. "He was a badass, that's what he was."

The fire crackled loudly in the fireplace in Moloch's office. He tapped his long talons on his desk, trying to piece together everything he knew about Pandora's sighting. He scribbled something on a piece of paper and held it up as he paced the room.

"She entered with seven others through a gate. They had some sort of equipment, and the two humans left early. The Damned, wearing special suits, fought off the demons. Pandora exited her human again, and grew to eighty feet tall and kicked my demon in the balls. Then they all left." Moloch scratched his head.

He read it over and over, not understanding what in the hell was going on. Finally, he balled up the piece of paper and chucked it hard into the fire, frustrated. Sparks shot up as it burned. He went to get a drink from his bar. He stopped and glanced at the television, quickly reading the headline at the bottom. "Massacre at Swiss Bar."

He grabbed the carafe of whiskey and the goblet of blood and hit the volume on the remote. A red-haired woman was bundled up in a jacket in front of a nightclub. There were police everywhere. "According to witnesses, this man came in for a drink, not knowing this is one of the more controversial clubs in this mountain town. It's a well-known neo-Nazi hangout, and they don't usually do well with strangers. The report says he got in a fight with a local, and things began to escalate from there. In the end, he left forty-three people dead, six critically injured with stab wounds, and a half-dozen being treated for broken bones and concussions."

A sketch popped up on the screen, and Moloch burst out laughing. The newscaster continued, "This is an artist's rendition of the assailant done with the assistance of the only conscious survivor, the bartender. They say he's about six feet tall, medium build, and has medium-length dark hair with a white stripe down the side. He has a thick accent as well."

The television switched over to the reporter standing beside the bartender. "We are here with Markus Khlur, the bartender in the establishment. Markus, I know this has been a shocking day for you and a crazy turn of events, but can you tell us what the man was like? Anything that can help us track him down?"

The bartender smiled and shook his head, a crazy chuckle under his breath. "He was like a Greek god!"

The reporter glanced nervously at the camera and held the microphone out to the guy. "A Greek god?"

The bartender nodded. "He never bled, never groaned, and never showed any weakness. He took down the whole place by himself. He took a shot before he left, and disappeared into the dark."

Moloch picked up the remote and clicked off the sound. He added whiskey to his blood and took a great gulp of the concoction. He started to laugh. "*There* you are, you sick bastard."

He clicked the sound back on as the bartender continued the story. "There were bodies everywhere. I don't know. He was probably one of the Damned who didn't like their politics."

Moloch leaned forward, almost spitting out his drink. "He's not Damned! He's a fucking Leviathan, you Swiss idiots! Goddamned humans can't even keep their species straight. He would come back and take a bite out of your ass if he heard you call him Damned. As if there's a drop of human blood in that man. Greek god is closer than Damned."

Moloch sighed and poured another drink. "What a prick."

24

Katie laid down on the squeaky bunk. Her whole body ached, but she was glad to be back in the barracks, even if it wasn't home. The guys had all been attended to by medical and were resting quietly in their own rooms. Calvin was the only one still up, watching the bay to make sure a portal didn't suddenly spring open.

Pandora yawned. *I don't know why that man doesn't try to get some sleep.*

He's always like that. Too jacked up after a fight to get any rest. He'll crash eventually, or round two will kick in, and then he'll crash. It's just the way he works.

Pandora grumbled something and then fell quiet.

Katie chuckled. *Good night to you, too.*

She curled her arms around the pillow and snuggled down. Just as she was almost asleep, her phone went off loudly. Pandora jumped into Katie. *Holy mother of Lucifer, a band is in your room.*

Katie groaned and threw back the covers. *It's just the phone.*

She picked it up when she saw the general's name on the screen. "Do you have someone watching me so that every time I lay down to sleep, you can call?"

The general chuckled but only momentarily. "I'm sorry, Katie, but I need to speak to Pandora."

"Oh sure, sure. I'm just Pandora's secretary. Hold, please."

Pandora quickly took Katie over without her having to ask. She held the phone to the side, addressing Katie. "It's about time you recognized that. I've been wondering if you're slow or just obstinate."

The general didn't say anything. He wasn't yet accustomed to the way the two of them addressed each other. He couldn't tell if they loved each other, hated each other, or if it oscillated between the two. Either way, it was usually entertaining.

Pandora rolled her eyes as Katie curled up in the background. "Yes, General. I'm sure whatever it is warrants a call right after a battle in hell."

The general let out a long dramatic breath. "Unfortunately, it does. We've had a weird sighting, and I need to know if you think this is a normal powerful Damned causing a problem or something else."

Pandora cringed. "Uh-oh, this sounds like it is a heavy one."

The general shook his head. "You have no idea. It would take something pretty badass to do this type of damage in the amount of time it was done. And apparently, the person or creature walked away without a scratch. Unfortunately, he is being hailed as a Greek god of sorts among some of the residents in the town where it occurred. I'm sending over pictures of the crime scene right now."

The phone buzzed in Pandora's ear. "Hold, please, while I look them over."

The first images were crime scene photos, then they changed to stills from the bar's security cameras. She flipped through them, watching Juntto as he fought off dozens of skinheads. The low lighting and the quick movements made it hard to see a clear image, but the puddles of blood on the floor were unmistakable. So was the last image. In it, the man smiled as he took a shot of liquor.

Pandora grunted. "Well, sonofabitch. Yeah, that's no Damned. That's Juntto, the Leviathan I told you about earlier. He's shrunk to human size, but that's him."

The general cleared his throat nervously. "Are you sure?"

Pandora nodded. "Mmhmm. If I didn't see it in the creepy smile or the way he moved, the silver streak in his hair is a dead giveaway. He has that no matter what he shifts into."

Pandora went silent for a moment, letting her mind wrap around the fact that Juntto was back. She had been told about it, but she hadn't wanted to believe it was true. Now that she saw it with her own eyes, she couldn't deny it.

He was a badass from what she could remember.

"General, we will go have a talk with Juntto. I cannot stress this enough, though. You need to try your best to avoid him until we get there. He's a wildcard, and he gives no fucks. He will fight us, and to be honest, he's not anyone I want to mess with right now."

The general rubbed his chin. "What kind of tactics are you saying to avoid?"

"The kind that would piss off anyone. No strike teams, no scrambling fighters. Don't even say his name in a snooty manner. Look, there's nothing really more to say about him at this point. Just know that he's not the dude to fuck with. I think Katie and I can take care of it if I play it right."

The general wanted to ask more questions, but it was obvious Pandora was done answering. "Okay. I understand. Let's talk about logistics, then. Can we get you, Calvin, and the military team together to find him? I don't want you and Katie going at this alone."

"Hey, the more, the merrier. Not like we just got back from hell or anything."

"I wouldn't ask if it wasn't important."

"I'm just screwing with you. Our team will be ready. We need to find him, sit down with him, and figure out what he wants. If it's something we can handle, then great—he should lay low for a while."

The general sat up straight in his chair. "Pandora, we do not negotiate or make deals with killers. I'm sure that after centuries on this planet, you know the United States does not negotiate with terrorists."

Pandora laughed. "Please. Don't give me that crap. Besides, that's like saying you're upset with a lion because he eats raw meat. He isn't from Earth, remember?"

The general was defiant. "I don't give a good goddamn what dimension or planet he's from. A killer is a killer just the same. Do you think we're going to give this guy what he wants and hope he doesn't kill anymore? Yeah, right. One thing I've learned is that once a killer, always one. It doesn't matter what you give them. I could see it in his eyes in the video. He is stone cold."

"That is definitely one thing you've got right. He is a stone-cold killer. Look, General, there *are* going to be more deaths. There's no way around it. At this point, we have to play our cards right. The question now is whether it will be from our side or the demons'. I can promise you, he dislikes us both equally. A body is a body. He probably threw that woman over the side of the mountain because she annoyed him. That's where his mind is."

It took the general by surprise when Pandora talked about their side versus the demons. She really *was* on the side of the humans, now, and she was in it to win it. She jumped in front of demons and protected humans, and never once had they seen her pause or question her actions. She had even taken the head off her own brother during the first major incursion.

Finally, the general replied, "I got you, Pandora. We will follow your lead. You know this guy better than any of us, and you are part of the team."

The team watched out the window as the plane began its descent into Switzerland. It touched down on the runway hard and came to a slow rolling stop on the snow. Turner groaned as he reached into the compartment over his seat and pulled out his jacket. "I got bruises on my bruises."

The tattooed soldier wrapped a scarf tightly around his neck. "We go from hotter than life to colder than a witch's titty. Wonderful."

Brock chuckled and slapped him on the back. "At least you know for sure you can survive it."

They grabbed their bags and stepped off the plane. Katie pulled her coat around her tightly and pulled her woolen cap over her ears. Suddenly, she longed for the coolness of the fall in New York. That was something she could live with. She wanted to run as far as she could from the bitter cold of Switzerland.

Calvin hopped down from the plane wearing just a T-shirt. He looked around excitedly. "I always wanted to come to Switzerland."

Katie rolled her eyes as she walked past him. "Too bad we're hunting a murderous Leviathan who may want to rip off your Röstis and flush them."

Calvin grimaced, putting his hand over his crotch. "That does not sound like a reasonable guy. Why do we always get stuck with the unreasonable guys?"

Katie laughed and followed the team to a fleet of waiting cars.

Juntto snored loudly. He had a pillow over his head to block out the light coming in around the edges of the window shade. His clothes, or the clothes of the hiker, were scattered on the floor. The hiker's credit cards were laid out on the table. Two empty pizza boxes were stacked by the trash can, and three empty bottles of tequila were lined up next to them.

Suddenly, Juntto sat straight up in the bed. There was a loud banging on his hotel room door, and it seemed to shake his brain. He rubbed his face and looked at the time. It was the middle of the day. "I fucking forgot about humans and their need for loud fucking *noises!*"

Whoever it was banged on the door again, this time rattling the mirror on the wall. Juntto scooted to the edge of the bed and growled. There was someone on the other side yelling at him in a language he didn't recognize. "What the fuck?"

He wandered to the door in a fog, more confused than angry. "Who knew that drinking the bar dry gave you such a fucking headache?"

He reached for the handle of the door and pulled it open. As he lifted his hand to his eyes to block the blinding light, a fist hit him so hard that he flew back into the room and slammed into the wall. The mirror wavered and teetered, but didn't fall.

Pandora strutted into the room. She was completely at ease in her body, and her eyes were a boiling red as she looked around. She spat at him in the demon tongue. "Nice to know your standards are still the same—low and disgusting."

Juntto lay on the floor, groaning. He raised a hand and felt blood oozing down his chin. Pandora walked over and kicked him in the side lightly. Juntto groaned and doubled over. "Heard you were back in town. Almost threw up when I heard, but whatever. Listen… Are you fucking listening?"

Juntto fought through his hangover fog, wondering how things had gone so badly so quickly. He mumbled something and nodded angrily.

Pandora smiled. "Good. I have a deal for you, one that gives you a chance to really cut loose. You interested?"

Juntto stood on shaking legs and looked at himself in the mirror. "Fuck my frozen ass." He raised his hands to either side of his nose and jerked it to the left. There was a sharp crack as his broken nose straightened. The blood trickling down his face was dark-green, and it stained the carpet wherever it landed. He popped his nose a little to the right. It was already starting to heal, so he had to work fast to make sure he put it back in the right place.

When he was done, he took a deep breath through his nose just make sure it was in working order. He held up a finger, telling Pandora to give him a second, and stumbled to the bathroom. He grabbed a towel off the sink and wiped the blood from his face, then looked Pandora up and down with a grin she wanted to smack right off his lips.

He could tell he was getting to her, but that was one of his favorite things to do. He chuckled and tossed the towel into the bathroom, standing there in all his glory, which didn't faze Pandora in the least. "Ah, still mad about that last remark, Lilith? I'd have thought you would have gotten over that by now."

Pandora gritted her teeth. "No. You let it fester, asshole."

Katie wasn't comfortable with how things were going, but she had to keep her faith in Pandora. *Why exactly are you being so arrogant right now? Aren't you the one who said not to do anything to piss him off?*

No. I told the military *not to do anything to piss him off. Arrogance is the only language Juntto understands. I could really care less if it makes him mad.*

Katie looked at him through Pandora's eyes. *He looks like he enjoys it. Can you have him put pants on?*

Hush. I'm working here.

Pandora picked up the ID on the dresser and looked it over. "So here's the deal...uh, Peter Cavanaugh. Shitty name, by the way. If we kick your ass, you work for me. You kick our asses, well, we'll probably try again."

Juntto chuckled. "That's what I've always appreciated about you, Lilith. You were willing to tell the truth...almost."

He took the ID from her and walked out the door. He glanced around the corner and saw a rank of soldiers with guns staring at him.

Calvin took one look at the naked man and shook his head. "Fuckin' Pandora."

Juntto yawned at the guns and went back inside, crossing his arms over his chest. "We have, what, six infected humans and you?"

Pandora shrugged, keeping her face neutral. "I'm infected too."

"I'm not even sure how that works."

"It's a long fucking story, one you don't need to worry about. It has nothing to do with you and never will."

Juntto smirked. "Man, you're still that same bitter old bitch you always were."

Pandora growled, "I am not old."

Pandora? About those pants?

Nope. I have him at a disadvantage.

He doesn't look *disadvantaged.*

Juntto walked closer to Pandora until he was pressing himself against her leg. "What can I say, I'm a sucker for a good fight. I'm in. Where are we meeting?"

Ew. Ew. Ew.

It's all part of the plan.

Leviathan dick on my leg is part of the plan?

It's a very complicated plan.

Pandora smiled and pulled out a piece of paper from her pocket. "Those are the coordinates, and there are directions, too, in case you're too far behind to understand coordinates."

"You got jokes. It's like foreplay."

Pandora bared her teeth. "Don't ever put me and you and foreplay in the same sentence again. I can feel the bile rising in my stomach."

He grinned. "Okay, get out. I still need my beauty sleep. I'll be there. I haven't had a good fight in forever."

"I think there's a fly on my leg. Clean your room. It's disgusting." Pandora spun away from him and left the room. She slammed the door behind her.

Juntto smiled in the dark. "Literally...like forever."

He plopped down on the bed and stretched out. Juntto was amused by what had just happened. Surprised, and amused. He really hadn't thought he would see Pandora. He certainly hadn't expected to walk away from that meeting with his balls attached.

He crossed his arms underneath his head and smiled. "Lucifer can suck it. That bitch will be mine."

The choppers flew low and fast as they made their way to the open field where Pandora would take Juntto on. It was a good place, away from the public and from prying eyes. And there was ample space for them to use really ferocious weapons. It was exactly the kind of place Pandora would have murdered him last time he had come to Earth.

The choppers landed and dropped the crew off near new .50 caliber gun turrets and several crates of rifles and handguns. A generous assortment of weapons had been donated by the Swiss military for their use. They had made an agreement with the US and were happy to do whatever they could to get Juntto out of their hair.

Pandora was already in control of Katie's body, with Katie paying close attention in the background.

She stood in front of her team. "All right, listen up. There are a lot of powerful weapons sitting here. They're what we'll need to injure this fool, but please make sure he doesn't get his grubby hands on them. We'll be completely fucked if he gets to the artillery, I promise."

Calvin cocked one of the guns. "Is he a good shot?"

Pandora scoffed. "Uh, yeah. He could shoot a flea off a horse's back from three hundred yards. And he's a double-fister, and I mean that in a non-sexual manner."

The guys wrinkled their noses, and Pandora chuckled. She loved messing with them. "Now, know this. The special metal probably won't wound him worse than normal bullets, but it doesn't hurt to try. The goal here is to beat him and not get fucking killed. He's extremely dangerous, and *not* a demon. He doesn't come from hell, he doesn't take stupid chances, and he doesn't have a conscience. He doesn't care if he could use you later, he will waste you where you stand and piss on your body."

Brock swallowed hard and gripped his gun tighter. "This guy sounds like he's never gotten his ass kicked.

Turner agreed. "He sounds like he *needs* his ass kicked."

Pandora smiled. "He doesn't even feel pain the way you do. Don't go toe to toe with him under any circumstances. Stay as far away as possible, okay?"

The team agreed, then set to work sorting through the weapons and gearing up.

Pandora snapped her fingers and waved to get their attention. "Almost forgot. One more thing. Don't fucking shoot me, please. There's nothing more embarrassing than friendly fire. If you aim for him and I'm in the way, you don't take the shot. It's simple. He is Billy Badass, and I'm going to have my hands full. So don't shoot my perfect posterior, okay?" The guys chuckled, but Pandora's face was serious. "I want everyone to walk away from this. Promise me, please, that if I die, you'll turn tail and get the fuck out of here. Do *not* try to save Katie or me, or you'll all end up dead. Now, get comfortable. He likes to make a late entrance."

Pandora sat in the snow, leaning her back against a .50 caliber turret. The guys were all sitting quietly, weapons ready, whispering to pass the time. It had been six hours since they'd arrived, and Juntto still hadn't gotten there. Calvin shuffled to Pandora. "How long do we wait before we decide he isn't going to show?"

Pandora, without looking, stuck up her hand and pointed into the field. "Speak of the douchebag. He's here now."

Calvin looked up to see Juntto, fully clothed this time, standing in the middle of the field. Pandora got up and stretched.

Calvin sniffed. "Are you gonna go talk to him or something?"

"In a minute. I'll make him wait. He hates waiting." She stood still and stared up at the sun. In the distance, Juntto raised a hand and waved to make sure she saw him. "All right, boys, stay safe. See you on the flip side."

Pandora made her way to the open field and stopped a hundred yards away from Juntto. She didn't trust him for a second.

He pointed to Pandora's crew. "What, no army?"

Pandora grinned maliciously. "Why would I bring one? You aren't that big a problem."

Juntto slapped his hand over his heart and feigned shock, stumbling back. "You wound me, Lilith. I see the puny men and their puny weapons. I can only assume it's you and me. Will they try to sting me?"

Pandora shrugged. "I guess so. Gotta give them something to do, right?"

"Right. Let me guess—you're planning on pouncing me and pulling me back to hell with you."

Pandora shook her head, looking innocent. "Nope, although I have to admit, the thought crossed my mind. I figured I wouldn't be doing myself any favors, though."

Juntto shook his finger at her. "You did that to Tiamat. I've been informed of your scare tactics. Poor Tiamat. You wounded her and then left her to Moloch. I mean, he fulfilled his promise, which was more than I would do, but he also sent her to her death. It was kind of fucked up."

Pandora circled around the frost giant, sizing him up. "All's fair, my friend. Besides, you're the one who works for those backstabbing weasels. You know they'll eventually do it to you, too. Poor Juntto never has any friends who stick by him."

"They told me you'd become a real bitch."

Pandora dug her heels into the snow and feigned injury. "Oh, no, someone squealed on me! That's so disappointing. Kind of makes me taking you down all the sweeter, though, don't you think?"

Juntto chuckled and crouched in the snow. "Only if you can do it."

They both jumped at the same time, clashing together brutally. They dropped to the ground in a whirlwind of punches and kicks, then separated and got to their feet. Pandora used her speed to knock his feet out from under him, but he was up faster than she could turn. He slammed his fist into her face and shoved a knee into her stomach. As she bent over in agony, he grabbed her by the back of the neck and flung her thirty feet.

Now that they were separated, the team opened up. They fired on Juntto, trying hard not to hit Pandora. Calvin held a hand up as Pandora launched herself back at him. She was all over the place, and moving so fast they could barely see her. They weren't getting as many shots off as they had hoped, but it was better than accidentally nailing their leader. The brawl moved from the field to a stand of trees.

Juntto lunged forward and elbowed Pandora in the nose. As she stumbled back, he spun and grabbed a fallen branch. He took a step toward the team and lobbed it as hard as he could at one of the guys.

They were spread out on the hill, so they were able to dodge the branch. But now Juntto knew he could reach them. Every time he got a good jab in on Pandora, he found something else to throw at the team. Calvin manned one of the .50s and let loose with a burst of gunfire.

"Ouch! *Fuck*! Those fucking bigger guns fucking hurt. I'm going to actually have a bruise on my skin for the first time in two centuries."

Pandora laughed at his pain. "You don't even know what's coming. That up there is just a taste of what we could unleash on your pathetic ass. Put you in a room with our gas, and you won't walk for three weeks. That is if I don't kill you while you're down."

He growled and raced forward. She tried to dodge, but he slapped her as hard as he could. She wobbled on her feet but caught herself, refusing to go down by his hand. He skipped around her in a circle, laughing wildly. "Wishing you were back in hell yet?"

Pandora glared at him, wiping the blood from her chin and flinging it into the snow. She raced forward and jabbed him hard in the stomach, then juked far enough away so that he couldn't easily retaliate. He choked and coughed, but there was laughter in his eyes. "I'll probably just bend you over and take you in front of your minions, you little slut."

Pandora growled and leaped at the frost giant. She ran through his flailing arms and grabbed him by the throat.

She heaved and lifted him, only to slam him back down into the snow. She tried to move quickly away from him, but he grabbed her ankle and yanked her foot right out from under her, then bounced to his feet, dragging her through the snow.

"You know what's wrong with you, Pandora? You think you're better than you are. You think that queen title ever actually meant anything? It didn't. You were just one of the lucky whores."

She kicked at him, but Juntto held firm. He spun her in a circle and grunted as he let go, hurling her into a nearby tree. Her back slammed into it and she fell to the ground, coughing blood onto the snow and speckling it red. She slowly put one hand on the ground and pushed herself back onto her feet. She wobbled from side to side, beat the fuck up and barely standing. It was the worst beating she had taken since she'd come back to Earth.

Juntto was confused. She obviously wasn't in his class. He was fucking her up, and something told him that she had expected it to be that way. He was powerful and from another planet, and she didn't stand a chance against him. Why was she still fighting? He just couldn't figure out what her angle was.

Juntto laughed loudly as Pandora stumbled toward him, wiping blood from her face. "No, please, don't move. Just stand very still for a moment. You might fall over otherwise."

She looked barely conscious. The frost giant snickered and ripped a skinny tree out of the ground. He slammed it against his leg and broke it into several pieces, then stuck the pieces into the ground like fence posts. He muttered under his breath, "Spears. Fuck you, Moloch. Spears are where it's at."

The guys watched from afar, not sure what he was doing. Suddenly, he ripped a piece of tree from the ground and launched it at them. Another. And another. The makeshift spears came crashing down around them, and they had no choice but to take cover. Splinters and shards of bark showered the team. Almost every single one of them was cut or impaled.

Juntto watched them retreating and knocked the dust off his hands. "I'm sorry, Pandora. Your friends fell back. They didn't like it when it rained sharp objects. Too bad they didn't love you enough to sacrifice themselves."

While Juntto was facing Pandora, Calvin snuck around the field toward the trees. He was making his way closer and closer to them, trying to help Pandora. He caught her eye, and she mouthed, "The plan."

Calvin's face turned grim, but he nodded. He began making his way back to the team. Juntto, with a shit-eating grin on his face, turned toward Pandora. "The plan? That's exciting, but I think I know what the plan was. It was for me to come here, beat the ever-loving shit out of you, get my rocks off, and piss Lucifer off because he can't come here while I'm banging his wife."

Pandora spat blood and held out both hands, steadying herself. She let herself giggle. "I'm not his woman. I divorced his ass."

Juntto threw his hands up, not bothered by her admission. "Okay, his *previous* woman. He'll still be pissed."

Juntto went to the side of the field and yanked another tree out of the ground, roots and all. He gave a few practice swings as he walked back toward her. "Any last pithy statements before I beat you?"

Pandora spoke through a mouth full of blood. "I've been hiding a secret."

Juntto set his tree on the ground. "What, you have a special weapon in your pants? I've had enough of that in my time. I'm not ruled by my other head, dear."

Pandora laughed maniacally. "Oh, you are, but that isn't my confession."

Juntto smiled, liking the game. He walked closer to her and leaned in. "What is it?"

Pandora grinned maniacally, showing off the blood covering her teeth. The smirk faded off Juntto's face as concern took over.

Pandora closed her eyes and let Katie come forward.

Juntto shook his head, not believing what he was seeing.

Katie was pissed. Her hand shot up, and she called her armor. In a heartbeat, she was clad in angelic metal. She stepped toward him, and the shock caused him to stumble. He dropped his tree.

Katie growled, "Spear, huh?" She extended her hand, and in another heartbeat her fist was gripping a gleaming golden spear. She moved like lightning. Her other hand grabbed Juntto by the shoulder, and she shoved the spear through his stomach and out his back.

His mouth dropped open. The frost giant wheezed wetly and ran his fingers down the long handle of the golden spear, trying to push himself off the thing. Katie grabbed the shaft with both hands and used it to pull him closer to her. She tilted her head to the side and hissed,

"How dare you threaten to force yourself on my sister!" She rammed her armored foot between his legs.

Juntto grunted and would have fallen if he were not impaled on the angelic spear.

Pandora coughed and whistled in excitement. *You know, if anyone else had done that I might like it. Kick that asshole a second time for me.*

You fucking got it.

Katie pulled her leg back and slammed it into his crotch again. His eyes grew wide, and a low wheeze creaked from his throat. Juntto was finally able to pull his lips together and mutter, "Angel?"

Katie smiled and reared back, slamming her fist into the side of his face. He struggled to move, but he couldn't pull the spear out no matter how hard he tried. All the strength he possessed was nothing compared to the might of angels.

Katie held him still with her spear. "You ready to die, asshole?"

Juntto coughed blood and spat at her feet, twisting his lips into a smile. "Wait until I get this out of me."

Katie reached up with one hand and pulled her angelic sword out of the air. She dropped her hand and effortlessly sliced off one of his legs. "Shall we go for dickless next?"

Pandora squealed with glee. *Yes, yes, yes.*

That was quite enough. Juntto pushed up on the spear, working to stand up straight on his one leg. He grunted and tried to force his body to grow and morph back into his frost giant form, but he remained human. The magic in the spear was limiting his abilities.

Katie carefully aimed her sword and thrust it forward,

sinking the blade deep into Juntto's chest. She leaned forward on the hilt. "Go ahead, grow a little larger. Then maybe I'll be able to find your prick, you murdering bastard."

Juntto growled and screamed, and with all his strength, he swung his arm and knocked Katie to the ground. Juntto collapsed on his one leg and struggled to stand. With both the sword and the spear buried in his torso, he looked like a pincushion.

Katie rolled away from him. As soon as she was out of the way, her team began blasting the frost giant with bullets. They had been waiting this entire time for their chance to light him up.

"Fuck, that dude can take some heat," Brock roared as the guys reloaded.

Calvin shook his head. "No shit. I can see him healing as we reload. This is insane. I don't know whether to be scared, pissed, or impressed."

Turner slotted his magazine into place. "Too bad he's on the other team. We could use an indestructible guy like that on our side. Hell, I want to *be* the indestructible guy. Fucking blow me up? Doesn't matter. Slice me with an angel sword? Who fucking cares?"

The tattooed soldier laughed. "I think Turner just fell in love."

Calvin held up a fist. "Hold up. Cease fire. Looks like Katie is back on her feet. This should be good."

Katie gritted her teeth angrily and stomped to Juntto. She whirled around and extended her leg, kicking him square in the face. Before he could recover, she pulled both Tom and Harry from her holsters and pulled the triggers, shooting him twice in the crotch. "They missed a spot."

Pandora bellowed with laughter. *Damn, girl, the twinsies. You are really pissed.*

Katie holstered the boys and grabbed the spear jutting from Juntto's stomach. She pulled his face close to hers. "Lilith made you an offer without asking me. You should have taken the deal. I'm going to spend all week ending your pathetic excuse for a life."

Juntto found himself gazing into crystal-blue angel eyes. He couldn't believe he'd let himself be conned. He hadn't seen it coming, but he should have. The reality of it was, angels had taken him out the last time he had been on Earth. He also knew he couldn't beat Lilith in hell, so on Earth or hell, he wasn't number one anywhere.

He swallowed his pride. "Let me talk to Lilith."

Katie pinned him to the ground with her spear. "She can talk through me. I don't trust your fucking ass."

Pandora's voice emerged from Katie, and the two began talking quickly in demon. It was a short conversation. From the look on Juntto's face, Katie knew things weren't going well for him. When their conversation was done, Pandora and Katie shared one voice.

Pandora nodded Katie's head. "I accepted his fealty, but there are rules he has to abide by. He has to stay human-sized. His frost giant form is outlawed. He can fight, but only demons. In exchange, he will fight with me, so there will be no shortage of battles. He will be given a place to live, and he will be well fed." Pandora said something else under her breath.

What was that?

Uh, he's requesting sex.

Katie choked a little. *"Uh, I'm not having sex with him. He's not only inhuman, but he's also a disgusting chauvinistic pig who thinks he can do whatever he wants. He was going to rape you/me. That's not okay. No woman should be with him."*

Pandora chuckled. *Not with you. I told him it depends on if he can woo a woman. That means not being his typical asshole self. If he can get someone to like him and offer sex to him in a normal fashion, I'm fine with it.*

Across the field, the team watched the two combatants have a conversation. Calvin looked at Brock. "What do you think?"

"We investigate?"

Calvin nodded. "Let's do it."

Pandora placed a hand on the spear impaling the fallen frost giant. "He can't force himself on anyone. No throwing women over the shoulder, clubbing them, or just taking what he wants. He can't just throw women away or impale them when they annoy him. They also can't be persuaded by magical means. He has a problem with using his charms to get a woman to cheat on her man. He went through a whole phase where those were the only women he would sleep with. It was fucking pathetic. Oh, and he can't hurt them. Did I say that already?" With that, she ripped the spear free. It disappeared from her hand.

Juntto groaned but sat up. His body started to heal faster, even with an angel sword still in his chest. "Their feelings always get hurt."

Pandora narrowed Katie's eyes at him. "No lying. If they don't accept you, that's their business. I understand that bitches can be crazy and think they can change a man.

Just be honest from the get-go, and I won't hold it against you."

Juntto shook his finger. "Oh, yeah, and I want one of those little tools they talk on. They make noises, and they are colorful."

Katie lifted an eyebrow. "Little tools they talk on?"

Juntto twirled his fingers around. "Yeah, they press the screens, and there are pictures and stuff. Then it makes a wild noise, and you can hear a person on the other side of the world."

"He wants a phone," Calvin suggested as the team joined them.

Juntto nodded. "One of the ones with the picture of an apple on the back."

Pandora laughed. "You want an iPhone. That's interesting. Of all the things Earth has to offer, you want a phone. They have made ungodly advances in technology since you've been here. Like flushing toilets and running water, battery-powered dildos, and microwaves that can reheat pizza in seconds. But you want a damn iPhone. Next thing I know, you'll be rolling around with headphones on listening to your MP3 player and working on your tablet. I bet you haven't even seen the internet yet. Strike that, it's probably not a good idea for you to use the internet. You could find yourself in all kinds of trouble on there. I barely go on it, and I have self-restraint."

Calvin scoffed. "Give him an android. See if he likes that."

Everyone looked at him like he was an alien, and he shrugged. "What? I'm not dissing the iPhone, but if he breaks an android, they're cheaper to replace."

Pandora nodded. "I have to agree with Calvin on that one."

Brock studied the frost giant skeptically. "I think he needs to change faces, too. Right now, he's wanted all over the entire world. He even looks like the guy he killed, which is fucking *Texas-Chainsaw-Massacre*-creepy."

Juntto looked confused. "What is that?"

Turner slapped his hands to his side. "This guy! Dude, the *Texas Chainsaw Massacre* was about this crazy guy who murdered a bunch of people with his chainsaw and wore their skins as a mask. Leatherface."

Juntto shook his head. "Fucking humans are weird. That would smell terrible. And by the way, it's fucking weird how you and Katie can talk out of the same face and control each other's facial movements. I don't like it."

Pandora wrinkled Katie's nose. "Deal with it. You have to pay for killing those people, too. It's obvious you have zero remorse for that."

Juntto opened his mouth to protest, but Pandora put her hand up. "I know that's you being you, but we don't take murder lightly in this group. Get up and get your big-boy pants on. Next week, we go to hell."

Juntto looked offended and slightly disgusted. "To do what?"

Pandora faded into the background, and Katie came forward. "That's easy, dummy." Katie grabbed her angelic sword and pulled it from his chest. She flicked green blood from the blade and grinned down at the frost giant. "To let them know Momma is back."

Thank you for not only reading this story, but also these *Author Notes* here at the back.

When the time came to work on this story, I was struggling with where to go from our Leviathan in the last book. I had set it up so there were multiple Leviathans, but did not want it to be the same type of beast over and over.

Then, the concept of Junnto in the ice, and a demon falling down an icy mountain came to mind. The nail in the coffin for me was when Moloch gated into his office in hell and smelled like Christmas.

Since I didn't want to go 'big,' I decided to go capable, smaller, and alien. Different enough that he is who he is, not because he is a horrible human, but rather that is what he knows. (For example, you don't get upset with an orca for eating a seal. That's what they do.)

Further, I wanted to have fun in this book. A lot of the time, the stories are a bit down, excluding some of the

Pandora banter. My sense of humor can be fairly wacked and dark, so I hope we didn't go overboard in places.

In this story, we see Pandora and Katie working together, feeling out their relationship and becoming a team in every sense of the word. I've heard of many comments (and those in the reviews) who enjoyed the ending to the last book with Pandora taking care of Katie. I enjoy knowing what you like about a previous story, since it encourages me to consider seeing if the next story has affords me opportunity to do more of the same.

My personal favorite scene in this story is when Pandora is thinking to herself in the restaurant on top of the building and Gabriel shows up.

However, the FUNNIEST scene for me is the beginning when Moloch and Baal are bitching about KatieDora fighting, and Pandora using the cold spell to kill the demons.

I chuckle about this (even now):

Baal put his large scaled foot on top of a frozen demon and rolled him over. He snarled as he looked down at the face frozen in fear. "We aren't even safe within our own walls of hell. The bitch started a goddamned blizzard down here. Now look at this fucking mess. These were good demons, and now we have a pile of fucking demonsicles."

The next book is almost complete—and if you liked the humor in this one? I think the next will tickle your funny bone as much or more.

Ad Aeternitatem,
Michael Anderle

SEPTEMBER 13, 2018

Well, hello! Hopefully, you're not in pumpkin-spice hell just yet. Man, when they open the doors to the fall's favorite flavor, they OPEN the doors!

Can't go anywhere without pumpkin spice in my face, beckoning me to try it. Just one bite, one sip, one time—and you're hooked forever. Don't let them drag you in. It's a cult.

Forgive me if you're a member. Ignore all that mad talk. *winks*

We're up in Canada! Lac Brom to be exact, which is in Quebec. I'm staring at a lake that's a few feet from the back door. My boys (hubs and the teenager) have been learning to kayak and paddle board. The water is most likely 50 degrees. And we're from Texas.

You get the humor in this.

It's been an interesting month of traveling for us. I opened up my clean romance traveling series from our adventures, and next month, we're jumping in paranormal romance, so yay. I've been waiting to do that for four years.

I'm writing more than sleeping, but life couldn't be better. Mike and I are loving The Damned series. OH! And great news: book 1 in our new spinoff, Damian, is done and in review. That was so much fun to write. I love our bad-ass priest and his trusty sidekick.

You should be hearing more about that this next month actually! Mike's been working on covers for it that blow my mind. I stay away from the art part as best I can. He's our homerun hitter there.

I hope you loved this book. It was an action-packed, humorous, good time for us. Appreciate you spending your hard-earned money on our entertainment. We're working hard to bring more of it to you as fast as we can. Thanks for the support. You're the reason we do what we do. Until next time.

Slave to Many Stories,
Laurie Starkey

CONNECT WITH MICHAEL TODD

Want more?

Find us On Facebook

https://www.facebook.com/Protected-by-the-Damned-193345908061855/